U0035174

NEW GEPT

新制全民英檢
初級 聽力測驗
必考題型

國際語言中心委員會、
李佳靜、林姿吟／著

全書MP3一次下載

9789864541515.zip

「iOS 系統請升級至 iOS 13 後再行下載，
此為大型檔案，建議使用 WIFI 連線下載，以免佔用流量，
並確認連線狀況，以利下載順暢。」

全民英檢常考的**生活場景**

情境融入＋題型剖析＝學習效果最佳！

Step 1

看圖辨義
迅速瀏覽圖中所有元素，先一步分析什麼樣的圖中元素可能會有什麼樣的出題方式，在題目音檔播出前不浪費任何一秒。

Step 2

問答
迅速瀏覽每個選項的答案，透過選項可猜測待會的出題方向是什麼，甚至可先以消去法把最不可能的答案排除。

Step 3

簡短對話
掌握五大疑問詞疑問句How? Who? What? Where? When? 的要領，仔細聆聽一段英文對話，面對問題時不會手忙腳亂，作答快速又正確。

Step 4

短文聽解
快速瀏覽題目提供的三張圖畫，掌握每張圖中可能的出題重點，推論可能的出題方式，只要鎖定答題關鍵字，就能順利作答！

Step 5

聽力測驗
高分通過！

「聽解能力」密集訓練

到底能幫我增強哪些能力呢？

自然反射訓練

每個主題情境都有3個經典問句與經典答句，每種出題方式皆有固定的回答句型，可訓練自己聽出句中的答題關鍵字，把回答變成一種自然而然的反射能力。課前先暖身一次，對稍後的聽力練習會有很大的幫助。

> **經典問句**
>
> 問法 **1** What is this?
> 問法 **2** What are these?
> 問法 **3** What can people find in here?
>
> **經典答句**
>
> 回答 **1** This/It is a/an _____ .
> 回答 **2** These/They are _____ .
> 回答 **3** People can find _____ .

快速上手句

每個主題情境中最重要的必備關鍵句，這些經常出現的生活慣用表達範例，也是最常出現在對話中的應對方式，句子簡短卻能貼切表達，文法、句型不再死背，開口跟著唸、回答更自然，同步提升口說能力。

> **Hint 快速上手句**
>
> A: How's it going? 最近好嗎？
> B: Not bad. 不錯。
>
> A: How are you doing these days? 最近過得怎麼樣？
> B: Pretty good. 很不錯。
>
> A: How's everything? 一切都好嗎？
> B: Everything's OK. 都還不錯。
>
> A: How's life? 過得怎麼樣？
> B: Same old thing. 老樣子。
>
> A: How are you getting along? 最近怎麼樣？
> B: Keeping busy. And you? 一直很忙。你呢？

看圖預測關鍵字

看圖辨義及短文聽解的題目內容沒有印在試卷上，因此必須先瀏覽插圖再依播放內容作答。這部分訓練你找出圖中的關鍵元素，並依經典問句的出題模式，預測待會題目會怎麼問，在等待中不浪費一分一秒，瀏覽插圖時，即可完成猜題。

Q2 （每題只播一次，請仔細聽。）
MP3 1-1

Q3 （每題只播一次，請仔細聽。）

答題時間提示

這可不是恐怖倒數！而是要讓你習慣考試節奏，平時練習時就能夠意識到每題的作答時間。只要掌握等待播出題目前的猜題技巧，在聽到播出的音檔前就可拿到60%的分數，只要根據題意做出最適切的回答，要拿高分絕對不是問題！

> **1**
> A. Well, about the same.
> B. They are the same.
> C. I don't know what I'm doing.
>
> 答題時間 約 **15** 秒/題
>
> **2**
> A. Yeah, how have you been?
> B. It's good to meet you.
> C. I'm O.K.
>
> MP3 2-1
>
> **3**
> A. It was wonderful.
> B. Wish you a happy holiday.
> C. No, it's good.

CONTENTS

第三部分 簡短對話

第四部分 短文聽解

解答篇

模擬測驗

全民英檢聽力測驗

第一部分　第二部分　第三部分　第四部分

看圖辨義

作答提示

▶ 試題冊上有數幅圖畫，每題請聆聽放音機播出的題目和三個英文句子之後，在選項 [A] [B] [C] 中選出與所看到的圖畫最相符的答案。（每題只播出一次，請仔細聆聽）

看圖辨義

主題 1　物品・動物 Things・Animals

課前暖身　以下是經典問句與經典答句，各有 3 句。請先瀏覽一次。對稍後的聽力訓練會有很大的幫助喔！

經典問句

問法 ① What is this?

問法 ② What are these?

問法 ③ What can people find in here?

經典答句

回答 ① This/It is a/an _____.

回答 ② These/They are _____.

回答 ③ People can find _____.

聽力練習　試題上有數幅圖畫，每題請聆聽放音機播出的題目和 3 個英語句子之後，在選項 A、B、C 中選出與所看到的圖畫最相符的答案。
☛（答案請見 P.146）

答題時間
約 **10** 秒/題

Q1

MP3 **1-1**

（每題只播一次，請仔細聽。）

Q2

MP3 **1-1**

（每題只播一次，請仔細聽。）

Q3

MP3 **1-1**

（每題只播一次，請仔細聽。）

主題 **2**	活動 Activities

課前暖身

以下是經典問句與經典答句，各有 3 句。請先瀏覽一次。對稍後的聽力訓練會有很大的幫助喔！

 經典問句

(問法**1**) What is she/he doing?

(問法**2**) What's happening here?

(問法**3**) What is she/he going to do?

 經典答句

(回答**1**) She/he is V-ing.

(回答**2**) People/They are V-ing.

(回答**3**) She/he is going to V.

聽力練習

試題上有數幅圖畫，每題請聆聽放音機播出的題目和 3 個英語句子之後，在選項 A、B、C 中選出與所看到的圖畫最相符的答案。
☞（答案請見 **P.147**）

答題時間
約 **10** 秒/題

Q1

MP3 **1-2**

（每題只播一次，請仔細聽。）

Q2

MP3 **1-2**

（每題只播一次，請仔細聽。）

Q3

MP3 **1-2**

（每題只播一次，請仔細聽。）

<table>
<tr><td>主題 3</td><td></td></tr>
</table>

主題 **3**	# 地點 Places

課前暖身 以下是經典問句與經典答句,各有 3 句。請先瀏覽一次。對稍後的聽力訓練會有很大的幫助喔!

 ## 經典問句

問法 **1** What is this place?

問法 **2** Where are these two girls?

問法 **3** Where are they probably going?

 ## 經典答句

回答 **1** This is a _____.

回答 **2** They are in/at/on a _____.

回答 **3** They are probably going to the _____.

聽力練習 試題上有數幅圖畫,每題請聆聽放音機播出的題目和 3 個英語句子之後,在選項 A、B、C 中選出與所看到的圖畫最相符的答案。
☛ (答案請見 **P.150**)

Q1

MP3 1-3

（每題只播一次，請仔細聽。）

Q2

MP3 1-3

（每題只播一次，請仔細聽。）

Q3

MP3 1-3

（每題只播一次，請仔細聽。）

以下是經典問句與經典答句，各有 3 句。請先瀏覽一次。對稍後的
聽力訓練會有很大的幫助喔！

 經典問句

問法① What is the time?

問法② What time is it?

問法③ When does the _____ start?

 經典答句

回答① It's _____ o'clock.

回答② It's _____ to/past _____.

回答③ It starts at _____ a.m./p.m..

試題上有數幅圖畫，每題請聆聽放音機播出的題目和 3 個英語句子
之後，在選項 A、B、C 中選出與所看到的圖畫最相符的答案。
☛（答案請見 **P.154**）

答題時間 約 **10** 秒/題

Q1

MP3 1-4

（每題只播一次，請仔細聽。）

Q2

MP3 1-4

（每題只播一次，請仔細聽。）

Q3

MP3 1-4

（每題只播一次，請仔細聽。）

情緒・外表 Feelings・Looks

課前暖身　以下是經典問句與經典答句，各有 3 句。請先瀏覽一次。對稍後的聽力訓練會有很大的幫助喔！

 經典問句

問法❶ How is she/he feeling?（問心情）

問法❷ How does she/he look?（問表情）

問法❸ What does she/he look like?（問身材、外表特徵）

經典答句

回答❶ She/He is _____.

回答❷ She/He looks _____.

回答❸ She's/He's _____.

She/He has _____.

She/He looks like _____.

聽力練習　試題上有數幅圖畫，每題請聆聽放音機播出的題目和 3 個英語句子之後，在選項 A、B、C 中選出與所看到的圖畫最相符的答案。
☞（答案請見 P.156）

答題時間
約 **10** 秒/題

Q1

MP3 **1-5**

（每題只播一次，請仔細聽。）

主題
5
情緒・外表
Feelings・Looks

Q2

MP3 **1-5**

（每題只播一次，請仔細聽。）

Q3

MP3 **1-5**

（每題只播一次，請仔細聽。）

課前暖身

以下是經典問句與經典答句,各有 3 句。請先瀏覽一次。對稍後的聽力訓練會有很大的幫助喔!

經典問句

問法 **1** What happened to him/her?

問法 **2** Why is she/he here?

問法 **3** What is wrong with him/her?

經典答句

回答 **1** She/He hurt her/his _____.

回答 **2** She/He has got _____.

回答 **3** She/He has a _____.

聽力練習

試題上有數幅圖畫,每題請聆聽放音機播出的題目和 3 個英語句子之後,在選項 A、B、C 中選出與所看到的圖畫最相符的答案。

☞（答案請見 **P.159**）

答題時間
約 **10** 秒/題

Q1

MP3 **1-6**

（每題只播一次，請仔細聽。）

Q2

MP3 **1-6**

（每題只播一次，請仔細聽。）

Q3

MP3 **1-6**

（每題只播一次，請仔細聽。）

食物 Food

課前暖身　以下是經典問句與經典答句，各有 3 句。請先瀏覽一次。對稍後的聽力訓練會有很大的幫助喔！

 經典問句

問法 **1** What is she/he eating/drinking?

問法 **2** What does she/he want?

問法 **3** What would she/he like?

 經典答句

回答 **1** She/He is eating ＿＿＿＿＿＿＿＿＿＿.

回答 **2** She/He wants ＿＿＿＿＿＿＿＿＿＿.

回答 **3** She/He would like ＿＿＿＿＿＿＿＿.

聽力練習　試題上有數幅圖畫，每題請聆聽放音機播出的題目和 3 個英語句子之後，在選項 A、B、C 中選出與所看到的圖畫最相符的答案。
☛（答案請見 **P.161**）

主題

7

食物

Food

Q1

MP3 **1-7**

（每題只播一次，請仔細聽。）

（每題只播一次，請仔細聽。）

Q2

MP3 **1-7**

（每題只播一次，請仔細聽。）

Q3

MP3 **1-7**

課前暖身 以下是經典問句與經典答句，各有 3 句。請先瀏覽一次。對稍後的聽力訓練會有很大的幫助喔！

 經典問句 ●

問法 **❶** What is she/he wearing?

問法 **❷** What is she/he carrying?

問法 **❸** What is she/he going to buy?

 經典答句 ●

回答 **❶** She/He is wearing _____.

回答 **❷** She/He is carrying _____.

回答 **❸** She/He is going to buy _____.

聽力練習 試題上有數幅圖畫，每題請聆聽放音機播出的題目和 3 個英語句子之後，在選項 A、B、C 中選出與所看到的圖畫最相符的答案。
☛（答案請見 P.164）

答題時間
約 **10** 秒/題

主題
8
服飾　Costumes & Accessories

Q1

MP3 **1-8**

（每題只播一次，請仔細聽。）

Q2

MP3 **1-8**

（每題只播一次，請仔細聽。）

Q3

MP3 **1-8**

（每題只播一次，請仔細聽。）

23

個人資訊 Personal Information

課前暖身　以下是經典問句與經典答句，各有 3 句。請先瀏覽一次。對稍後的聽力訓練會有很大的幫助喔！

 經典問句

(問法①) How old is she/he?

(問法②) How heavy is she/he?

(問法③) How tall is she/he?

 經典答句

(回答①) She/He is _____ year(s) old.

(回答②) She/He is _____ kilogram.

(回答③) She/He is _____ tall.

聽力練習　試題上有數幅圖畫，每題請聆聽放音機播出的題目和 3 個英語句子之後，在選項 A、B、C 中選出與所看到的圖畫最相符的答案。
☛（答案請見 P.166）

主題 9 個人資訊 Personal Information

Q1

MP3 1-9

（每題只播一次，請仔細聽。）

Q2

MP3 1-9

（每題只播一次，請仔細聽。）

Q3

MP3 1-9

（每題只播一次，請仔細聽。）

主題 **10**	季節・月分 Seasons・Months

以下是經典問句與經典答句，各有 3 句。請先瀏覽一次。對稍後的聽力訓練會有很大的幫助喔！

課前暖身

 經典問句

問法 **1** What season is it?

問法 **2** What month is it?

問法 **3** What time of the year is it?

 經典答句

回答 **1** It's winter/spring/summer/fall.

回答 **2** It's January/February/....

回答 **3** It's New Year's Day/Halloween/Christmas/....

聽力練習

試題上有數幅圖畫，每題請聆聽放音機播出的題目和 3 個英語句子之後，在選項 A、B、C 中選出與所看到的圖畫最相符的答案。

☛（答案請見 P.169）

答題時間
約 **10** 秒/題

主題
10
季
節
‧
月
分

Seasons‧Months

Q1

MP3 **1-10**

（每題只播一次，請仔細聽。）

Q2

MP3 **1-10**

（每題只播一次，請仔細聽。）

Q3

MP3 **1-10**

（每題只播一次，請仔細聽。）

主題 11　　日期 Dates

課前暖身　以下是經典問句與經典答句，各有 3 句。請先瀏覽一次。對稍後的聽力訓練會有很大的幫助喔！

經典問句

問法 **1** What day is today/it?

問法 **2** What is the date today?

問法 **3** What date is _____?

經典答句

回答 **1** Today/It is （Monday~Sunday）.

回答 **2** Today/It is （Month/date）.

回答 **3** It is (on) （Month/date）.

聽力練習　試題上有數幅圖畫，每題請聆聽放音機播出的題目和 3 個英語句子之後，在選項 A、B、C 中選出與所看到的圖畫最相符的答案。
☛（答案請見 **P.171**）

Q1

MP3 **1-11**

（每題只播一次，請仔細聽。）

Q2

MP3 **1-11**

（每題只播一次，請仔細聽。）

Q3

MP3 **1-11**

（每題只播一次，請仔細聽。）

NOTE	
Jane's birthday	1979/10/15
Annie's birthday	1975/8/30
Terry's birthday	1976/6/11
Mary's birthday	1974/3/7

以下是經典問句與經典答句,各有 3 句。請先瀏覽一次。對稍後的
聽力訓練會有很大的幫助喔!

經典問句

問法 **1** Where is _____?

問法 **2** Where does _____ live?

問法 **3** What is under/on/ ... the _____?

經典答句

回答 **1** It is _____.

回答 **2** She/He lives _____ the _____.

回答 **3** A/The _____ is under/on ... the _____.

試題上有數幅圖畫,每題請聆聽放音機播出的題目和 3 個英語句子
之後,在選項 A、B、C 中選出與所看到的圖畫最相符的答案。
☞(答案請見 **P.173**)

答題時間
約 **10** 秒/題

Q1

MP3 **1-12**

（每題只播一次，請仔細聽。）

Q2

MP3 **1-12**

（每題只播一次，請仔細聽。）

Q3

MP3 **1-12**

（每題只播一次，請仔細聽。）

課前暖身

以下是經典問句與經典答句,各有 3 句。請先瀏覽一次。對稍後的聽力訓練會有很大的幫助喔!

經典問句

問法 **1** What number is it?

問法 **2** How many _____ are there?

問法 **3** Who is first?

經典答句

回答 **1** It is number _____ .

回答 **2** There are _____ .

回答 **3** _____ is first.

聽力練習

試題上有數幅圖畫,每題請聆聽放音機播出的題目和 3 個英語句子之後,在選項 A、B、C 中選出與所看到的圖畫最相符的答案。
☞(答案請見 **P.175**)

答題時間
約 **10** 秒/題

Q1

MP3 **1-13**

（每題只播一次，請仔細聽。）

Q2

MP3 **1-13**

（每題只播一次，請仔細聽。）

Q3

MP3 **1-13**

（每題只播一次，請仔細聽。）

價錢 Prices

課前
暖身

以下是經典問句與經典答句,各有 3 句。請先瀏覽一次。對稍後的
聽力訓練會有很大的幫助喔!

經典問句

問法 **1** How much is it?

問法 **2** How much does it cost?

問法 **3** How much did she/he spend?

經典答句

回答 **1** _____ dollars.

回答 **2** It costs _____ dollars.

回答 **3** She/He spent _____ dollars.

聽力
練習

試題上有數幅圖畫,每題請聆聽放音機播出的題目和 3 個英語句子
之後,在選項 A、B、C 中選出與所看到的圖畫最相符的答案。
☞(答案請見 **P.176**)

Q1

MP3 **1-14**

（每題只播一次，請仔細聽。）

Ticket Fare

To Tainan................$856
To Taichung...........$412
To Keelung..............$165

（每題只播一次，請仔細聽。）

Q2

MP3 **1-14**

（每題只播一次，請仔細聽。）

Q3

MP3 **1-14**

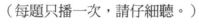

主題 **15**	天氣 Weather

課前暖身 以下是經典問句與經典答句，各有 3 句。請先瀏覽一次。對稍後的聽力訓練會有很大的幫助喔！

 經典問句 ━━━━━━━━━━━━━━━━━━━━━━━━━━━━━━━━●

問法**1** How's the weather?

問法**2** What will the weather be like?

問法**3** What's the temperature?

 經典答句 ━━━━━━━━━━━━━━━━━━━━━━━━━━━━━━━━●

回答**1** It's _____.

回答**2** It will be _____.

回答**3** The temperature is _____ degree.

聽力練習 試題上有數幅圖畫，每題請聆聽放音機播出的題目和 3 個英語句子之後，在選項 A、B、C 中選出與所看到的圖畫最相符的答案。
☛（答案請見 **P.178**）

答題時間
約 **10** 秒/題

Q1

MP3 **1-15**

（每題只播一次，請仔細聽。）

Q2

MP3 **1-15**

（每題只播一次，請仔細聽。）

Q3

MP3 **1-15**

（每題只播一次，請仔細聽。）

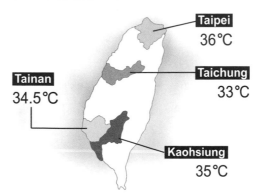

主題	16	職業 Occupations

課前暖身 以下是經典問句與經典答句，各有 3 句。請先瀏覽一次。對稍後的聽力訓練會有很大的幫助喔！

經典問句

問法 ❶ What is she/he?

問法 ❷ What does she/he do?

問法 ❸ Whom should they call?

經典答句

回答 ❶ She/He is a _____.

回答 ❷ She/He works as a _____.

回答 ❸ They should call _____.

聽力練習 試題上有數幅圖畫，每題請聆聽放音機播出的題目和 3 個英語句子之後，在選項 A、B、C 中選出與所看到的圖畫最相符的答案。
☞（答案請見 **P.179**）

答題時間
約 **10** 秒/題

主題
16
職業 Occupations

Q1

MP3 1-16

（每題只播一次，請仔細聽。）

（每題只播一次，請仔細聽。）

Q2

MP3 1-16

（每題只播一次，請仔細聽。）

Q3

MP3 1-16

比較 Comparisons

課前暖身

以下是經典問句與經典答句,各有 3 句。請先瀏覽一次。對稍後的聽力訓練會有很大的幫助喔!

經典問句

問法 1 What is more expensive?

問法 2 What is the cheapest way to _____?

問法 3 Who should pay the most?

經典答句

回答 1 _____ is more expensive.

回答 2 By _____. / Take a/the_____.

回答 3 The _____ should pay the most.

聽力練習

試題上有數幅圖畫,每題請聆聽放音機播出的題目和 3 個英語句子之後,在選項 A、B、C 中選出與所看到的圖畫最相符的答案。
☛(答案請見 **P.182**)

答題時間 約 **10** 秒/題

Q1

MP3 1-17

（每題只播一次，請仔細聽。）

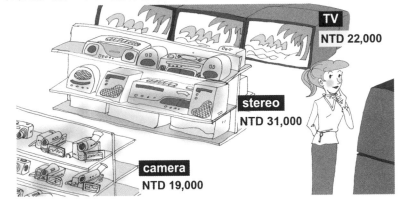

TV
NTD 22,000

stereo
NTD 31,000

camera
NTD 19,000

（每題只播一次，請仔細聽。）

Q2

MP3 1-17

3 Ways to Kaohsiung

By Plane.................$2000
By Train.................$600
By Bus...................$550

（每題只播一次，請仔細聽。）

Q3

MP3 1-17

$80

$40

$50

人際關係 Relationships

課前暖身 以下是經典問句與經典答句,各有 3 句。請先瀏覽一次。對稍後的聽力訓練會有很大的幫助喔!

經典問句

問法**1** Who is the person ...?

問法**2** Who is the woman/man in _____ ?

問法**3** What is their relationship?

經典答句

回答**1** She/He is _____.

回答**2** She/He is her/his _____.

回答**3** They are _____ and _____.

聽力練習 試題上有數幅圖畫,每題請聆聽放音機播出的題目和 3 個英語句子之後,在選項 A、B、C 中選出與所看到的圖畫最相符的答案。
☛(答案請見 P.184)

答題時間
約 **10** 秒/題

Q1

MP3 **1-18**

（每題只播一次，請仔細聽。）

Q2

MP3 **1-18**

（每題只播一次，請仔細聽。）

Q3

MP3 **1-18**

（每題只播一次，請仔細聽。）

43

日常用品（1）Things for Daily Use (1)

課前暖身　以下是經典問句與經典答句，各有 3 句。請先瀏覽一次。對稍後的聽力訓練會有很大的幫助喔！

經典問句

問法 **1** Where can people probably find this?

問法 **2** Where should this/these be put?

問法 **3** What goes with this?

經典答句

回答 **1** People can probably find this in _____.

回答 **2** It/They should be put in _____.

回答 **3** _____ goes with _____.

聽力練習　試題上有數幅圖畫，每題請聆聽放音機播出的題目和 3 個英語句子之後，在選項 A、B、C 中選出與所看到的圖畫最相符的答案。
☛（答案請見 P.186）

答題時間
約 **10** 秒/題

Q1

MP3 **1-19**

（每題只播一次，請仔細聽。）

Q2

MP3 **1-19**

（每題只播一次，請仔細聽。）

Q3

MP3 **1-19**

（每題只播一次，請仔細聽。）

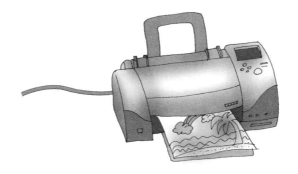

課前暖身 以下是經典問句與經典答句,各有 3 句。請先瀏覽一次。對稍後的聽力訓練會有很大的幫助喔!

經典問句

問法 ① What does she/he need most?

問法 ② Who needs/uses this most?

問法 ③ What's her/his trouble?

經典答句

回答 ① She/He needs _____ most.

回答 ② A _____ needs/uses this most.

回答 ③ She/He _____.

聽力練習 試題上有數幅圖畫,每題請聆聽放音機播出的題目和 3 個英語句子之後,在選項 A、B、C 中選出與所看到的圖畫最相符的答案。
☛(答案請見 **P.188**)

答題時間
約 **10** 秒/題

Q1

MP3 1-20

（每題只播一次，請仔細聽。）

Q2

MP3 1-20

（每題只播一次，請仔細聽。）

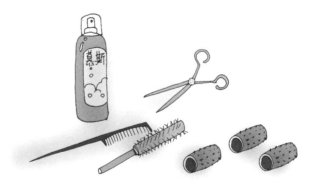

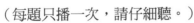

（每題只播一次，請仔細聽。）

Q3

MP3 1-20

全民英檢聽力測驗

第一部分　**第二部分**　第三部分　第四部分

問答

作答提示

▶ 每題請先聆聽放音機播出的英文句子，再從試題冊上的 [A] [B] [C] 選項中，選出一個最相符的回應。
（每題只播出一次，請仔細聆聽）

問答

第一類 招呼與問候

主題 1　見　面

Hint 快速上手句 *important sentences*

A: How's it going? 最近好嗎？
B: Not bad. 不錯。

A: How are you doing these days? 最近過得怎麼樣？
B: Pretty good. 很不錯。

A: How's everything? 一切都好嗎？
B: Everything's OK. 都還不錯。

A: How's life? 過得怎麼樣？
B: Same old thing. 老樣子。

A: How are you getting along? 最近怎麼樣？
B: Keeping busy. And you? 一直很忙。你呢？

A: Hey, What's up? 嘿，最近好嗎？
B: Nothing new. 差不多吧。

A: Hi, what's new (with you)? 嗨，最近怎麼樣？
B: Nothing much. 不怎麼樣。

每題請聆聽放音機播出的英文句子之後，再從試題冊上的選項 A、B、C 三個選項中，選出一個與題意最相符的答案。（每題只播一次，請仔細聽。）☛（答案請見 **P.190**）

主題 1 招呼與問候 ∨ 見面

1
A. Well, about the same.
B. They are the same.
C. I don't know what I'm doing.

答題時間 約 **15** 秒/題

2
A. Yeah, how have you been?
B. It's good to meet you.
C. I'm OK.

MP3 2-1

3
A. It was wonderful.
B. Wish you a happy holiday.
C. No, it's good.

4
A. How do you do, Ms. Davis?
B. Who is Betty Davis?
C. Do you know her?

5
A. Goodbye, Rose.
B. Hi, Rose. It's nice to meet you.
C. It's nice of you, Rose.

道 別

■機場道別的表達方式■

1. It's very nice of you to come and see me off.
   你人真好，還特地來送我。

2. I hope to see you again.
   希望能再見到您。

3. I'll be seeing you.
   再見。
   ※〔註〕這是美國人喜歡使用的道別用語。

4. Happy landing.
   旅途平安。
   ※〔註〕這是送行的人對上飛機的人說的道別用語。

5. Bon voyage!
   一路順風！
   ※〔註〕本句是法語，但英美人士在日常生活中常會使用。

聽力練習 每題請聆聽放音機播出的英文句子之後，再從試題冊上的選項 A、B、C 三個選項中，選出一個與題意最相符的答案。（每題只播一次，請仔細聽。）☞（答案請見 **P.191**）

主題
2
招呼與問候 ∨ 道別

1
A. Go away.
B. I come here sometimes.
C. Thanks, I will.

答題時間
約 **15** 秒/題

MP3 2-2

2
A. Happy birthday.
B. Enjoy yourself!
C. Who is coming?

3
A. You, too.
B. It's a nice day, isn't it?
C. Hi, I'm back.

4
A. Sure thing.
B. Here you are.
C. I will get there by three.

5
A. Same here.
B. I missed the bus.
C. Did I miss anything?

主題 3 邀約與招待

🗒️ **聽力練習** 每題請聆聽放音機播出的英文句子之後,再從試題冊上的選項A、B、C三個選項中,選出一個與題意最相符的答案。(每題只播一次,請仔細聽。) ☛(答案請見 **P.193**)

1
A. Sorry, I don't have time.
B. Of course I can count.
C. Yes, I am Ken.

答題時間 約 **15** 秒/題

2
A. I'd love to.
B. I am with you.
C. We are together.

MP3 **2-3**

3
A. I like drinking tea.
B. No, thanks. I'm fine for now.
C. Be careful with what you eat.

4
A. I can make it home.
B. Thanks, I will.
C. Nobody's home.

5
A. Let me see you out.
B. Welcome. Please come in.
C. Thank you for the great party!

主題 **4** 祝賀與道喜

聽力練習 每題請聆聽放音機播出的英文句子之後,再從試題冊上的選項A、B、C 三個選項中,選出一個與題意最相符的答案。(每題只播一次,請仔細聽。)☛(答案請見 **P.195**)

1
A. Happy birthday!
B. How are you?
C. Oh! How nice.

答題時間 約 **15** 秒/題

2
A. Why were you off for a week?
B. Have a nice trip.
C. That's too bad. I hope you get well soon.

MP3 **2-4**

3
A. That's very kind of you to say so.
B. Can I get past, please?
C. I'm afraid not.

4
A. What do you believe?
B. I hope we have the key to this lock.
C. Honey, I'm so happy for you.

5
A. Same to you.
B. I saw the news.
C. How are you?

每題請聆聽放音機播出的英文句子之後,再從試題冊上的選項A、B、C三個選項中,選出一個與題意最相符的答案。(每題只播一次,請仔細聽。) ☛(答案請見 P.196)

1
A. You have the wrong number.
B. It's not correct.
C. I broke my tooth.

答題時間
約 **15** 秒/題

2
A. It will take you three days.
B. Three times a day; after meal, please.
C. I have three meals a day.

MP3 **2-5**

3
A. I have a cold.
B. What can go wrong?
C. You'd better see a doctor.

4
A. Too bad.
B. You need to blow your nose.
C. You have bad teeth.

5
A. My nose is running.
B. Not much.
C. Please call an ambulance.

主題 6 電話用語

Hint 快速上手句

important sentences

電話號碼的唸法及技巧

★ 在電話號碼中 "0" 讀作字母 "O"，就像在單字 "go" 中的 "O" 的發音。

★ 一個特定地區的電話，一般來說只有 7 位或 8 位數字。7 位的號碼，讀的時候前三位一組連在一起，後四位一組連在一起，中間有一個停頓，比如：
625-4598 讀作："six-two-five，four-five-nine-eight"；8 位的號碼，可以用 4 個一組來讀。

★ 兩個或三個相同的數字放在一起，可以用 "double" 或 "triple" 來代替，比如 224-6555 可以讀作："double-two-four，six-triple-five"。

★ 若號碼末尾出現 3 個零，可以用「thousand（千）」來發音，如：
979-6000 讀作："nine-seven-nine，six-thousand"。

聽力
練習
每題請聆聽放音機播出的英文句子之後,再從試題冊上的選項A、B、C 三個選項中,選出一個與題意最相符的答案。（每題只播一次,請仔細聽。）☛（答案請見 P.198）

1

A. I'm here.

B. This is Grace.

C. Hi, how are you?

答題時間 約 **15** 秒/題

MP3 **2-6**

2

A. Hello, May.

B. I'm pleased.

C. I'm sorry, but he is out.

3

A. I'll be right back.

B. Thank you. I'll call back later.

C. OK, tell me later.

4

A. Yes, please.

B. Yes, take it.

C. No, you can't.

5

A. Don't be afraid.

B. I'm terribly sorry.

C. You look terrible.

第二類 稱謂與關係

主題 7　名字、人名與職業

聽力練習 每題請聆聽放音機播出的英文句子之後，再從試題冊上的選項A、B、C 三個選項中，選出一個與題意最相符的答案。（每題只播一次，請仔細聽。）☛（答案請見 **P.200**）

1
A. It's a lucky dog.
B. We call him "Lucky."
C. My father gave him a name.

答題時間
約 **15** 秒/題

2
A. It's name is "Micky."
B. It's a "mouse."
C. I don't like it.

MP3 2-7

3
A. I'm fine. Thank you.
B. How do you do?
C. I'm a computer engineer.

4
A. Neither, I'm a vet.
B. Either a doctor or a dentist.
C. Both of them.

5
A. I am a firefighter.
B. I want to be a teacher.
C. I want to grow up.

主題 **8** 所有格關係

聽力 練習 每題請聆聽放音機播出的英文句子之後,再從試題冊上的選項A、B、C 三個選項中,選出一個與題意最相符的答案。(每題只播一次,請仔細聽。)☞(答案請見 **P.201**)

1
  A. Yes, it's new.
  B. We have a few.
  C. I think so.

答題時間 約 **15** 秒/題

2
  A. Yes, this is Jim.
  B. I don't know.
  C. I didn't know it's James'.

MP3 **2-8**

3
  A. Which one?
  B. Never think about it.
  C. It's no use.

4
  A. Yes, very well.
  B. No, he doesn't.
  C. I know what you mean.

5
  A. No. Wife.
  B. It's him.
  C. Not me.

主題 **9** 自 己

聽力練習 每題請聆聽放音機播出的英文句子之後,再從試題冊上的選項A、B、C 三個選項中,選出一個與題意最相符的答案。(每題只播一次,請仔細聽。)☛(答案請見 **P.203**)

1
A. I'm not.
B. This is Bryan calling.
C. It's me, Bryan.

答題時間 約 **15** 秒/題

2
A. Yes, I see.
B. Here I am.
C. I heard from Cathy yesterday.

MP3 **2-9**

3
A. I will.
B. I did. Sorry.
C. I brought it.

4
A. Help yourself, please.
B. Yes, I did.
C. Didn't you?

5
A. What else?
B. No, I'm the only one.
C. Yes, I need glasses.

聽力練習 每題請聆聽放音機播出的英文句子之後,再從試題冊上的選項A、B、C三個選項中,選出一個與題意最相符的答案。(每題只播一次,請仔細聽。)☛(答案請見 **P.205**)

1
A. No, I live alone in Taipei.
B. We live in Taipei.
C. Yes, I love my family.

答題時間 約 **15** 秒/題

MP3 **2-10**

2
A. Yes, with two children.
B. Yes, I'm Marian.
C. No, I'm not single.

3
A. So it's near your house?
B. So you're going for a walk?
C. So you're off now?

4
A. I want to have a computer.
B. I love surfing the net.
C. I think it's wasting time.

5
A. Why not me?
B. Sure. I'm a good swimmer.
C. Yes, she's sweet.

第三類 情境

主題 11 餐廳

Hint 快速上手句

important sentences

西餐常用字彙

牛排熟度	咖啡	可樂/披薩
rare 生的/一分熟	black 純/黑咖啡	small 小
medium rare 三分熟	with cream/milk 加奶精/加牛奶	regular 中
medium 五分熟	with sugar 加糖	large 大
medium well 七分熟	**牛排醬料**	
	black pepper 黑胡椒	
well-done 全熟	mushroom 蘑菇	
用餐地點	to go = take out　外帶 for here = eat in　內用	

聽力練習 每題請聆聽放音機播出的英文句子之後，再從試題冊上的選項A、B、C 三個選項中，選出一個與題意最相符的答案。（每題只播一次，請仔細聽。）☞（答案請見 **P.206**）

1
A. Three, please.
B. Yes, sir.
C. Are you sure?

2
A. Yes, I'll have a Sirloin steak.
B. No, you may not.
C. Here, take it.

MP3 **2-11**

3
A. Medium level.
B. In the medium.
C. Medium rare, please.

4
A. Well, I like black pepper.
B. I like sausages.
C. Yes, I sold it.

5
A. Never mind.
B. Nothing else.
C. I'll have coffee, please.

主題12 外表打扮

聽力練習 每題請聆聽放音機播出的英文句子之後，再從試題冊上的選項A、B、C三個選項中，選出一個與題意最相符的答案。（每題只播一次，請仔細聽。）☛（答案請見 **P.208**）

1
A. He's 23 years old.
B. He's very fat.
C. He's 172 cm.

答題時間 約**15**秒/題

MP3 **2-12**

2
A. My brother is taller than me.
B. He is as tall as me.
C. The tall one.

3
A. He likes sports.
B. He is a tall young man with long hair.
C. He is fine.

4
A. A purse.
B. A dress.
C. Luggage.

5
A. You're gown up.
B. Go to get a belt.
C. You should wear a tie.

結 帳

付款時的口語表達方式

1. We'll go Dutch. 我們要分開付。

2. Let me take care of the check. 我來付。

3. This is on me. 這次算我的。

4. This is on the house. 本店請客。

5. The company will pay for it. 公司會付。

6. Bill, please. （我要）買單，謝謝。

7. Where is the cashier? 在哪裡結帳？

8. Does this price include tax? 這個價錢有含稅嗎？

9. Is it duty free? 這個免稅嗎？

10. Can't you give me a discount?
    你不能給我個折扣嗎？

主題
13
情境
v
結帳

每題請聆聽放音機播出的英文句子之後，再從試題冊上的選項A、B、C三個選項中，選出一個與題意最相符的答案。（每題只播一次，請仔細聽。）☛（答案請見 **P.210**）

聽力練習

1
A. Oh, no. Let me get it.
B. Got it?
C. You'll pay for it.

答題時間
約 **15** 秒/題

2
A. Oh, thank you. I'll get the next one.
B. You can't cheat.
C. Oh, no. It's too bad.

MP3 **2-13**

3
A. One moment.
B. Is it the right amount of money?
C. I'll pay by check.

4
A. I don't want to change it.
B. Oh, keep the change.
C. Grab the chance.

5
A. Yes, it is.
B. I got a flu.
C. We have good service.

主題 14 個人好惡

聽力練習 每題請聆聽放音機播出的英文句子之後,再從試題冊上的選項A、B、C 三個選項中,選出一個與題意最相符的答案。(每題只播一次,請仔細聽。)☛(答案請見 **P.211**)

1
A. Not so good.
B. The record store is having a sale.
C. I can't sing.

答題時間 約 **15** 秒/題

MP3 **2-14**

2
A. I'd rather wear jeans than a dress.
B. What choices do we have?
C. It's on me.

3
A. I love it very much.
B. This university is famous.
C. You're unlike me.

4
A. Just a haircut.
B. Cut it short all over.
C. I'd like a shampoo.

5
A. Yes, I do. I'll go there one day.
B. I'll be there in a second.
C. I visited the city several times.

第四類 數字

主題 15　　　　詢　價

Hint
快速上手句

討價還價的慣用表達

1. Would you lower the price?
   你可以算便宜一點嗎？

2. Could you cut the price a little?
   你可以少算一點嗎？

3. Can you give me a discount?
   你可以給我個折扣嗎？

4. Sorry, it's one price for all.
   抱歉，大家都是付這個價的。

5. Our price are all fixed.
   我們都是不二價。

6. I'll buy it if it's under 50 dollars.
   如果這不到 50 元我就買。

聽力
練習 每題請聆聽放音機播出的英文句子之後，再從試題冊上的選項A、B、C三個選項中，選出一個與題意最相符的答案。（每題只播一次，請仔細聽。）☛（答案請見 **P.213**）

1
A. It's about $1,200 for one night.
B. We'll stay for 3 nights.
C. This is for rent.

MP3 2-15

2
A. Three meals a day.
B. $100 a meal.
C. No, they aren't.

3
A. Can I change to another room?
B. I have a 25-cent coin.
C. US$25.00 a week.

4
A. Oh, it's free.
B. Oh, you have to pay in cash.
C. Should I?

5
A. You're worth it.
B. I have a lot of it.
C. Yes, I bought you a coat.

主題 16 例行時間

聽力練習 每題請聆聽放音機播出的英文句子之後,再從試題冊上的選項A、B、C三個選項中,選出一個與題意最相符的答案。(每題只播一次,請仔細聽。)☛(答案請見 **P.215**)

1
A. Why did you get up so early?
B. It's time to go to bed.
C. I usually get up at six thirty.

答題時間 約 **15** 秒/題

MP3 **2-16**

2
A. At the store.
B. At ten o'clock, sir.
C. The store is open.

3
A. Keep early hours.
B. It is 9:00 a.m. to 5:30 p.m.
C. I worked from 9:00 a.m. to 5:30 p.m. yesterday.

4
A. 9:25 on Platform 2.
B. It takes 9 hours by train.
C. We will leave Los Angeles by 9 o'clock.

5
A. About ten minutes.
B. About ten meters.
C. About ten long ropes.

主題 17	時間約定

聽力
練習
每題請聆聽放音機播出的英文句子之後,再從試題冊上的選項A、B、C 三個選項中,選出一個與題意最相符的答案。(每題只播一次,請仔細聽。)☞(答案請見 P.217)

1
A. At 9:00 last night.
B. Nothing is right.
C. I'm afraid not.

答題時間 約 **15** 秒/題

MP3 **2-17**

2
A. The house is made out of wood.
B. Just a second. I'll have to check.
C. OK. I'll check the house.

3
A. Yeah, I will be here.
B. Will you come tonight?
C. Yes, I can hear.

4
A. OK, bye.
B. I come back home at 5:00 in the evening.
C. Did you see?

5
A. You name the time.
B. Ten times.
C. In old times.

主題 18 詢問時間

聽力練習 每題請聆聽放音機播出的英文句子之後,再從試題冊上的選項A、B、C三個選項中,選出一個與題意最相符的答案。(每題只播一次,請仔細聽。)☛(答案請見 **P.218**)

1
A. It's one o'clock sharp.
B. Don't touch. It's sharp.
C. Don't ask.

答題時間 約 **15** 秒/題

2
A. Can't you?
B. Are you sure?
C. Sure. It's twenty to nine.

MP3 **2-18**

3
A. It's two hundred and twenty.
B. It's two twenty.
C. Two times twenty is forty.

4
A. I don't think it is five o'clock yet.
B. I don't think so.
C. No wonder.

5
A. My watch says two o'clock.
B. Watch what you say.
C. Watch out.

第五類 慣用句型

聽力練習 每題請聆聽放音機播出的英文句子之後,再從試題冊上的選項A、B、C三個選項中,選出一個與題意最相符的答案。(每題只播一次,請仔細聽。)☞(答案請見 **P.220**)

1
A. I'm in Hualian.
B. I live in Korea.
C. I live in school housing.

約 **15** 秒/題

答題時間

MP3 **2-19**

2
A. Not me.
B. Not yet.
C. I can't.

3
A. We're on the bus.
B. You're right.
C. We're right here.

4
A. Do you like spaghetti?
B. I know that place.
C. How pretty!

5
A. People around the world know about it.
B. Indonesia has the most islands in the world.
C. Is it China?

主題 20 詢問方法

聽力練習

每題請聆聽放音機播出的英文句子之後,再從試題冊上的選項A、B、C 三個選項中,選出一個與題意最相符的答案。(每題只播一次,請仔細聽。)☛(答案請見 **P.222**)

1
A. Just take a chance.
B. My father drives me to school.
C. Take it easy.

答題時間 約 **15** 秒/題

2
A. Go ahead.
B. I'll take it.
C. Take bus 202.

MP3 2-20

3
A. By MRT.
B. It's by the zoo.
C. By heart.

4
A. Here is $2,000 cash.
B. Here you come!
C. Here we are!

5
A. You can leave now.
B. I'm doing housework.
C. I'd like to see the ties.

主題 21　詢問原因

Hint 快速上手句

important sentences

解釋語氣的開頭表達方式

1. There's a (good) reason for this...
   我做這件事的理由是……。

2. Here's what happened...
   事情是這樣的，……。

3. Let me tell you why...
   讓我來告訴你為什麼……。

4. Let me explain...
   讓我來解釋……。

5. The reason is...
   理由是……。

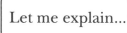

Let me explain...

聽力練習 每題請聆聽放音機播出的英文句子之後，再從試題冊上的選項A、B、C三個選項中，選出一個與題意最相符的答案。（每題只播一次，請仔細聽。）☛（答案請見 P.223）

答題時間 約 **15** 秒/題

MP3 2-21

主題 **21** 慣用句型 v 詢問原因

1
A. Excuse me.
B. You'll be sorry.
C. Did you catch a cold?

2
A. I did it myself.
B. That sounds great.
C. Nothing.

3
A. I was ... um ... busy.
B. I came by a taxi.
C. Yeah, sure.

4
A. Why me again?
B. That's right.
C. Don't mention it.

5
A. It's cool!
B. Why not use a comb?
C. Why not?

感官動詞

感官動詞的慣用表達方式

◆常見的感官動詞：
see/hear/smell/taste/watch/feel

❶ 感官動詞的用法：

1. 感官動詞＋形容詞：
   I **feel** cold. 我覺得冷。

2. 感官動詞＋名詞：
   I **heard** the thunder. 我聽到了雷聲。

3. 感官動詞＋受詞＋原形動詞／V-ing：
   I **saw** the train come/coming into the platform.
   我看到火車進站了。

❷ 特殊用法：

4. 感官動詞＋like＋名詞：……起來像～
   You **look like** a doctor. 你看起來像個醫生。
   She **felt like** a fool. 她覺得自己像個笨蛋。

聽力練習 每題請聆聽放音機播出的英文句子之後,再從試題冊上的選項A、B、C 三個選項中,選出一個與題意最相符的答案。(每題只播一次,請仔細聽。) ☞ (答案請見 **P.225**)

1
A. OK. I'm here.
B. Yes, very well.
C. I'm pretty well, thank you.

答題時間
約 **15** 秒/題

MP3 2-22

2
A. I can't hear it.
B. It smells good.
C. It smells like garbage.

3
A. Never. You just surprised me.
B. I'll never see you again.
C. I have a sore throat.

4
A. How does it feel?
B. Then why not stay longer?
C. How do you feel?

5
A. Yeah, I can't feel my feet anymore.
B. It's not good for you.
C. I'm not feeling well.

主題 **22** 慣用句型 Ⅴ ⒋感官動詞+to+名詞……起來像~

主題 **23** 驚訝與驚喜

important sentences

Hint
快速上手句

驚呼的口語慣用表達

Oh, my goodness!

1. Hooray! = Yippee!
   萬歲！(歡呼聲)

2. Oops! = Oh, no!
   糟糕！

3. Ouch!
   唉唷！痛啊！

4. Yuck! = Gross!
   討厭！噁心！

5. Oh, my goodness!
   噢，天啊！

每題請聆聽放音機播出的英文句子之後,再從試題冊上的選項A、B、C 三個選項中,選出一個與題意最相符的答案。(每題只播一次,請仔細聽。)☞(答案請見 P.227)

1
A. What a surprise!
B. You can't do this.
C. It's mine.

答題時間 約 **15** 秒/題

MP3 2-23

2
A. What's the matter?
B. Do you believe it?
C. How can you do this?

3
A. That's surprising. He's never late.
B. Why were you late?
C. Give me one second.

4
A. Are you joking? She looks so young.
B. No kidding? She's your sister?
C. Wow. What a good kid!

5
A. I'm afraid it is.
B. Yes, it's real.
C. For real this time?

主題 24 命令與警告

聽力練習　每題請聆聽放音機播出的英文句子之後，再從試題冊上的選項A、B、C 三個選項中，選出一個與題意最相符的答案。（每題只播一次，請仔細聽。）☛（答案請見 **P.228**）

1
A. You're too careful.
B. I do care.
C. Yes. What is it?

答題時間 約 **15** 秒/題

MP3 **2-24**

2
A. OK. OK.
B. Come on. Let's leave.
C. Go away.

3
A. Would you hand me that vase?
B. Hey, take it easy.
C. It's as easy as pie.

4
A. I won't.
B. I'm sorry.
C. I forgot.

5
A. Oh, thank you.
B. Better safe than sorry!
C. How are you?

主題 25 　　　　催促與延緩

聽力練習 每題請聆聽放音機播出的英文句子之後，再從試題冊上的選項A、B、C 三個選項中，選出一個與題意最相符的答案。（每題只播一次，請仔細聽。）☛（答案請見 **P.230**）

1
A. OK, coming.
B. Good luck!
C. Take your time.

答題時間 約 **15** 秒/題

2
A. Sure. What is it?
B. Slow down.
C. Don't push me.

MP3 **2-25**

3
A. Oh, I'm sorry.
B. How could you?
C. Wait a minute.

4
A. Oh, good. We still have time.
B. The game is over now.
C. Where are we going?

5
A. Don't worry.
B. Don't take too long.
C. I'm late for the bus.

主題 **26**　　　　　　拒　絕

每題請聆聽放音機播出的英文句子之後,再從試題冊上的選項A、B、C 三個選項中,選出一個與題意最相符的答案。(每題只播一次,請仔細聽。)☞(答案請見 **P.232**)

1
  A. No way.
  B. That's nothing.
  C. That's not true.

2
  A. We need to get help.
  B. No way.
  C. No, but thank you anyway.

MP3 **2-26**

3
  A. That's too bad!
  B. Do you need a hand?
  C. Any questions?

4
  A. That's not possible.
  B. See you tomorrow.
  C. I haven't finished it.

5
  A. No, that's all for now.
  B. I'm tired now.
  C. Excuse me.

主題27 道謝

聽力練習 每題請聆聽放音機播出的英文句子之後,再從試題冊上的選項A、B、C 三個選項中,選出一個與題意最相符的答案。(每題只播一次,請仔細聽。) ☞(答案請見 **P.233**)

1
　A. Anytime.
　B. I'm glad to hear that.
　C. No, I didn't do anything.

答題時間 約 **15** 秒/題

2
　A. It's my pleasure.
　B. As you pleased.
　C. You are wonderful.

MP3 2-27

3
　A. What do you like to play?
　B. I'm glad to hear that.
　C. I'm so glad for you.

4
　A. It's just what I want. Thank you.
　B. I will do what I can.
　C. It was nothing like that.

5
　A. Don't worry. I will help you.
　B. Sit down, please.
　C. Thanks. You're very kind.

主題 28　讚　美

讚嘆的慣用表達方式

1. Good job! 做得好！
2. (Very) well done! 做得好！
3. Way to go! 真棒！
4. Nice going! 真棒！
5. Looking good! 看起來很棒！
6. How nice! 真棒！

Way to go!!

快速上手句

Hint

important sentences

聽力
練習

每題請聆聽放音機播出的英文句子之後,再從試題冊上的選項A、B、C 三個選項中,選出一個與題意最相符的答案。(每題只播一次,請仔細聽。) ☞(答案請見 **P.235**)

1

A. That's nice.

B. You're nice.

C. It's a nice boat.

MP3 **2-28**

2

A. Good for you!

B. Great. Let's do together.

C. OK, that's all.

3

A. Um, it smells good.

B. I'm dying for a drink.

C. What would you like for dinner?

4

A. Just look at what you've done.

B. Take it or leave it.

C. It's delicious!

5

A. Really? You are?

B. Well done.

C. Cheer up!

道 歉

聽力練習　每題請聆聽放音機播出的英文句子之後，再從試題冊上的選項 A、B、C 三個選項中，選出一個與題意最相符的答案。（每題只播一次，請仔細聽。）☛（答案請見 **P.236**）

1
A. You'll be sorry.
B. What kept you so long?
C. What for?

答題時間 約 **15** 秒/題

MP3 **2-29**

2
A. OK, see you tomorrow.
B. I had better go by myself.
C. I'm out of here.

3
A. I'll give you a call.
B. What do you call it?
C. OK, put it through.

4
A. Let me think about it.
B. Forget it.
C. Never.

5
A. I will do my best.
B. Sorry. Let me treat you a coffee.
C. You got it.

主題 30 安撫與鼓勵

Hint
快速上手句

important sentences

鼓勵的慣用表達方式

1. Have a try! 試試看吧！

2. Have a go! 試試看吧！

3. Try again! 再試一次吧！

4. Go for it! 就去做吧！

5. You can do it (if you try)!
   試試看，你可以做到的！

6. Trust me! You can make it!
   相信我！你可以做到的！

You can do it!

聽力練習　每題請聆聽放音機播出的英文句子之後，再從試題冊上的選項A、B、C 三個選項中，選出一個與題意最相符的答案。（每題只播一次，請仔細聽。）☞（答案請見 P.238）

MP3 **2-30**

1
A. That's good news.
B. Did he agree?
C. I'm fine.

2
A. That's OK. Did you get hurt?
B. Please don't hurt me!
C. The cup is broken.

3
A. Surly you will.
B. Come on this way.
C. Come on. Give it a try.

4
A. Go ahead. Don't worry about me.
B. Sure. Take a chance.
C. You'll never know until you do it.

5
A. Better late than never.
B. Hurry up.
C. What's this for?

主題 31 表示不介意

聽力練習 每題請聆聽放音機播出的英文句子之後,再從試題冊上的選項 A、B、C 三個選項中,選出一個與題意最相符的答案。(每題只播一次,請仔細聽。)☛(答案請見 **P.239**)

1
A. It's okay.
B. Please say it again.
C. You're welcome.

答題時間 約 **15** 秒/題

MP3 2-31

2
A. Never mind.
B. What would you like?
C. Don't talk to me.

3
A. It happens.
B. I'm doing fine.
C. It's nothing important, really.

4
A. Don't talk too much.
B. It's not important.
C. No, go ahead.

5
A. Oh, that's no problem.
B. I just want to help.
C. I have no idea.

聽力練習　每題請聆聽放音機播出的英文句子之後，再從試題冊上的選項A、B、C三個選項中，選出一個與題意最相符的答案。（每題只播一次，請仔細聽。）☛（答案請見 **P.241**）

1
A. It's all done.
B. I guess so.
C. I'll write it down.

答題時間 約 **15** 秒/題

2
A. That all depends on what it is.
B. You're welcome.
C. I'm fine.

MP3 **2-32**

3
A. There's only half an hour left.
B. Sooner or later.
C. I guess "forever".

4
A. I just want to help people.
B. Well, I did get an A.
C. I will cheer for you!

5
A. We should work hard everyday.
B. I don't go to work on weekends.
C. No, but maybe the teacher won't ask for it.

主題 33 尋求認同

聽力練習 每題請聆聽放音機播出的英文句子之後,再從試題冊上的選項A、B、C 三個選項中,選出一個與題意最相符的答案。(每題只播一次,請仔細聽。) ☞（答案請見 P.242）

1
A. I can't believe it, either.
B. But it's true.
C. But we are leaving.

答題時間 約 **15** 秒/題

2
A. You did a great job.
B. May I take a picture of you?
C. I'd like some more, please.

MP3 **2-33**

3
A. Yes, go ahead.
B. Do you play golf?
C. It's better than nothing.

4
A. Sure. He's our friend.
B. I'm sorry.
C. It's terrible.

5
A. Do you think I'm stupid?
B. Why are you doing this?
C. Of course you can.

表達認同

聽力練習 每題請聆聽放音機播出的英文句子之後，再從試題冊上的選項Ａ、Ｂ、Ｃ三個選項中，選出一個與題意最相符的答案。（每題只播一次，請仔細聽。）☛（答案請見 **P.244**）

1
A. I want some cookies.
B. I like to read a book on weekends.
C. You're right.

2
A. It was great.
B. Yeah, I went.
C. What a great idea.

3
A. Yeah, it's my plan.
B. It seems great!
C. I agree.

4
A. Yes, very much.
B. Yes, it's very noisy.
C. Yes, we're alike.

5
A. Yes, Luke won the first place in the game.
B. Yes, she has a warm heart.
C. Yes, I think so too.

主題 35 不完全肯定

聽力練習 每題請聆聽放音機播出的英文句子之後,再從試題冊上的選項A、B、C三個選項中,選出一個與題意最相符的答案。(每題只播一次,請仔細聽。) ☛(答案請見 **P.246**)

1
A. I don't know she's divorced.
B. Is she getting better?
C. Is that true?

答題時間 約 **15** 秒/題

2
A. Thanks. Don't bother.
B. I'm not myself today.
C. Do you think so?

MP3 **2-35**

3
A. Yes, we'll be there.
B. I hope so.
C. Are you sure?

4
A. I like Seattle best.
B. Oh, I've been to lots of countries.
C. It's hard to say. Each country is different.

5
A. It seemed that way at first.
B. Are they?
C. I'm not Chinese.

不認同

Hint 快速上手句

Important sentences

不認同對方看法的表達方式

1. I can't go along with what you say.
   我無法同意你所說的。

2. I don't agree with your point.
   我不同意你的論點。

3. I don't think so.
   我不這麼認為。

4. I don't see it that way.
   我不這麼想。

5. I'm not sure.
   我不確定。

每題請聆聽放音機播出的英文句子之後,再從試題冊上的選項A、B、C三個選項中,選出一個與題意最相符的答案。(每題只播一次,請仔細聽。)☞(答案請見 P.247)

主題
36
強調短句 v 不認同

1

A. Of course we can.

B. Trust me, you can make it.

C. Believe it or not.

答題時間 約 **15** 秒/題

MP3 2-36

2

A. No, you may not.

B. It's no use. He won't listen to you.

C. He kept on smoking all the time.

3

A. It's the right time.

B. She will never sell her car.

C. It's impossible.

4

A. Sorry to let you down.

B. No, I don't have a fax machine.

C. I believe in you.

5

A. Never think about it.

B. OK, I'll give it a try.

C. I can't forgive you.

提供或尋求協助

提供協助

- Do you need any help? 你需要幫忙嗎？
- How can I help you? 我可以怎麼幫你？
- Would you like me to...? 你要我……嗎？
- Let me... 讓我……。

接受

- I'd appreciate it. 我很感激。
- Would (could) you...? 你可以……嗎？

回絕

- It's OK, I can do it. 沒關係，我可以。
- No, but thank you anyway. 不用，但還是謝謝你。
- I'd rather/I'd better do it myself.
  我寧可／最好自己做。
- Thanks, I can manage. 謝謝，我可以應付。

主題
37
強調短句 ∨

提供或尋求協助

每題請聆聽放音機播出的英文句子之後，再從試題冊上的選項A、B、C三個選項中，選出一個與題意最相符的答案。（每題只播一次，請仔細聽。）☞（答案請見 **P.249**）

1
A. No, do it yourself.
B. This will help.
C. There's no hope for me.

答題時間
約 **15** 秒/題

2
A. Let me think it over.
B. Sorry, I don't have a watch.
C. I've got plenty of time.

MP3 **2-37**

3
A. No, don't bother.
B. Turn right here.
C. You have no right to do this.

4
A. Yes, please. That would be very kind of you.
B. We need to get help.
C. This is difficult.

5
A. It's not the answer.
B. I'll help you.
C. If you wouldn't mind.

主題 **38** 請求許可與允諾

每題請聆聽放音機播出的英文句子之後，再從試題冊上的選項 A、B、C 三個選項中，選出一個與題意最相符的答案。（每題只播一次，請仔細聽。）☞（答案請見 **P.250**）

1
A. It's tea time.
B. It depends on you.
C. The tea is really hot.

2
A. Get me some, please.
B. I'd love some. Thanks.
C. Please help yourself.

MP3 **2-38**

3
A. Sure. Come follow me.
B. Oh, I can't believe you're saying this.
C. We don't have enough money.

4
A. No, go ahead.
B. Save it!
C. I didn't mean to do it.

5
A. Try me.
B. It fitted you very well.
C. Why not?

100

主題 39 建議

聽力練習 每題請聆聽放音機播出的英文句子之後，再從試題冊上的選項A、B、C三個選項中，選出一個與題意最相符的答案。（每題只播一次，請仔細聽。）☞（答案請見 **P.252**）

1
A. We'll have dinner at 7:00.
B. How about watching a movie?
C. How about eating out?

答題時間 約 **15** 秒/題

2
A. Come out and play!
B. I'll buy the tickets.
C. That's a good idea.

MP3 **2-39**

3
A. Why don't you learn?
B. You knew it.
C. How did you know?

4
A. Bring an umbrella.
B. I don't like this.
C. You might want to try this.

5
A. Yes, I'll go.
B. No. It's only a three-minute walk.
C. You should take the chance.

主題 40　　　　　　　　確　認

聽力練習　每題請聆聽放音機播出的英文句子之後，再從試題冊上的選項 A、B、C 三個選項中，選出一個與題意最相符的答案。（每題只播一次，請仔細聽。）☞（答案請見 P.254）

1
A. He didn't say.
B. He'll be back.
C. I happened to overhear what he said.

答題時間 約 **15** 秒/題

MP3 **2-40**

2
A. I'll start right away.
B. No chance at all.
C. How many?

3
A. This shirt is very colorful.
B. Can you order one for me?
C. No more excuses.

4
A. I mean it's expensive.
B. I know what you mean.
C. I really mean it.

5
A. How was your show?
B. Can't you see me?
C. Yeah? Tell me more about it.

全民英檢聽力測驗

第一部分　第二部分　第三部分　第四部分

簡短對話

作答提示

▶ 每題請聆聽放音機播出的一段對話和相關問題之後，再從試題冊上 [A] [B] [C] 三個選項中，選出一個與題意最相符的答案。
（每題只播出一次，請仔細聆聽）

簡短對話

主題 **1** 問 > 什麼地方

聽力練習 每題請聆聽放音機播出的一段對話和相關問題後,再從試題冊上 A、B、C 三個選項中,選出一個與題意最相符的答案。(每題只播一次,請仔細聽。) ☛(答案請見 **P.256**)

Conversation 1.

A. Taipei Train Station.

B. The taxi stand.

C. The bus stop.

答題時間 約 **15** 秒/題

MP3 **3-1**

Conversation 2.

A. At Cindy's home.

B. At his home.

C. At the park.

Conversation 3.

A. Paris.

B. Beijing.

C. She hasn't decided where to go yet.

Conversation 4.

A. In Taiwan.

B. In London.

C. In America.

主題 2 問 > 什麼人

聽力練習 每題請聆聽放音機播出的一段對話和相關問題後,再從試題冊上 A、B、C 三個選項中,選出一個與題意最相符的答案。(每題只播一次,請仔細聽。)☞(答案請見 P.258)

Conversation 1.

A. Jenny.

B. The library.

C. Ted.

答題時間 約 **15** 秒/題

MP3 3-2

Conversation 2.

A. The man.

B. The woman.

C. Neither of them.

Conversation 3.

A. The woman.

B. The man.

C. Both of them.

Conversation 4.

A. Both of them like it.

B. Neither of them liked it.

C. His mother liked it, but his father didn't.

問 > 什麼種類

聽力練習 每題請聆聽放音機播出的一段對話和相關問題後,再從試題冊上 A、B、C 三個選項中,選出一個與題意最相符的答案。(每題只播一次,請仔細聽。)☛(答案請見 **P.260**)

Conversation 1.

A. Math.

B. A novel.

C. A test paper.

約 **15** 秒/題 答題時間

MP3 3-3

Conversation 2.

A. Soda.

B. Milk.

C. Fruit juice.

Conversation 3.

A. She is good at English spelling.

B. The spelling contest.

C. Betty is nervous.

Conversation 4.

A. Find a bookstore.

B. Write homework.

C. Get some food.

主題 **4**

問 > 做什麼

聽力練習 每題請聆聽放音機播出的一段對話和相關問題後，再從試題冊上 A、B、C 三個選項中，選出一個與題意最相符的答案。（每題只播一次，請仔細聽。） ☞（答案請見 **P.262**）

Conversation 1.

A. Go to the movie theater.
B. Watch TV.
C. Play volleyball.

答題時間
約 **15** 秒/題

Conversation 2.

A. He had dinner with Ann.
B. He went to Ann's party.
C. He threw a birthday party.

MP3 3-4

Conversation 3.

A. To go shopping with her.
B. To get more money.
C. To buy some fruit.

Conversation 4.

A. To help him get some food.
B. To have some more food.
C. To drink some tea.

主題 5 　問 > 點鐘・時間

聽力練習　每題請聆聽放音機播出的一段對話和相關問題後，再從試題冊上 A、B、C 三個選項中，選出一個與題意最相符的答案。（每題只播一次，請仔細聽。）☛（答案請見 P.264）

Conversation 1.

    A. At 5:45.

    B. At 5:35.

    C. At 5:30.

答題時間 約 **15** 秒/題

MP3 3-5

Conversation 2.

    A. It's ten o'clock.

    B. It's a quarter past ten.

    C. It's a quarter to ten.

Conversation 3.

    A. At 10:00 p.m.

    B. At 9:00 a.m.

    C. At 9:00 p.m.

Conversation 4.

    A. 9:00 a.m. to 6:00 p.m.

    B. 9:00 a.m. to 12:00 a.m.

    C. It is closed.

主題 6 | 問 > 日期

每題請聆聽放音機播出的一段對話和相關問題後,再從試題冊上 A、B、C 三個選項中,選出一個與題意最相符的答案。(每題只播一次,請仔細聽。) ☞ (答案請見 P.266)

Conversation 1.
A. It's Monday.
B. It's Sunday.
C. It's Saturday.

答題時間 約 **15** 秒/題

MP3 3-6

Conversation 2.
A. Today.
B. Not Friday.
C. On Friday.

Conversation 3.
A. On Wednesday.
B. Any day.
C. Next week.

Conversation 4.
A. In March.
B. In April.
C. On March 4.

問 > 季節 · 月分 · 氣候

聽力
練習 每題請聆聽放音機播出的一段對話和相關問題後,再從試題冊上 A、B、C 三個選項中,選出一個與題意最相符的答案。(每題只播一次,請仔細聽。)☛(答案請見 P.268)

Conversation 1.

A. Spring and summer.

B. Spring.

C. Summer.

約 **15** 秒/題

MP3 **3-7**

Conversation 2.

A. It's freezing and rainy.

B. It's sunny and hot.

C. It's freezing but sunny.

Conversation 3.

A. December.

B. January.

C. February.

Conversation 4.

A. January.

B. February.

C. November.

主題 8　問 > 數字與計算問題

聽力練習 每題請聆聽放音機播出的一段對話和相關問題後，再從試題冊上 A、B、C 三個選項中，選出一個與題意最相符的答案。（每題只播一次，請仔細聽。）☞（答案請見 **P.270**）

答題時間 約 **15** 秒/題

MP3 **3-8**

Conversation 1.

A. 3218-5467.
B. 3218-6574.
C. 3281-6547.

Conversation 2.

A. She is fifteen years old.
B. She is 3 years younger than Tim.
C. She is 3 years older than Tim.

Conversation 3.

A. $200.
B. $300.
C. $150.

Conversation 4.

A. Seven thirty.
B. Seven twenty-three.
C. Seven thirty-seven.

比 較

每題請聆聽放音機播出的一段對話和相關問題後，再從試題冊上 A、B、C 三個選項中，選出一個與題意最相符的答案。（每題只播一次，請仔細聽。）☛（答案請見 **P.273**）

Conversation 1.

    A. Ben is younger.

    B. Mary is younger.

    C. They're of the same age.

MP3 **3-9**

Conversation 2.

    A. Jane.

    B. Mary.

    C. Rebecca.

Conversation 3.

    A. He wants a sheep.

    B. He wants a bigger sheet of paper.

    C. He wants a smaller sheet of paper.

Conversation 4.

    A. The dress.

    B. The blouse.

    C. The handbag.

主題 10　Yes-No 問題

聽力練習 每題請聆聽放音機播出的一段對話和相關問題後，再從試題冊上 A、B、C 三個選項中，選出一個與題意最相符的答案。（每題只播一次，請仔細聽。）☛（答案請見 **P.275**）

Conversation 1.

    A. Yes, he did.

    B. No, he didn't.

    C. We don't know.

答題時間 約 **15** 秒/題

MP3 **3-10**

Conversation 2.

    A. No, she didn't.

    B. Yes, she did.

    C. Yes, she worked in a library for three months.

Conversation 3.

    A. No, she doesn't like working.

    B. Yes, she has to work.

    C. No, she has to work.

Conversation 4.

    A. He can't find his mother.

    B. Yes, he can.

    C. No, he can't.

主題 11 混淆音

每題請聆聽放音機播出的一段對話和相關問題後，再從試題冊上 A、B、C 三個選項中，選出一個與題意最相符的答案。（每題只播一次，請仔細聽。）☛（答案請見 P.277）

Conversation 1.

A. Stephen.

B. Ms. Smith.

C. Sandy.

Conversation 2.

A. Blake.

B. Frank.

C. Eric.

Conversation 3.

A. A dog.

B. A coat.

D. A cat.

Conversation 4.

A. A cellphone.

B. A pair of shoes.

C. We don't know.

答題時間
約 **15** 秒/題

MP3 3-11

主題 12 推 測

聽力
練習 每題請聆聽放音機播出的一段對話和相關問題後，再從試題冊上 A、B、C 三個選項中，選出一個與題意最相符的答案。（每題只播一次，請仔細聽。）☛（答案請見 P.279）

Conversation 1.

    A. In a restarant.

    B. In a toy shop.

    C. In a shoe store.

Conversation 2.

    A. He will open the door.

    B. He will answer the door.

    C. He will close the door.

MP3 **3-12**

Conversation 3.

    A. She's a student.

    B. She's a teacher.

    C. She studies English.

Conversation 4.

    A. She works at midnight.

    B. She works at home.

    C. She works as a writer.

健 康

每題請聆聽放音機播出的一段對話和相關問題後，再從試題冊上 A、B、C 三個選項中，選出一個與題意最相符的答案。（每題只播一次，請仔細聽。）☛（答案請見 **P.282**）

Conversation 1.

A. He's bad.

B. He's a doctor.

C. He got a stomachache.

MP3 3-13

Conversation 2.

A. She is sick.

B. She is wrong.

C. She is not home.

Conversation 3.

A. The man.

B. The woman.

C. The man's mother.

Conversation 4.

A. Father and daughter.

B. Doctor and patient.

C. Teacher and student.

主題 14 會面與道別

聽力練習 每題請聆聽放音機播出的一段對話和相關問題後,再從試題冊上 A、B、C 三個選項中,選出一個與題意最相符的答案。(每題只播一次,請仔細聽。) ☛(答案請見 **P.284**)

Conversation 1.
A. Clair.
B. Lisa.
C. Holly.

答題時間 約 **15** 秒/題

MP3 3-14

Conversation 2.
A. At Julie's home.
B. At the party.
C. In Joe's car.

Conversation 3.
A. He's saying goodbye.
B. He's driving.
C. He is going to stay longer.

Conversation 4.
A. She will be leaving by 3 o'clock.
B. She has a piano class.
C. She has a piano.

用　餐

聽力練習　每題請聆聽放音機播出的一段對話和相關問題後，再從試題冊上 A、B、C 三個選項中，選出一個與題意最相符的答案。（每題只播一次，請仔細聽。）☞（答案請見 **P.287**）

Conversation 1.

A. Some bread and water.

B. Some cake and coffee.

C. Some cake and water.

Conversation 2.

A. She feels hungry.

B. She feels like eating some dessert.

C. She feels full.

MP3 **3-15**

Conversation 3.

A. Pizza and spaghetti.

B. Fried chicken and soda.

C. Rice and fish.

Conversation 4.

A. Cola and coffee.

B. Coffee and cake.

C. Pancake and sandwiches.

主題 16 購 物

聽力
練習
每題請聆聽放音機播出的一段對話和相關問題後,再從試題冊上 A、B、C 三個選項中,選出一個與題意最相符的答案。(每題只播一次,請仔細聽。) ☛(答案請見 P.290)

Conversation 1.

　　A. A shirt.

　　B. A jacket.

　　C. A coat.

答題時間 約 **15** 秒/題

Conversation 2.

　　A. He's a police officer.

　　B. He's a shop salesman.

　　C. He's a fashion designer.

MP3 3-16

Conversation 3.

　　A. He doesn't look good on them.

　　B. They are too big.

　　C. They are too small.

Conversation 4.

　　A. In a book shop.

　　B. In a library.

　　C. In a record store.

約定・預約

每題請聆聽放音機播出的一段對話和相關問題後,再從試題冊上 A、B、C 三個選項中,選出一個與題意最相符的答案。(每題只播一次,請仔細聽。)☛(答案請見 **P.292**)

Conversation 1.

A. She is Miss Yu.

B. She is the man's Miss Right.

C. We don't know.

MP3 **3-17**

Conversation 2.

A. Mr. Ford.

B. No. 4.

C. The dentist.

Conversation 3.

A. The day after tomorrow.

B. Tomorrow.

C. Today.

Conversation 4.

A. On June 6.

B. By plane.

C. Ride a train.

主題 18 學 校

聽力練習 每題請聆聽放音機播出的一段對話和相關問題後，再從試題冊上 A、B、C 三個選項中，選出一個與題意最相符的答案。（每題只播一次，請仔細聽。）☞（答案請見 **P.295**）

Conversation 1.

A. Neither English nor math is interesting.

B. Math.

C. English.

MP3 **3-18**

Conversation 2.

A. She begins to learn Japanese.

B. She has learned Japanese for two years.

C. She met a very good Japanese teacher.

Conversation 3.

A. To the English teachers' office.

B. To the third floor.

C. To the Chinese teachers' office.

Conversation 4.

A. It was 95.

B. It was less than 95.

C. It was 98.

主題 19　工　作

每題請聆聽放音機播出的一段對話和相關問題後，再從試題冊上 A、B、C 三個選項中，選出一個與題意最相符的答案。（每題只播一次，請仔細聽。）☞（答案請見 P.297）

Conversation 1.

    A. She is a nurse.

    B. She is looking for a job.

    C. She is a housewife.

答題時間 約 **15** 秒/題

MP3 3-19

Conversation 2.

    A. He has a meeting on Tuesday.

    B. He is unhappy with the meeting.

    C. The manager is angry.

Conversation 3.

    A. About finding a job.

    B. About hopes.

    C. About running a company.

Conversation 4.

    A. An artist.

    B. A pianist.

    C. We don't know.

主題 20 社交

聽力練習 每題請聆聽放音機播出的一段對話和相關問題後,再從試題冊上 A、B、C 三個選項中,選出一個與題意最相符的答案。(每題只播一次,請仔細聽。) ☛ (答案請見 **P.299**)

答題時間 約 **15** 秒/題

MP3 **3-20**

Conversation 1.

A. Cookies and cake.

B. Some drinks.

C. Bread.

Conversation 2.

A. To help him get some food.

B. To have some more food.

C. To leave some food.

Conversation 3.

A. She doesn't like dancing.

B. She doesn't like people in there.

C. She doesn't like people smoking in there.

Conversation 4.

A. Singer and audience.

B. Shop owner and customer.

C. Host and guest.

全民英檢聽力測驗

第一部分　第二部分　第三部分　第四部分

短文聽解

作答提示

▶ 每題請聆聽放音機播出的英文內容之後，再從試題冊上的選項 [A] [B] [C] 三張圖片中，選出一個最適當的答案。

（每題只播出一次，請仔細聆聽）

短文聽解

第 一 類 廣播

主題 1　交通工具上

課前暖身　以下是這類題型的經典問句。請先瀏覽一次，對稍後的聽力訓練會有很大的幫助喔！

經典問句

問法 ❶ Where does the talk take place?

單字補充 take place 發生；舉行

聽力練習　每題請聆聽放音機播出的英文內容之後，再從試題冊上的選項 A、B、C 三張圖片中，選出一個最適當的答案。☛（答案請見 P.302）

答題時間
約 **10** 秒/題

Q1

MP3 **4-1**

（每題只播一次，請仔細聽。）

A.

B.

C.

Q2

MP3 **4-1**

（每題只播一次，請仔細聽。）

A.

B.

C.

Q3

MP3 **4-1**

（每題只播一次，請仔細聽。）

A.

B.

C.

課前
暖身

以下是這類題型的經典問句。請先瀏覽一次，對稍後的聽力訓練會
有很大的幫助喔！

經典問句

問法 **1** Where can you hear this talk?

問法 **2** What might be the background?

　　　單字補充 background 背景

聽力
練習

每題請聆聽放音機播出的英文內容之後，再從試題冊上的選項 A、
B、C 三張圖片中，選出一個最適當的答案。☛（答案請見 **P. 305**）

答題時間
約 **10** 秒/題

Q1

MP3 **4-2**

（每題只播一次，請仔細聽。）

A.

B.

C.

Q2

MP3 **4-2**

（每題只播一次，請仔細聽。）

A.

B.

C.

Q3

MP3 **4-2**

（每題只播一次，請仔細聽。）

A.

B.

C.

主題 **3**	**百貨公司・賣場**

課前暖身 以下是這類題型的經典問句。請先瀏覽一次，對稍後的聽力訓練會有很大的幫助喔！

 經典問句

問法① Where will you most probably hear this announcement?

　　單字補充 probably 大概，可能

問法② At what place might you hear this announcement?

　　單字補充 announcement 公告；宣布

聽力練習 每題請聆聽放音機播出的英文內容之後，再從試題冊上的選項 A、B、C 三張圖片中，選出一個最適當的答案。☞（答案請見 **P.308**）

答題時間
約 **10** 秒/題

Q1

MP3 **4-3**

（每題只播一次，請仔細聽。）

A.

B.

C.

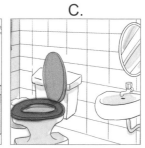

Q2

MP3 **4-3**

（每題只播一次，請仔細聽。）

A.

B.

C.

Q3

MP3 **4-3**

（每題只播一次，請仔細聽。）

A.

B.

C.

第二類 留言

主題 4 親友間

課前暖身 以下是這類題型的經典問句。請先瀏覽一次,對稍後的聽力訓練會有很大的幫助喔!

 經典問句

問法 1 What will (someone) probably do?

問法 2 What might (someone) do next?

聽力練習 每題請聆聽放音機播出的英文內容之後,再從試題冊上的選項 A、B、C 三張圖片中,選出一個最適當的答案。☛(答案請見 **P.311**)

答題時間
約 **10** 秒/題

Q1

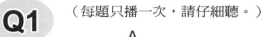（每題只播一次,請仔細聽。）

主題
4
留言
∨
親友間

A.　　　　　　　　B.　　　　　　　　C.

Q2

（每題只播一次,請仔細聽。）

A.　　　　　　　　B.　　　　　　　　C.

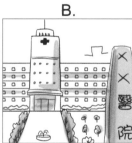

Q3

（每題只播一次,請仔細聽。）

A.　　　　　　　　B.　　　　　　　　C.

課前暖身　以下是這類題型的經典問句。請先瀏覽一次，對稍後的聽力訓練會有很大的幫助喔！

 經典問句

問法 **1** How is (someone) going to do?

聽力練習　每題請聆聽放音機播出的英文內容之後，再從試題冊上的選項 A、B、C 三張圖片中，選出一個最適當的答案。☛（答案請見 **P.314**）

答題時間
約 **10** 秒/題

Q1

MP3 4-5

（每題只播一次，請仔細聽。）

A.

B.

C.

主題
5
留言
∨
公
事

Q2

MP3 4-5

（每題只播一次，請仔細聽。）

A.

B.

C.

Q3

MP3 4-5

（每題只播一次，請仔細聽。）

A.

B.

C.

主題 6	提 醒

課前暖身 以下是這類題型的經典問句。請先瀏覽一次,對稍後的聽力訓練會有很大的幫助喔!

經典問句

問法 **1** What is suggested?

問法 **2** What is reminded?

聽力練習 每題請聆聽放音機播出的英文內容之後,再從試題冊上的選項 A、B、C 三張圖片中,選出一個最適當的答案。☛(答案請見 **P.317**)

Q1

MP3 4-6

（每題只播一次，請仔細聽。）

A.

B.

C.

Q2

MP3 4-6

（每題只播一次，請仔細聽。）

A.

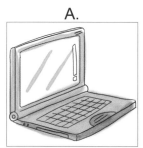

B.

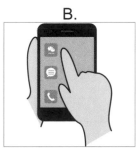

C.

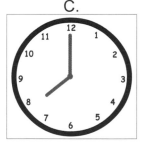

Q3

MP3 4-6

（每題只播一次，請仔細聽。）

A.

B.

C.

第三類 簡短談話

主題 7 問「什麼地方」

課前暖身 以下是這類題型的經典問句。請先瀏覽一次，對稍後的聽力訓練會有很大的幫助喔！

 經典問句

問法① Where is probably mentioned?

單字補充 mention 提及，說及

問法② What might be the place?

問法③ Which place suits the description best?

單字補充 suit 符合，適合
description 描述

聽力練習 每題請聆聽放音機播出的英文內容之後，再從試題冊上的選項 A、B、C 三張圖片中，選出一個最適當的答案。☛（答案請見 P.320）

答題時間
約 **10** 秒/題

Q1

MP3 4-7

（每題只播一次，請仔細聽。）

A. 　　B. 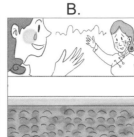　　C.

Q2

MP3 4-7

（每題只播一次，請仔細聽。）

A. 　　B. 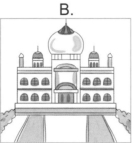　　C.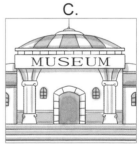

Q3

MP3 4-7

（每題只播一次，請仔細聽。）

A. 　　B. 　　C.

| 主題 **8** | 問「做什麼」 |

課前暖身　以下是這類題型的經典問句。請先瀏覽一次,對稍後的聽力訓練會有很大的幫助喔!

經典問句

問法 1 What will (someone) do later?

問法 2 What did (someone) do yesterday/last week?

問法 3 What might (someone) plan to do?

聽力練習　每題請聆聽放音機播出的英文內容之後,再從試題冊上的選項 A、B、C 三張圖片中,選出一個最適當的答案。☛（答案請見 **P.323**）

答題時間
約 **10** 秒/題

主題
8
簡短談話 v 問「做什麼」

Q1

MP3 4-8

（每題只播一次，請仔細聽。）

A.   B.   C.

Q2

MP3 4-8

（每題只播一次，請仔細聽。）

A.   B.   C.

Q3

MP3 4-8

（每題只播一次，請仔細聽。）

A.   B.   C.

課前暖身

以下是這類題型的經典問句。請先瀏覽一次，對稍後的聽力訓練會有很大的幫助喔！

經典問句

問法 ❶ What can be expected from (someone)?

問法 ❷ What can be told from the short talk?

聽力練習

每題請聆聽放音機播出的英文內容之後，再從試題冊上的選項 A、B、C 三張圖片中，選出一個最適當的答案。☞（答案請見 **P.326**）

答題時間
約 **10** 秒/題

Q1

MP3 4-9

（每題只播一次，請仔細聽。）

A. 　B. 　C.

Q2

MP3 4-9

（每題只播一次，請仔細聽。）

A. 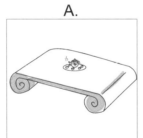　B. 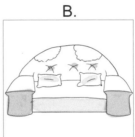　C.

Q3

MP3 4-9

（每題只播一次，請仔細聽。）

A. 　B. 　C.

第四類 其他

主題 10　綜合問題

課前暖身

以下是這類題型的經典問句。請先瀏覽一次,對稍後的聽力訓練會有很大的幫助喔!

經典問句

問法 ❶ Which one is _____?

問法 ❷ Which picture matches the talk?

問法 ❸ Which picture is the best match?

單字補充 match 符合

聽力練習

每題請聆聽放音機播出的英文內容之後,再從試題冊上的選項 A、B、C 三張圖片中,選出一個最適當的答案。☛(答案請見 P.329)

答題時間
約 **10** 秒/題

主題
10
其他 ∨
綜合問題

Q1

（每題只播一次，請仔細聽。）

A.   B.   C.

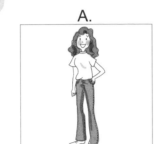  

Q2

（每題只播一次，請仔細聽。）

A.   B.   C.

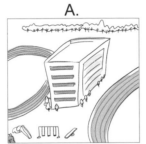 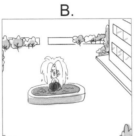 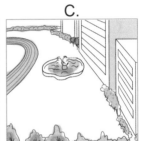

Q3

（每題只播一次，請仔細聽。）

A.   B.   C.

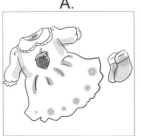 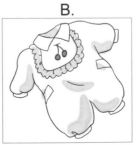 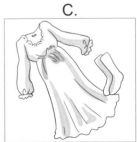

解答　看圖辨義

主題 **1**　物品・動物 Things・Animals

Q1　What is this? 這是什麼？

A:＿＿＿＿＿＿＿＿＿＿＿＿＿＿＿

A. It's a book. 這是一本書。
B. This is a sheet of paper. 這是一張紙。
C. It's a sheep. 這是一隻羊。

解答　B

※〔註〕選項 B. 中 a sheet of（一張～）的 sheet 和選項 C. 的 sheep（羊）發音容易混淆，是聽力常考重點。

Q2　What are these? 這些是什麼東西？

A:＿＿＿＿＿＿＿＿＿＿＿＿＿＿＿

A. They are chairs. 它們是椅子。
B. They are furniture. 它們是家具。
C. These are beds and desks. 這些是床和桌子。

解答　B

※〔註〕畫面中 chair（椅子）、bed（床）和 desk（書桌）都出現了，這些物品可統稱為 furniture（家具），因此答案要選 B.

Q3　What can people find in here?
人們可以在這裡發現什麼？

A:＿＿＿＿＿＿＿＿＿＿＿＿＿＿＿

A. Zoo animals. 物園裡的動物。
B. Sea animals. 海中動物。
C. Pets. 寵物。

解答　B

※〔註〕在海洋世界裡常見的 seal（海豹）和 dolphin（海豚），都是 sea animals（海中動物）的一種，因此答案為 B.。

統稱性的名詞

物品	furniture 家具	food 食物
	stationery 文具	fruit 水果
	clothes 衣服	vegetables 蔬菜
	footwear 鞋子	

生物	animals 動物	plants 植物
	pets 寵物	insects 昆蟲

主題 **2**　　活動 Activities

Q1　What is he doing?　他在做什麼？

A:＿＿＿＿＿＿＿＿＿＿＿＿＿＿＿＿＿＿＿

A: He is sleeping. 他在睡覺。
B: He is taking a bath. 他在泡澡。
C: He is washing his face. 他在洗臉。

解答　B

※〔註〕場景是在「浴室」裡面，男子正在這裡泡澡，即為美語中的 taking a bath（泡澡），taking a shower 則為「淋浴」之意。

如何描述進行中的動作

身體清潔	taking a shower 淋浴
	washing his hair 洗頭
	brushing his teeth 刷牙

Q2 What's happening here? 這裡發生了什麼事？

A: _____

A: People are watching a game. 人們正在看比賽。
B: They are playing basketball. 他們正在打籃球。
C: Students are playing the musical instruments.
　　學生們正在彈奏樂器。

解答　A

※〔註〕這些人正在 watching a game（看比賽），電視畫面轉播
的是 soccer game（足球比賽）。

Column

加分
必背

watching + 節目

watching TV 看電視
watching a movie 看電影
watching a game 看比賽
watching a show 看表演

playing + 運動

playing baseball 打棒球
playing basketball 打籃球
playing soccer 踢足球
playing volleyball 打排球
playing tennis 打網球
playing badminton 打羽球
playing ping-pong 打乒乓球

playing + the + 樂器

playing the piano 彈鋼琴
playing the violin 拉小提琴
playing the drums 打鼓
playing the flute 吹笛子

Q3 What is she going to do? 她要去做什麼？

A: _____

A. She is going to cook. 她要去煮飯。
B. She is going to go shopping. 她要去購物。
C. She is going to go swimming. 她要去游泳。

解答 B

※〔註〕由畫面中的女子揹著 bag（包包）的模樣來看，可推測
她正在前往某處，打算去 shopping（購物）的可能性最高。

"go V-ing" 表示去做某事

go shopping 去購物
go swimming 去游泳
go surfing 去衝浪
go fishing 去釣魚
go jogging 去慢跑
go hiking 去健行
go bowling 去打保齡球
go picnicking 去野餐

主題 3 地點 Places

Q1 What is this place? 這是什麼地方？

A: _____

A. This is a museum. 這是博物館。
B. This is a library. 這是圖書館。
C. This is an office. 這是辦公室。

解答 B

※〔註〕從構圖可輕易看出，這個地方是 library（圖書館），只要對單字熟悉，就很容易可以選對。

Column 加分必背

參觀地點

museum 博物館
art gallery 美術館
zoo 動物園
aquarium 水族館

學術地點

library 圖書館
school 學校
classroom 教室
auditorium 禮堂；講堂

工作地點

company 公司
office 辦公室
conference room 會議室
factory 工廠

Q2 Where are these two girls? 這兩個女孩在哪裡？

A: _____

A. They're in a restaurant. 她們在餐廳裡。
B. They're in a supermarket. 她們在超市裡。
C. They're in a stadium. 她們在體育館裡。

解答 C

※〔註〕題目利用疑問詞 Where 發問，因此答案必須選擇地點，從在圖片背景中出現的物品來看，只有選項 C. 是可能的正確答案。

購物地點

supermarket 超市

mall 大賣場

grocery store 雜貨店

department store 百貨公司

shoe store 鞋店

flower store 花店

stationery store 文具店

book shop 書店

toy shop 玩具店

sporting goods store 運動用品店

飲食地點

restaurant 餐廳
fast food restaurant 速食餐廳
cafeteria 自助餐廳；小餐館
café 咖啡廳
bakery 烘焙坊

休閒地點

stadium 體育館
gym 健身房
park 公園
amusement park 遊樂園
movie theater 電影院
theater 劇院

Q3 Where are they probably going?
他們有可能是要去哪裡？

A: _____

A. They are probably going to the airport.
   他們可能是要去機場。
B. They are probably going to the hospital.
   他們可能是要去醫院。
C. They are probably going to the barbershop.
   他們可能是要去理髮店。

解答 B

※〔註〕這題必須從圖中主角的情況來判斷答案，由於懷孕的婦人似乎快要生產了，因此在此情況下，最可能前往的地點當然就是 hospital（醫院）了。

搭乘交通工具的地點

airport 機場
port 港口
train station 火車站
MRT station 捷運站
bus stop 公車站牌
taxi stand 計程車招呼站

醫療相關的地點

hospital 醫院
clinic 診所
pharmacy 藥局

美容健康相關的地點

barbershop 理髮店
hair salon 美髮店
beauty salon 美容院
fitness center 健身中心
spa 水療館
drug store 藥妝店

主題 **4**　　**時刻** Time

Q1 What is the time? 現在是什麼時間？

A: _____

A. It's six-o-five. 現在是 6 點 05 分。
B. It's six o'clock. 現在是 6 點鐘。
C. It's five-o-six. 現在是 5 點 06 分。

解答　C

※〔註〕注意！當問題詢問 "what time" 時，回答應該是一個時間點，而非一段時間。根據畫面中的數字 5:06 即可選出正確的答案。

6:00 ～ 6:30 英文怎麼說？

◆ 6 點鐘
(6:00)　six o'clock.
◆ 6 點 01 分 ～ 6 點 09 分
(6:01 ～ 6:09)　six-o-one ～ six-o-nine
◆ 6 點 10 分 ～ 6 點 19 分
(6:10 ～ 6:19)　six ten ～ six nineteen
◆ 6 點 20 分 ～ 6 點 29 分
(6:20 ～ 6:29)　six twenty ～ six twenty-nine
◆ 6 點 30 分
(6:30)　six thirty

Q2 Look at the clock on the wall. What time is it?
請看牆上的時鐘。現在是幾點？

A: _____

A. It's a quarter to three. 差 15 分鐘 3 點
B. It's half past two. 兩點半。
C. It's a quarter after two. 2 點 15 分。

解答 A

主題 **4** 時刻 Time

時刻的表示法

◆ a quarter（一刻鐘）
   = 15 minutes（15 分鐘）
◆ half（半小時）= 30 minutes（30 分鐘）
◆ a quarter to three
   = a quarter before three
   = 2:45
◆ half past two = half before three = 2:30
◆ a quarter past two
   = a quarter after two
   = 2:15

Q3 When does the show start? 表演什麼時候開始？

A: _____

A. It starts at 6:30 p.m. 晚上 6:30 開始。
B. It starts at noon. 中午開始。
C. It starts at 6:00 p.m. 晚上 6:00 開始。

解答 C

※〔註〕p.m. 是拉丁文 after noon（中午以後）的意思，由插圖可知表演是在「晚上六點鐘」開始的。
※ 補充：a.m.（拉丁文 Ante Meridiem）=before noon 中午前

Column

加分 必背

午別：上午、下午、晚上

(1) a.m.（拉丁文 Ante Meridiem）
    = before noon 正午前
    p.m.（拉丁文 Post Meridiem）
    = after noon 午後
    ※"a.m." 和 " p.m." 常出現在時間數字之後。
    如：(x) p.m. 6:00 ==> (o) 6:00 p.m.。

(2) noon = 12:00 a.m.
    midnight = 12:00 p.m.
    ※ 注意： noon/midnight 之後不可以再加
    a.m. 或 p.m.。

主題 **5** **情緒・外表** Feelings・Looks

Q1 How is the girl feeling? 這個女孩覺得怎樣？

A: _____

A. She is happy. 她很開心。
B. She's worried. 她很擔心。
C. She's angry. 她很生氣。

解答 B

※〔註〕從女孩和圖畫中男子及女子的表情來判斷，女孩應該是
在 worried（擔心）父母生氣，因此選項 B. 是合理的正確答案。

關於情緒的常用表達

1. 情緒相關的疑問句：

   How do you feel?/How are you feeling?

   你覺得如何？

2. 情緒相關的回答方式：

   I feel sad./I'm feeling sad./I am sad.

   我覺得很傷心。

Q2 How does the man look?

這名男子看起來如何？

A: _____

A. She looks tired. 她看起來很累。

B. He looks excited. 他看起來很興奮。

C. They are bored. 他們覺得很無聊。

解答　B

※〔註〕題目問的是單數的 the man（這名男子），因此答案的主詞應該是 he（他），而男子的表情看起來應該是 excited（興奮的），正確答案應為選項 B.。

人的分類

man 男人

woman 女人

kid 小孩

baby 嬰兒

elder 老人

youth 青年

adult 成年人

情緒形容詞

angry 生氣的
nervous 緊張的
bored 無聊的
sad 傷心的
worried 擔心的
tired 累的
sleepy 睏的
happy 開心的
excited 興奮的

Q3 What does the girl look like? 這個女生看起來如何？

A: _____

A. She is short and fat. 她又矮又胖。
B. She has a thin face. 她有張瘦瘦的臉。
C. She looks heavy. 她看起來胖胖的。

解答 B

※〔註〕畫面中的女生體型瘦瘦的（thin），一點也不胖（fat/heavy），答案很容易選。

身材相關的形容詞

tall 高的
short 矮的
thin/skinny 瘦的
fat/heavy 胖的
slim/slender 苗條的

關於外型的其他回答方式

◆ She/He has＿＿＿＿＿＿.
　替換字：long legs 長腿
　　　　　big ears 大耳朵
　　　　　short curly hair 短的捲髮
　　　　　brown eye 棕色眼睛

※ 注意：我們常說東方人有著「黑眼睛」，但是在英語裡卻常用 brown eyes 或 dark eyes 來表達。

主題 6 疾病・不適症狀 Diseases・Symptoms

Q1 What happened to the boy? 這個男孩發生了什麼事？

A: ＿＿＿＿＿＿＿＿＿＿＿＿＿＿＿

A. He hurt his toes. 他傷了腳趾頭。
B. He heard bad news. 他聽到了壞消息。
C. He happened to pass by. 他碰巧經過。

解答 A

※〔註〕畫面中可看出男孩 hurt his toes（傷了腳趾頭）。必須要注意的是選項 B. 所使用的動詞 heard（聽到）和正確選項中的 hurt 的發音很接近，這種容易混淆的發音是聽力測驗的常見題型。

Q2 Why is Kyle here? 凱爾為什麼在這裡？

A: ＿＿＿＿＿＿＿＿＿＿＿＿＿＿＿

A. He has hurt his nose. 他傷了鼻子。
B. He is sick. 他生病了。
C. He hurt his leg. 他傷了他的腿。

解答 C

※〔註〕選項 B. 不可選，因為男子是腿受傷，而不是生病（sick/ill）。

「～受傷」的說法

He (has) hurt his _____.
= He got hurt in his _____.
= His _____ was/got hurt.

Q3 What is wrong with the boy? 這個男孩怎麼了？

A: _____

A. He has a toothache. 他的牙痛。
B. He hurt his finger. 他傷了手指。
C. He has a cold. 他感冒了。

解答 A

※〔註〕畫面中的男孩把手按在自己的嘴上，因此他很可能是「牙痛」而去看醫生。

感冒常見症狀與表達

a cold 感冒

a flu 流行性感冒

a cough 咳嗽

a sore throat 喉嚨痛

a runny nose 流鼻水

a stuffy nose 鼻塞

※〔註〕感冒 = have a cold/flu
　　　　　 caught a cold/flu

一般疼痛

a toothache 牙痛
an earache 耳朵痛
a stomachache 胃痛
a sore eye 眼睛痛或不舒服

主題 7 食物 Food

Q1 What is the girl eating? 這個女孩正在吃什麼？

A: _____

A. She is eating a lunch box. 她正在吃午餐便當。
B. He is having fried chicken. 他正在吃炸雞。
C. She is eating fast food. 她正在吃速食。

解答 C

※〔註〕再次提醒，當題目問的主角是 the girl，主詞是 he 的選項就千萬不可選。由圖畫內容可知正確選項應該是 C.。

速食 fast food

◆ have = eat/drink
have 可以用來表示「吃」或「喝」。

	fried chicken 炸雞
	French fries 薯條
	hamburger 漢堡
速食 fast food	chicken nuggets 雞塊
	orange juice 柳橙汁
	milk shake 奶昔
	coke 可樂

Q2 What does the daughter want to have?
這個女兒想要吃什麼？

A: _____

grandfather

A. She wants to have some rice. 她想要吃飯。
B. She wants to have some bread. 她想要吃麵包。
C. She wants some noodles. 她想要吃麵。

解答 B

家庭成員

mother 媽媽	parents 雙親
father 爸爸	brother 兄；弟
son 兒子	sister 姐；妹
daughter 女兒	cousin 堂、表兄弟姐妹
grandfather 祖父	uncle 伯、叔、舅、姑父
grandmother 祖母	aunt 嬸、姨、姑母

中式＆西式主食

rice 米飯
noodles 麵
cereal 麥片
oatmeal 燕麥粥
rice porridge 稀飯
bread 麵包
dumpling(s) 水餃
spaghetti 義大利麵
pizza 披薩

Q3 What would the man like? 這個男子想要點什麼？

A: _____

A. He would like a cup of coffee with cream and sugar. 他想要點一杯加奶精和糖的咖啡。
B. He would like a piece of cake and a glass of juice. 他想要點一片蛋糕和一杯果汁。
C. He would like a cup of black coffee. 他想要點一杯黑咖啡。

主題 **7** 食物 Food

解答 C

※〔註〕問「某人想吃什麼」，回答方式有：「主詞＋would like ＋食物」、「主詞＋want＋食物」、「主詞＋want to have＋食物」。

Column
加分必背

咖啡 coffee

black coffee 黑咖啡（不加奶精或糖）
cream 奶精　　　sugar 糖

計量詞＋不可數名詞

a cup of 一杯
　coffee 咖啡
　tea 茶
a glass of 一杯
　juice 果汁
　milk 牛奶
　water 水
a cup/glass of 一杯
　wine 葡萄酒
　whisky 威士忌

a spoonful of 一匙
　cream powder 奶精粉
　salt 鹽
　sugar 糖
a piece of 一片
　cake 蛋糕
　apple pie 蘋果派

※〔註〕點餐的時候，經常會省略計量詞，直接說 a coffee、two coffees 等等。

主題 8 服飾 Costumes & Accessories

Q1 What's the man wearing? 這名男子穿著什麼？

A: _____

A. He's wearing shorts. 他穿著短褲。
B. He's wearing jeans. 他穿著牛仔褲。
C. He's wearing a jacket. 他穿著夾克。

解答 A

※〔註〕題目中出現的男子身上穿著 shirt（襯衫）和 shorts（短褲），因此答案應選 A.。

服裝 clothing

全身	a suit 套裝 sportswear/sweat suit 運動服 a jacket 夾克 a coat 大衣
上半身	a shirt 襯衫 a T-shirt T 恤 a sweater 毛衣
下半身	shorts 短褲 /pants 長褲 jeans 牛仔褲 a skirt 短裙

※〔註〕所有的褲子都以「複數形態」出現，因為褲子是兩隻褲管。

purse 女用包包　　　　wallet 皮夾

Q2 What is the third person in line carrying?
隊伍裡的第三個人拿著什麼？

A: _____

A. He is wearing a necktie. 他打著領帶。
B. He is carrying a suitcase. 他拿著一個公事包。
C. He is carrying a book bag. 他拿著一個書包。

解答 B

※〔註〕選項 A. C. 描寫的都是隊伍中的第一個人，但題目詢問的是第三個人，因此選項 B. 是正確答案。

各式包包

briefcase 公事包
book bag 書包
handbag 手提包
backpack 後背包
wallet 皮夾
pouch 化妝包

服裝配件

a necktie --> neckties 領帶
a scarf --> scarves 圍巾
a handkerchief --> handkerchiefs 手帕
a pair of glasses 一副眼鏡
a belt 皮帶
glove(s) 手套
sock(s) 短襪
stockings 長襪

Q3 What is she going to buy? 她要買什麼？

A: _____

A. They are wearing shoes. 她們穿著鞋子。
B. She is going to buy shoes. 她要買鞋子。
C. They are going to buy glasses. 她們要買眼鏡。

解答 B

※〔註〕題目問句的主詞是 She，所以答句的主詞也應為 She，所以答案選 B.。

各種鞋子

shoes 鞋子	sandal 涼鞋
sneakers 運動鞋	slipper 室內拖鞋
high heels 高跟鞋	mule 穆勒鞋
boots 靴子	pump 平底淺口女鞋

主題 9 個人資訊 Personal Information

Q1 How old is the child? 這個小孩幾歲？

A: _____

A. He is seventy years old. 他七十歲。
B. He is seven years old. 他七歲。
C. She is seventeen years old. 她十七歲。

解答 B

※〔註〕這題主要是測驗考生對數字唸法的熟悉程度，尤其是字尾 -teen（thirteen 到 nineteen）和 -ty（thirty 到 ninety）的唸法，這部分相當容易混淆，平時必須要多聽、多說，才能在正式測驗時一聽就明白。透過插圖中蛋糕上的數字 7 蠟燭可知，答案是選項 B.。

另一種年齡詢問方式

◆ What is his/her age?
她／他的年齡多大？

◆ She/He is _____ year(s) of age.
她／他是～歲。

Q2 How heavy is the woman? 這個女人有多重？

A: _____

A. She is fifty-six kilograms. 她五十六公斤。
B. She is heavy. 她很重／胖。
C. She is a woman. 她是個女人。

解答 A

另一種體重詢問方式

◆ What is her/his weight?
她／他體重多少？

◆ She/He weights _____kg.
她／他的體重是～公斤。

◆ She/He is _____kg in weight.
她／他的體重有～公斤。

※〔註〕英國和美國在重量單位上多半使用 pound（磅）。

Q3 How tall is the boy? 這個男孩多高？

A: _____

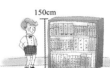

A. He is one meter tall. 他 1 公尺高。
B. He is one hundred and fifteen centimeters.
　 他 115 公分。
C. He is one-point-five meters tall. 他 1.5 公尺高。

解答　C

公尺、公分的換算

◆ 1 M = one meter 1 公尺 = 100 cm
　 = one hundred centimeters 100 公分
◆ 1.5 M = one-point-five meters 1.5 尺 =
　 150 cm = one hundred and fifty centimeters

※〔註〕當回答身高有多高時，句尾的 tall 說不說都可以。例
如： He is one meter (tall).。

另一種身高的詢問方式

◆ What is her/his height?
　 她／他身高多少？
◆ She/He is _____ cm in height.
　 她／他的身高是～公分。

※〔註〕英國和美國在長度單位上多半使用「foot（複數
feet）英呎」、「inch（複數 inches）英吋」。

主題 10 季節・月分 Seasons・Months

Q1 What season is it? 這是什麼季節？

A: _____

A. It is windy. 風很大。
B. It is winter. 冬天。
C. It is a cold day. 很冷的一天。

解答 B

※〔註〕問 What season（什麼季節），就一定要回答四季之一，也就是 spring（春）、summer（夏）、fall/autumn（秋）或 winter（冬）。

Q2 What month is it? 這是幾月？

A: _____

April

A. It is April. 這是四月。
B. It is not April. 這不是四月。
C. It is raining. 正在下雨。

解答 A

※〔註〕問 What month（什麼月分），就應該回答十二個月分之一，把以下的韻文背下來，就可以記熟十二月分的說法了。

Column 加分必背

月分

Months of the Year
一年的月分
January, February, March, and April,
一月、二月、三月和四月，
May, June, July, and August,
五月、六月、七月和八月，
September, October, November, December,
九月、十月、十一月、十二月，
Twelve months make a year.
十二個月組成了一年。

Q3 What time of the year is it? 這是一年中的什麼時候？

A: _____

A. It is New Year's Day. 這是元旦。
B. It is a new day. 這是新的一天。
C. It is a new year. 這是新的一年。

解答 A

※〔註〕問 what time of the year（一年中的什麼時候），可以回答某個季節、某個月分或某一天。這題只有選項 A. 明確道出是 New Year's Day（新年）這一天，其他兩個選項都不對。

美國重要節慶

日期	節日英文	節日中文
1 月 1 日	New Year's Day	元旦
2 月 14 日	Valentine's Day	情人節
3 月中旬	St. Patrick's Day	聖派翠克節
7 月 4 日	Independence Day	獨立紀念日（美國國慶）
10 月 31 日	Halloween	萬聖節
11 月第 4 個禮拜四	Thanksgiving Day	感恩節
12 月 25 日	Christmas	聖誕節

台灣農曆重要節慶

日期	節日中文	節日英文
1 月 1 日	大年初一	Chinese New Year's Day
1 月 15 日	元宵節	Lantern Festival
5 月 5 日	端午節	Dragon-Boat Festival
7 月 7 日	七夕情人節	Chinese Valentine's Day
7 月 15 日	中元節	Ghost Festival
8 月 15 日	中秋節	Moon Festival
9 月 9 日	重陽節	Double Ninth Festival

※〔註〕新曆 (solar) calendar
農曆 lunar calendar

主題 **11** 日期 Dates

主題 **11** 日期 Dates

Q1 What day is today? 今天星期幾？

A: _____

A. It is Tuesday. 是星期二。
B. Today is Thursday. 今天星期四。
C. Today is Saturday. 今天星期六。

解答 B

※〔註〕圖中的小女孩在跳舞，由牆上的課程表可知，跳舞課是在星期四，故答案選 B.。

Calendar Song 日曆頌

There are 7 days, there are 7 days,
有七天、有七天，
There are 7 days in a week.
一星期有七天
Sunday, Monday, Tuesday, Wednesday.
星期日、星期一、星期二、星期三
Thursday, Friday, Saturday.
星期四、星期五、星期六

Q2 What is the date today? 今天是幾月幾日？

A: _____

A. It is the girl's birthday. 今天是這個女孩的生日。
B. Today is Sunday. 今天是星期日。
C. It is February 2. 今天是二月二日。

解答 C

※〔註〕問 What is the date today?，回答一定要是明確的日期。
如果這題問的是 What day is today?，則選項 A. 和 C. 就都是正確
答案了。

Q3 When is Terry's birthday? 泰瑞的生日在什麼時候？

A: _____

NOTE
Jane's birthday 1979/10/15
Annie's birthday 1975/8/30
Terry's birthday 1976/6/11
Mary's birthday 1974/3/7

A. It is on April 14th. 是在四月十四日。
B. On June 11th. 在六月十一日。
C. Her birthday is August 30th.
　她的生日是八月三十日。

解答 B

※〔註〕講一個人的生日或某個節日，可以直接說出月分和日期
（如選項 C.），或在這之前加上一個介系詞 on（如選項 A. 或
B.）。由圖畫可知 Terry 的生日在六月十一日（June 11th）。

主題 12 位置 Positions

Q1 Where is bus 220? 220 公車在哪裡？

A: _____

A. It's between a car and a motorbike.
   在一輛汽車和一台機車之間。
B. It's in front of a car. 在一輛汽車前面。
C. It's behind a motorbike. 在一台機車後面。

解答 B

※〔註〕這題要能順利作答，一定得熟悉道路交通工具的說法，也必須知道相對位置的表達方式。

交通工具

bus 巴士
car 汽車
taxi 計程車
van 廂型車
motorbike/motorcycle 機車
scooter 輕型機車
bike/bicycle 腳踏車
sports car 跑車
coach 客運
train 火車
High Speed Rail 高鐵
Metro = MRT 捷運

Q2 Where does Peter live? 彼得住在哪裡？

A: _____

A. He lives in the school. 他住在學校裡。
B. He lives next to the theater. 他住在戲院隔壁。
C. He lives across from the school. 他住在學校對面。

解答 C

※〔註〕題目要求考生找出彼得家和社區內其他建築物的相對位置，選項 A. 的內容與圖畫內容不符，而圖畫中出現的是 movie theater（電影院），而非戲院，因此選項 B. 也不是正確答案，在參考題目圖畫後，可知正確答案是選項 C.。

常見建築物

school 學校
library 圖書館
swimming pool 游泳池
bank 銀行
post office 郵局
police station 警察局
fire station 消防局

Q3 What is under the chair? 椅子下面是什麼？

A: _____

A. The breakfast is under the table. 早餐在桌子下面。
B. The cat is under the chair. 貓在椅子下面。
C. The toy is on the table. 玩具在桌子上面。

解答 B

※〔註〕under 和 on 這兩個介系詞，乍聽之下發音有些相似，因此常有考生會混淆，必須特別注意。圖畫中 under the chair 的是 cat（貓），而 on the table 的則是 breakfast（早餐）和 newspaper（報紙）。

主題 13 數量 Quantity

Q1 What number is it? 號碼是多少？

A: _____

A. It is number thirty. 是 30 號。
B. Thirty-one. 31。
C. Thirteen. 13。

解答 B

※〔註〕這題想考的是 thirteen 和 thirty 間的發音差異，是常出的聽力陷阱。

Q2 How many children are there? 那裡有幾個小孩？

A: _____

A. They are on the beach. 他們在沙灘上。
B. There are two children. 有兩個小孩。
C. They are wearing swimming suits.
   他們穿著泳衣。

解答 B

※〔註〕題目詢問 How many（幾個）就一定要回答出一個明確的數字，選項 B. 回答了 "two" children（「兩個」小孩），所以是正確答案。

Q3 Who is first? 誰是第一名？

A: _____

A. Sally is running. 莎莉正在跑步。
B. Emily is second. 艾蜜莉第二。
C. Sally is first. 莎莉第一。

解答 C

※〔註〕題目不是問誰是第二，而是問誰是第一，因此選項 C. 是正確答案。

序數的唸法

1st = first	11th = eleventh
2nd = second	12th = twelfth
3rd = third	13th = thirteenth
4th = fourth	14th = fourteenth
5th = fifth	15th = fifteenth
6th = sixth	16th = sixteenth
7th = seventh	17th = seventeenth
8th = eighth	18th = eighteenth
9th = ninth	19th = nineteenth
10th = tenth	20th = twentieth

※〔註〕序數 4 到 20 的唸法都是基數後面加上 "th"，但是字尾拼法有些必須稍作改變，必須特別注意。

主題 **14**　　　價錢 Prices

Q1 How much is the ticket to Taichung?
到台中的票多少錢？

A: _____

Ticket Fare	
To Tainan	$ 856
To Taichung	$ 412
To Keelung	$ 165

A. NTD412. 412 元。
B. NTD865. 865 元。
C. NTD165. 165 元。

解答 A

※〔註〕題目詢問 How much（多少錢），因此一定要回答明確的價錢，根據圖畫內容可知正確答案是 A. 。

Q2 How much does a watermelon cost? 一粒西瓜多少錢？

A: _____

A. Six for ninety-nine dollars. 六粒 99 元。
B. One hundred and eighty-nine dollars. 189 元。
C. A kilo of grapes costs forty-five dollars.
   葡萄一公斤 45 元。

解答 B

※〔註〕透過題目圖畫，可以看到西瓜一粒賣 189 元。

Q3 How much did she spend? 她花了多少錢？

A: _____

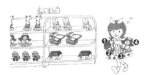

A. $50. 50 元。
B. She bought 5 toys. 她買了五個玩具。
C. She spent $200. 她花了 200 元。

解答 C

※〔註〕由標示可知每件玩具是 50 元，小女孩買了 4 個，所以總共是 200 元。

Column

加分必背

花費金錢的說法

※〔註〕動詞三態 cost/cost/cost
　　　　　　　 spend/spent/spent

◆物＋cost＋錢

ex: The toy costs two hundred dollars.

這個玩具要兩百元。

◆物＋cost＋人＋錢

ex: The toy cost me two hundred dollars.

這個玩具花了我兩百元。

※〔註〕cost 是過去式。

◆人＋spend＋錢＋on＋物

ex: I spent two hundred dollars on this toy.

我花了兩百元在這個玩具上。

※〔註〕spent 是過去式。

主題 **14** 價錢 Prices

主題 15　天氣 Weather

Q1 How's the weather? 天氣如何？

A: _____

A. It's cold and windy. 又冷又颳風。
B. It's hot and sunny. 又熱又出太陽。
C. It's cool and rainy. 又涼又下雨。

解答 A

※〔註〕題目問的是天氣，通常都會用 It 當代名詞。從畫面中看得出來天氣十分寒冷（cold）而且有風，故選 A.。

Q2 What will the weather be like on Thursday?
星期四天氣會如何？

A: _____

A. More rain will come. 雨會下得更大。
B. It will be cloudy. 多雲。
C. We'll have clear skies. 晴朗無雲。

解答 B

※〔註〕從氣象預報圖可以看到，Thursday（星期四）應該是多雲（cloudy）的天氣，而選項 C. 的 clear sky（晴朗無雲）就是晴天的另一種說法，而且通常以第一人稱複數 "We" 當主詞。

Q3 What's the temperature in Tainan? 台南的溫度是多少？

A: _____

A. The temperature is 34.5℃.
　溫度是攝氏 34.5 度。
B. It is 36℃. 攝氏 36 度。
C. It is hot. 天氣很熱。

解答 A

※〔註〕正確溫度是 34.5 ℃（thirty-four point five degree Celsius）。所以答案是選項 A.。

溫度的說法

◆ Celsius 攝氏；Fahrenheit 華氏
35.5℃/℉ 唸做 thirty-five point five degree
Celsius [`sɛlsɪəs] / Fahrenheit [`færən‚haɪt]。

※〔註〕degree 後面不可以加複數 -s。

主題 16 職業 Occupations

Q1 What is the woman?
這個女人是做什麼的？

A: _____

A. She is a woman.
　她是個女人。
B. He's a policeman.
　他是個警察。
C. She's a police officer.
　她是個警察。

解答 C

※〔註〕穿著制服的女子正在指揮交通（direct traffic），題目問句的意思等於 "What is the woman's job?"，問的是這名女子的職業，故選 C.。

不同職業的新、舊名稱

舊職業名	新職業名
policeman 警察	police officer 警員
fireman 消防員	firefighter 消防員
mailman 郵差	mail carrier 郵務士
salesman 業務員	salesperson 業務員
businessman 商人	business person 商人

※〔註〕近來英文中的職業名稱多半會避免使用「-man」或
「-woman」來限定從業者的性別，意在使單字更加中性、避
免歧視。

Q2　What does Andrew do? 安德魯是做什麼工作的？

A: _____

A. It is an automatic teller machine.
　　這是一部自動櫃員機。
B. He works as a teller. 他做的是銀行櫃員。
C. He is a banker. 他是個銀行家。

解答 B

※〔註〕bank teller 和 banker 之間的差異常會有人搞混。其實
bank teller（銀行櫃員）是受銀行聘雇的員工，而 banker（銀行家）
則是資金投入者，小心不要搞錯囉。

銀行相關用語

◆ automatic teller machine
　　= ATM 自動櫃員機
◆ teller = bank teller 銀行櫃員
◆ banker 銀行家
◆ name of account 戶名

Q3 Whom should people call for help?
人們應該打電話向誰求助？

A: _____

A. They should call a reporter.
　他們應該打電話給記者。
B. Call 119. 打給 119。
C. Call the library. 打給圖書館。

解答 B

※〔註〕由圖中的火災可知當時應該打電話向 119 求助。

求助相關用語

求助電話	求助單位	求助對象
110 警察局	police station	the police
	警察局	警方
119 消防局	fire station	the firefighters
	消防局	消防隊員
	hospital	paramedics
	醫院	急救人員

※〔註〕美國的緊急電話號碼是 911，不要搞錯囉！

主題 17 比較 Comparisons

Q1 What is more expensive? 什麼比較貴？

A: _____

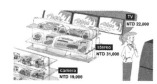

A. The stereo is more expensive. 音響比較貴。
B. The TV is more expensive than the stereo.
 電視比音響貴。
C. The stereo is less expensive. 音響比較不貴。

解答 A

※〔註〕形容詞比較級 more 表示「更多」，less 表示「更少」，
透過題目圖畫可以知道 stereo set（音響）比 TV set（電視）貴，
所以答案為 A.。

形容詞比較級

more expensive = less cheaper
less expensive = cheaper

相反詞

expensive 貴 ↔ cheap 便宜
fast/quick 快 ↔ slow 慢
tall 高 ↔ short 矮
high 高 ↔ low 低
thick 厚 ↔ thin 薄
strong 強 ↔ weak 弱
hot 熱 ↔ cold 冷
big 大 ↔ small/little 小
young 年輕 ↔ old 老
new 新 ↔ old 舊
wide 寬 ↔ narrow 窄

Q2 What is the cheapest way to Kaohsiung?
去高雄最便宜的方法是什麼？

A: _____

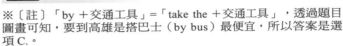

3 Ways to Kaohsiung	
By Plane	$2000
By Train	$600
By Bus	$550

A. By train. 搭火車。
B. Take the plane. 搭飛機。
C. By bus. 搭巴士。

解答 C

※〔註〕「by＋交通工具」＝「take the＋交通工具」，透過題目圖畫可知，要到高雄是搭巴士（by bus）最便宜，所以答案是選項 C.。

運輸方式

1. by＋交通工具 ＝ take the＋交通工具
2. by sea ＝ by boat （貨物等）船運
   by air ＝ by plane （貨物等）空運
   by land （貨物等）陸運

Q3 Who should pay the most? 誰應該付最多錢？

A: _____

A. The old man should pay. 老人應該付。
B. The woman. 女人。
D. The kid should pay the most. 小孩應該付最多錢。

解答 B

※〔註〕kid（小孩）和 old man/woman（老人）的票價比 woman（女人）的票價 $80 要便宜，因此答案是選項 B.。

the＋形容詞最高級 → 最～的

the most 最多的
the least 最少的
the best 最好的
the worst 最差的

主題 **18** 人際關係 Relationships

Q1 Who's the person behind Maria?
在瑪莉亞後面的人是誰？

A: _____

A. She is Lily. 她是莉莉。
B. He is Philip. 他是菲力浦。
C. Maria is between Mark and Rosa.
　　瑪莉亞是在馬克和羅莎之間。

解答 B

※〔註〕behind 是「在……之後」的意思。圖畫中在 Maria 後面
的是 Philip，故答案是 B.。

Q2 Who is the man in a black tie?
打著黑色領帶的男子是誰？

A: _____

A. He is probably the woman's doctor.
　　他可能是這個女子的醫生。
B. He is probably the boss. 他可能是老闆。
C. He is probably the woman's classmate.
　　他可能是這個女子的同學。

解答 B

※〔註〕聽到題目詢問「Who is＋主詞」的句子，應回答所詢問
對象的「身分」或與配角間的「關係」。因為這張圖畫的場景是
在辦公室，因此選項 B. 是正確答案。

Q3 What is their relationship? 他們的關係是什麼？

A: _____

A. They're a rider and a passenger.
   他們是騎士和乘客。
B. They're strangers to each other.
   他們彼此是陌生人。
C. They're a family. 他們是一家人。

解答 B

※〔註〕題目若詢問 relationship（關係），答案有可能只是一個名詞，例如 family（家人），但此時這個名詞的前面不會加上冠詞 a/an 或 the。

常見的人際關係

family 家人
relative 親戚
classmate 同學
roommate 室友
housemate 住同屋但不同房的朋友
friend 朋友
co-worker/colleague 同事
rival 競爭對手

主題 **18**
人際關係 Relationships

相對應的人際關係

parents 父母 ↔ children 子女
teacher 老師 ↔ student 學生
coach 教練 ↔ athlete 運動員
director 導演 ↔ actor 男演員
　　　　　　　　actress 女演員
conductor 指揮家 ↔ musician 音樂家
taxi/bus driver 計程車／公車司機
　　　　　　　　　　　↔ passenger 乘客
doctor 醫生 ↔ patient 病人
store clerk 店員 ↔ customer 顧客

主題 19 日常用品(1) Things for Daily Use (1)

Q1 Where can you probably find these things?
你可能會在哪裡發現這些東西？

A: _____

A. In a pencil box. 在鉛筆盒裡。
B. In a closet. 在衣櫃裡。
C. In a refrigerator. 在冰箱裡。

解答 A

※〔註〕圖畫中這些物品是文具，最合理的地方就是 pencil box
（=pencil case「鉛筆盒」）裡了。

Q2 Where should these things be put?
這些東西應該放在哪裡？

A: _____

A. They should be put away. 應該把它們收好。
B. They should be put in the office.
   應該把它們放在辦公室裡。
C. They should be put in the bathroom.
   應該把它們放在浴室裡。

解答 C

主題 **19** 日常用品 (1) Things for Daily Use (1)

Column

加分必背

房屋格局

bathroom 浴室	dining room 餐廳
bedroom 臥室	study 書房
living room 客廳	balcony 陽台
kitchen 廚房	storeroom 儲藏室

Q3 What goes with this machine? 這個機器要和什麼一起用？

A: _____

A. A vase. 一個花瓶。
B. A computer. 一台電腦。
C. A pair of shoes. 一雙鞋子。

解答 B

※〔註〕這台 machine（機器）正確的名稱是 printer（印表機），
必須搭配 computer（電腦）一起使用，故選 B.。

Column 加分必背

電腦配備

monitor 螢幕	printer 印表機
keyboard 鍵盤	scanner 掃描器
speaker 喇叭	mouse 滑鼠

主題 20 日常用品(2) Things for Daily Use (2)

Q1 What does the man need most? 這名男子最需要什麼？

A: _____

A. A public phone. 公共電話。
B. He needs a pay card. 他需要一張電話卡。
C. He needs to pay. 他必須付錢。

解答 B

※〔註〕pay card 儲值卡 =phone card 電話卡，是圖畫中站在公共電話前的男子最需要的東西。

Column 加分必背

各類電話

phone/telephone 電話
cell/mobile phone 手機
car phone 汽車電話
pay/public phone 公共電話
intercom 室內對講機
walkie-talkie 行動對講機

Q2 Who needs these tools most? 誰最需要這些工具？

A: _____

A. A hair dresser needs them most.
髮型設計師最需要它們。
B. This is a school. 這是一所學校。
C. These tools are for musicians.
這些工具是給音樂家用的。

解答 A

※〔註〕題目詢問 who 就要回答「人物」，所以只有 A. 會是正確答案。

Q3 What's the boy's trouble? 這個男孩遇上了什麼麻煩？

A: _____

A. He can't get down to the ground.
他無法回到地面上。
B. He can't fly. 他無法飛。
C. He can climb the tree. 他會爬樹。

解答 A

※〔註〕由畫面中小男孩的表情及整體情境來判斷：他應該是被困在樹上了，故答案選 A.。

問答

第一類 招呼與問候

主題 1　見 面

Q1 Hi, Tom. How have you been?
嗨，湯姆。最近過得怎麼樣？

正解 A. Well, about the same. 嗯，差不多吧。

B. They are the same. 他們是一樣的。

C. I don't know what I'm doing. 我不知道我在做什麼。

※〔註〕題目問句是「在一段時間沒見面後」的常見問候語，選項 A. 的意思是和之前差不多，沒什麼特殊的事發生。選項 C. 是用來回答 What are you doing now?（你現在在做什麼？）的答案。

Q2 Hi, good to see you again.
嗨，能再見到你真好。

正解 A. Yeah, how have you been? 是啊，你最近好嗎？

B. It's good to meet you. 很高興認識你。

C. I'm OK. 我還不錯。

Q3 Did you have a good holiday?
假期愉快嗎？

正解 A. It was wonderful. 很棒。

B. Wish you a happy holiday. 祝你佳節愉快。

C. No, it's good. 不，這很好。

Q4 You must be Dr. Evans. Let me introduce myself. I'm Betty Davis.
你一定是伊凡斯醫生了。請容我自我介紹,我是貝蒂·戴維斯。

正解 A. How do you do, Ms. Davis? 妳好嗎?戴維斯小姐。

B. Who is Betty Davis? 誰是貝蒂·戴維斯?

C. Do you know her? 你認識她嗎?

※〔註〕當一個人要自我介紹時,一定會說出自己的名字,這位向 Dr. Evans 自我介紹的女人叫做 Betty Davis,這時因為不知道對方是已婚還是未婚,所以 Dr. Evans 會以 Ms. Davis 來稱呼她。

Q5 Frank, this is Rose, my classmate.
法蘭克,這位是羅絲,我的同學。

A. Goodbye, Rose. 再見,羅絲。

正解 B. Hi, Rose. It's nice to meet you. 嗨,羅絲。很高興認識妳。

C. It's nice of you, Rose. 妳人真好,羅絲。

主題 **2** 　　　道　別

Q1 Come over again.
有空再來。

A. Go away. 走開。

B. I come here sometimes. 我有時會來這裡。

正解 C. Thanks, I will. 謝謝,我會的。

Q2 I'm going to a party now.
我現在要去派對了。

A. Happy birthday. 生日快樂。

正解 ► B. Enjoy yourself! 好好去玩啊！

C. Who is coming? 誰要過來？

※〔註〕正確答案為 B.，意思是希望對方能在派對中玩得盡興。

Q3 Have a nice day.
祝你有美好的一天。

正解 ► A. You, too. 你也是。

B. It's a nice day, isn't it? 天氣很好，不是嗎？

C. Hi, I'm back. 嗨，我回來了。

※〔註〕如果有人比你早說出這句話，那你也要趕快用 You, too. 來回應對方，祝福他一整天都順遂。選項 B. 和 C. 所對應的回應主題與題目內容不符，題目談的是「一天的心情」，但選項 B. 回應的是「天氣」，C. 的主題則是「人」。

Q4 Give me a call when you get there, okay?
你到那裡的時候打個電話給我，好嗎？

正解 ► A. Sure thing. 當然。

B. Here you are. 這給你。

C. I will get there by three. 我三點以前會到那裡。

※〔註〕正確答案 "Sure thing." 等於 "Sure./Certainly./OK." 的意思。選項 B. 應該是你要拿東西給對方時的表達方式，選項 C. 則是回答對方問你 "When will you get there?" 問題時的回答方式。

Q5 I will miss you.
我會想你的。

正解 A. Same here. 我也是。

B. I missed the bus. 我錯過了巴士。

C. Did I miss anything? 我錯過了什麼嗎？

※〔註〕正確答案 "Same here." 的意思等於 "I will miss you, too."。這裡的 miss 是「思念」之意，而選項 B. 和 C. 裡的 miss 則都是「錯過」的意思。

主題 **3**　　　　邀約與招待

Q1 Can you come?
你可以來嗎？

正解 A. Sorry, I don't have time. 對不起，我沒有時間。

B. Of course I can count. 我當然會算。

C. Yes, I am Ken. 是，我是肯恩。

※〔註〕有人向你提出邀約，你卻必須拒絕時，除了要說 "sorry." 表示歉意之外，最好能明確說出理由，例如 "I don't have time. I have to work late tonight.（我沒有時間，我今晚得工作到很晚。）"。

Q2 Would you like to have lunch together?
你想要一起吃午餐嗎？

正解 A. I'd love to. 好啊。〔我很樂意。〕

B. I am with you. 我同意你說的。

C. We are together. 我們在一起了。

Q3 Would you care for something to drink?
你要不要喝點什麼？

A. I like drinking tea. 我喜歡喝茶。

正解 B. No, thanks. I'm fine for now. 不用了，謝謝。我現在還好。

C. Be careful with what you eat. 要小心你吃了什麼。

Q4 Please make yourself at home.
請不要拘束。

A. I can make it home. 我有辦法到家的。

正解 B. Thanks, I will. 謝謝，我會的。

C. Nobody's home. 沒人在家。

※〔註〕「Please make yourself at home.」是主人希望來訪的客人「放輕鬆、當成像在自己家一樣、不要拘束」時會說的話，這時候客人可以回答「Thanks, I will.」來感謝主人的體貼。

Q5 It's too bad that you have to go.
真可惜你必須要走了。

A. Let me see you out. 讓我送你出去。

B. Welcome. Please come in. 歡迎，請進。

正解 C. Thank you for the great party! 謝謝你辦這場很棒的派對！

※〔註〕在聚會還沒結束、卻有人必須先離開時，主人在挽留不成後，便會說「It's too bad that you have to go.」，所以這句話是「主人」說的，而對應的就會是要離開的「客人」所說的話，三個選項中只有 C. 正確，選項 A.、B. 都是「主人」才會說的話。

主題 4 祝賀與道喜

Q1 Happy birthday! This is for you.
生日快樂！這個是給你的。

A. Happy birthday! 生日快樂！

B. How are you? 你好嗎？

正解 C. Oh! How nice! 噢！真棒！

※〔註〕壽星聽到別人的祝福，又收到禮物，一定很開心，覺得對方人真好，選項 C. "How nice" 的完整意思就是 "How nice of you for giving me this present."，對於對方送自己禮物表示感謝。

Q2 I've had this cough for a week now.
我已經這樣咳嗽咳一個禮拜了。

A. Why were you off for a week? 你為什麼離開了一週？

B. Have a nice trip. 旅途愉快。

正解 C. That's too bad. I hope you get well soon.
那真是太糟糕了。祝你早日康復。

Q3 I hope you will pass the exam.
我希望你會通過考試。

正解 A. That's very kind of you to say so. 謝謝你這麼說。

B. Can I get past, please? 可以請你讓我過一下嗎？

C. I'm afraid not. 恐怕不行。

※〔註〕當別人擋住了你要走的地方時，就可以說選項 B. 的這句慣用表達，這句話的前面通常會加上「Excuse me.（不好意思）」，而選項 C. 則會在「覺得對方的意見不可行」時使用，這是一種比較委婉的表達方式，例如在以下情境中使用：

A: Can I get a discount? 可以給我打個折嗎？

B: I'm afraid not. 恐怕不行。

Q4　I can't believe my luck.
我不敢相信我的好運。

A. What do you believe? 你相信什麼？

B. I hope we have the key to this lock.

　　我希望我們有這個鎖的鑰匙。

正解── C. Honey, I'm so happy for you. 親愛的，我真為你高興。

※〔註〕當出乎意料的事發生時，就可以說「I can't believe ~」來表達「震驚」或「驚喜」的情緒。當 luck（好運）降臨在你身上，你的親朋好友當然也會為你高興，所以就會對你說「happy for you」。選項 A. 中的 believe 意思是「相信」、「信仰」，選項 B. 則是企圖利用發音相似的 luck/lock 來混淆你的判斷。

Q5　Happy New Year.
新年快樂。

正解── A. Same to you. 你也是。

B. I saw the news. 我看過那則新聞。

C. How are you? 你好嗎？

※〔註〕只要有人祝你佳節愉快，無論是 "Happy New Year." 還是 "Merry Christmas." 都可以這樣回答。

主題 **5**　　　　　　　　　　　**健康狀況**

Q1　What's wrong? You look pale.
怎麼了？你看起來很蒼白。

A. You have the wrong number. 你打錯（電話號碼）了。

B. It's not correct. 這不對。

正解── C. I broke my tooth. 我弄斷我的牙齒了。

※〔註〕"What's wrong?" 一般都是在「關心」對方發生了什麼「不好」的事。
pale [pel] 蒼白的；灰白的。

Q2 How often do I take the medicine?
這個藥我多久要吃一次？

A. It will take you three days. 它會花你三天的時間。

正解 B. Three times a day; after meal, please.
一天三次，請在飯後吃。

C. I have three meals a day. 我一天吃三餐。

Q3 Do you have some medicine for a stomachache?
你有胃痛的藥嗎？

A. I have a cold. 我感冒了。

B. What can go wrong? 不會出錯的啦！

正解 C. You'd better see a doctor. 你最好去看醫生。

Q4 My tooth hurts when I eat.
我吃東西的時候牙齒會痛。

正解 A. Too bad. 真糟糕。

B. You need to blow your nose. 你需要擤鼻涕。

C. You have bad teeth. 你牙齒很差。

※〔註〕當別人就原因與你無關的事向你抱怨時，可以用「Too bad.」來回應對方來表示與對方同理。

【補充】常出現的感冒症狀
a running nose 流鼻水
a caugh 咳嗽
a headache 頭痛
a sore throat 喉嚨痛

Q5 Does it hurt when I press it here?
我按這裡會不會痛？

A. My nose is running. 我在流鼻水。

正解 B. Not much. 不太會。

C. Please call an ambulance. 請叫救護車。

※〔註〕ambulance [ˋæmbjələns] 救護車。

主題 **6**	電話用語

Q1 Hello, is Grace there?
喂，葛蕾絲在嗎？

A. I'm here. 我在這裡。

正解 B. This is Grace. 我是葛蕾絲。

C. Hi, how are you? 嗨，你好嗎？

※〔註〕在對方無法看見自己的時候，比如說在電話上，不能直接以 I am... 回答，必須說 This is.../It's...，並加上自己的名字，或用受格代名詞 her, him, me。在門口透過對講機對話時的情形也是一樣，例：
A: Who is it? 是誰？
B: It's me. 是我。

Q2 May I speak to Tom, please?
可以請湯姆聽電話嗎？

A. Hello, May. 哈囉，梅。

B. I'm pleased. 我很高興。

正解 C. I'm sorry, but he is out. 不好意思，他不在

※〔註〕因為無法確定打電話來的人是不是 May，因此選項 A. 不能選，題目裡出現的 May 是助動詞而不是 A. 選項中的人名，因此是「同音異義字」。選項 B. 中則出現了「同形異義字」的 pleased，題目句子中的 please 是表示「請～」的副詞；be pleased 則是動詞的被動語態用法，表示「（被）取悅」，有些字典或文法書會把這種動詞的被動語態用法視為形容詞。

Q3 Sorry. He's not here. Please call back.
抱歉，他不在這裡。請你之後再打。

A. I'll be right back. 我馬上回來。

正解 — B. Thank you. I'll call back later. 謝謝你，我晚點再打。

C. OK, tell me later. 好，晚點和我說。

Q4 Can I take a message?
你要留言嗎？

正解 — A. Yes, please. 好的，謝謝。

B. Yes, take it. 是，拿去。

C. No, you can't. 不，你不可以。

※〔註〕來電者要求留言時會說 leave a message，把動詞 leave 改成 take 後，就變成受話者詢問對方是否要留言的表達方式了，例如 I'm sorry, he's out. Can I take a message for you?（抱歉，他出去了。你要我幫你留言嗎？）。

Q5 I'm afraid you have the wrong number.
恐怕你打錯電話了。

A. Don't be afraid. 別害怕。

正解 — B. I'm terribly sorry. 我相當抱歉。

C. You look terrible. 你看起來真糟。

主題
6
招呼與問候 ∨ 電話用語

第二類 稱謂與關係

主題 7　名字、人名與職業

Q1 What do you call your dog?
你叫你的狗什麼？〔你的狗叫什麼名字？〕

A. It's a lucky dog. 這是一隻幸運狗。

正解 ─ B. We call him "Lucky." 我們叫他「Lucky」。

C. My father gave him a name. 我爸給他取了個名字。

Q2 How do you say this in English?
這個東西的英文怎麼說？

A. It's name is "Micky." 牠的名字是「米奇」。

正解 ─ B. It's a "mouse." 這是一個「mouse〔老鼠 → 滑鼠〕」。

C. I don't like it. 我不喜歡這個。

Q3 What do you do?
你是做什麼的？

A. I'm fine. Thank you. 我很好，謝謝你。

B. How do you do? 你好嗎？〔初次見面時的問候語〕

正解 ─ C. I'm a computer engineer. 我是電腦工程師。

Q4 Are you a doctor or a dentist?
你是醫生還是牙醫？

正解 A. Neither, I'm a vet. 都不是，我是獸醫。

B. Either a doctor or a dentist. 不是醫生就是牙醫。

C. Both of them. 他們兩個都是。

※〔註〕詢問「X or Y」時，答案就會是這兩個選項的其中一個，因此沒有回答到問題的 B.、C. 都是錯的。如果不選擇題目提供的兩個選項，則會用 Neither 回答，並提供第三個選項。

Q5 What do you want to be when you grow up?
你長大想做什麼？

A. I am a firefighter. 我是消防員。

正解 B. I want to be a teacher. 我想當老師。

C. I want to grow up. 我想長大。

※〔註〕在玩遊戲時也會用到 What do you want to be? 這句話，意思是「你要當什麼角色？」。題目在這句話的後面加上了副詞子句 when you grow up，因此可以知道詢問的是「未來」的事，A.、C. 表達的都是「現在」的情況，因此都是錯誤選項。

主題 **8**   **所有格關係**

Q1 Is that our new teacher?
那是我們的新老師嗎？

A. Yes, it's new. 是，這是新的。

B. We have a few. 我們有一些。

正解 C. I think so. 我想是這樣沒錯。

※〔註〕回答 Yes-No 疑問句時，除了直接以 Yes 或 No 來回答，也可以用不確定的表達方式來回答，例如 I think so.（我想是這樣沒錯）、I'm not sure.（我不確定）、Maybe.（也許）。

Q2 Is this Jim's?
這是吉姆的嗎？

A. Yes, this is Jim. 是，這位是吉姆。

正解 — B. I don't know. 我不知道。

C. I didn't know it's James'. 我之前不知道這是詹姆士的。

※〔註〕A. 不對，題目是問「是～的嗎？」，這裡回答的卻是「誰」。C. 不對，因為 Jim 的所有格是 Jim's，而 James 的所有格是 James'，因為發音類似，所以極有可能會聽錯，要小心！

Q3 Use mine.
用我的吧。

正解 — A. Which one? 哪一個？

B. Never think about it. 想都別想。

C. It's no use. 這沒用。

※〔註〕這段對話的背景情境可能是甲要把東西借給乙，但是乙不確定甲要出借的是哪一個，因此向甲確認。此外，選項 C. 中出現的 use，在題目句子裡是動詞「使用」的意思，這裡則是名詞「效用」的意思。

Q4 Do you know him?
你認識他嗎？

正解 — A. Yes, very well. 認識，很熟。

B. No, he doesn't. 不，他沒有。

C. I know what you mean. 我懂你的意思。

Q5 Is she his girlfriend?
她是他的女朋友嗎？

正解► A. No. Wife. 不。是老婆。

B. It's him. 是他。

C. Not me. 不是我。

※〔註〕B. 和 C. 談論的對象都不符合題意，題目談論的是 she ，這裡卻是 he (him) 及 I (me)。

主題 9　　　　　　　　　**自　己**

Q1 Who's there?
誰在那裡？

A. I'm not. 我不是。

B. This is Bryan calling. 我是布萊恩。〔電話情境下〕

正解► C. It's me, Bryan. 是我，布萊恩。

※〔註〕突然發現有人在周圍，卻不知道是誰，就可以說 Who's there?。對方如果是你聽到聲音就知道是誰的人，通常就會回應你 "It's me."。

Q2 Let's see who's here. Cathy?
我們來看看是誰來了。凱西？

A. Yes, I see. 是，我懂了。

正解► B. Here I am. 是我〔在這兒〕。

C. I heard from Cathy yesterday. 昨天凱西跟我聯絡了。

Q3 Who broke the window?
是誰打破了窗戶？

A. I will. 我會。

正解 — B. I did. Sorry. 是我。對不起。

C. I brought it. 我帶來的。

※〔註〕"broke [brok] / brought [brɔt]" 發音相似。

Q4 Did you do this all by yourself?
這全是你自己做的嗎？

A. Help yourself, please. 請自行取用。

正解 — B. Yes, I did. 沒錯，我自己做的。

C. Didn't you? 你沒有嗎？

※〔註〕問話者問的是「過去」發生的事，A. 的時間點不對；C. 回答的主詞錯了，應改成 I 才有可能會是正確答案。

Q5 Is there anyone else at home?
還有其他人在家嗎？

A. What else? 還有什麼？

正解 — B. No, I'm the only one. 沒有，只有我。

C. Yes, I need glasses. 是，我需要眼鏡。

※〔註〕發問者問的是「人」，選項 A.、C. 回答的則都是「物」，故不可選。

主題 10　個人資訊

Q1 Do you live with your family?
你和家人同住嗎？

正解▶ A. No, I live alone in Taipei. 不，我自己住在台北。

B. We live in Taipei. 我們住在台北。

C. Yes, I love my family. 是，我愛我的家人。

※〔註〕題目問的是「是否同住」的問題，而不是「愛不愛」的問題，因此 C. 與題目主旨不符。題目問「與誰」住，而不是問住「哪裡」，故 B. 也不對。

Q2 Are you married?
你結婚了嗎？

正解▶ A. Yes, with two children. 是的，有兩個小孩。

B. Yes, I'm Marian. 是，我是瑪利安。

C. No, I'm not single. 不，我不是單身。

※〔註〕選項 B. 答非所問，這裡利用發音相似的 married/Marian 來設下陷阱。選項 C. 沒有回答到問題，因此是錯誤選項。正確答案是選項 A.，表示自己不但結了婚，而且連孩子都有兩個了。

Q3 I walk to the office.
我走路到辦公室。

正解▶ A. So it's near your house? 所以辦公室離你家很近？

B. So you're going for a walk? 所以你要去散步囉？

C. So you're off now? 所以你現在要走？

※〔註〕go for a walk = take a walk = have a walk 散步
be off = be leaving = go 離開

Q4 What do you think of computer games?
你對電腦遊戲有什麼看法？

A. I want to have a computer. 我想要有一部電腦。

B. I love surfing the net. 我喜歡上網。

正解 C. I think it's wasting time. 我認為那是在浪費時間。

※〔註〕surf 衝浪；surf the net 上網

Q5 Can you swim?
你會游泳嗎？

A. Why not me? 為什麼不是我？

正解 B. Sure. I'm a good swimmer. 當然。我很會游泳。

C. Yes, she's sweet. 是的，她很甜美。

※〔註〕利用相似發音 "swim [swɪm]/sweet [swit]" 造成混淆。

※〔註〕swim 游泳；swimmer 游泳者；go swimming 去游泳；swimming pool 游泳池；swimming suit = bathing suit 泳衣

第三類 情境

主題 11 　　　　　　　　　　　餐　廳

Q1 How many persons, sir?
先生，請問幾位？

正解 A. Three, please. 三位，謝謝。

B. Yes, sir. 是，長官。

C. Are you sure? 你確定嗎？

Q2 May I take your order now?
您現在要點餐了嗎？

正解 A. Yes, I'll have a Sirloin steak. 是的，我要一客沙朗牛排。

B. No, you may not. 不，你不行。

C. Here, take it. 這裡，拿去。

※〔註〕order 當動詞時是「點菜；訂購」的意思；名詞則是「訂購的東西；訂單」的意思。不過，常常看到的片語 in order，意思是「照順序；就緒」，這裡的 order 則是名詞「順序；秩序」的意思。

Q3 How would you like your steak, sir?
先生，您的牛排要幾分熟？

A. Medium level. 中級。

B. In the medium. 在中等。

正解 C. Medium rare, please. 三分熟，謝謝。

※〔註〕「幾分熟」是一種慣用表達，例如五分熟說 medium、全熟說 well-done，像這種固定的慣用表達，一定要牢牢記住喔！

Q4 Which sauce would you want?
你想要哪一種醬？

正解 A. Well, I like black pepper. 這個嘛，我喜歡黑胡椒。

B. I like sausages. 我喜歡香腸。

C. Yes, I sold it. 是，我把它賣了。

※〔註〕sauce/sausage/sold 三個字的發音相當類似，但選項 B、C. 都不是題目要問的內容，因此正確答案是 A.。

主題
11
情境 v
餐廳

Q5 Would you like anything to drink?
你想要喝點什麼嗎？

A. Never mind. 別在意。

B. Nothing else. 沒有其他的了。

正解 C. I'll have coffee, please. 我要咖啡，謝謝。

※〔註〕選項 A. 通常是用來回應 I'm sorry. 等道歉表達，選項 B. 則會被用來回應 Anything else...? 的句子，皆與題目主題不符，故正確答案是選項 C.。

主題 **12** 　　　　　　　　**外表打扮**

Q1 How tall is your boyfriend?
妳男朋友多高？

A. He's 23 years old. 他 23 歲。

B. He's very fat. 他非常胖。

正解 C. He's 172 cm. 他 172 公分。

Q2 Which is your brother, the tall one or the short one?
哪個是你哥哥？是高的還是矮的那個？

A. My brother is taller than me. 我哥哥比我高。

B. He is as tall as me. 他和我一樣高。

正解 C. The tall one. 高的那個。

※〔註〕題目要求在兩個選項（高的或矮的）中二選一，且比較的對象不是你自己和你哥哥，而是某個和你哥哥站在一起的人，因此正確答案是選項 C.。

Q3 What does he look like?
他長什麼樣子？

A. He likes sports. 他喜歡運動。

正解► B. He is a tall young man with long hair.
他是個留著長髮、很高的年輕人。

C. He is fine. 他很好。

Q4 What did the woman wear?
那個女子穿了什麼？

A. A purse. 皮包。

正解► B. A dress. 洋裝。

C. Luggage. 行李。

※〔註〕若是描述手提的東西則要使用動詞 "carry"。

Q5 My pants are way too big.
我的長褲大太多了。

A. You're gown up. 你長大了。

正解► B. Go to get a belt. 去拿條皮帶。

C. You should wear a tie. 你該繫條領帶。

※〔註〕題目中出現的 way 是用來「強調程度」的副詞，意思是「相當地；大大地」，常用於美式英語。

主題 13　　　　　　　　　結 帳

Q1 Let me pay this time.
這次我來付。

正解 — A. Oh, no. Let me get it. 噢，不。我來付。

B. Got it? 懂了嗎？

C. You'll pay for it. 你會為此付出代價的。

Q2 It's my treat.
我請客。

正解 — A. Oh, thank you. I'll get the next one. 噢，謝謝你。下次我來付。

B. You can't cheat. 你不能作弊。

C. Oh, no. It's too bad. 噢，不。這太糟了。

※〔註〕出現在題目裡的 treat 和選項 B. 中的 cheat 發音相似，只有字首發音不同，但選項 B. 答非所問，而選項 C. 則通常會被用來回應「糟糕」的情況，因此不是正確答案。

Q3 Check, please.
結帳，謝謝。

正解 — A. One moment. 馬上來。

B. Is it the right amount of money? 金額對嗎？

C. I'll pay by check. 我要用支票付。

※〔註〕題目中的 check，意思是「帳單」，而選項 C. 中出現的 check，意思是「支票」。B. 則應該是顧客已經拿了帳單且把錢付出去之後才會說的話。

Q4 Here is your change.

這是您的零錢。

A. I don't want to change it. 我不想改變它。

正解 B. Oh, keep the change. 噢,零錢不用找了。

C. Grab the chance. 抓住機會。

※〔註〕出現在選項 A. 裡的 change 是動詞「改變」的意思,而題目中的 change 則是名詞「零錢」的意思。選項 C. 中的 chance,發音與 change 接近,小心不要聽錯囉。

主題 **13** 情境 ∨ 結帳

Q5 Is the service charge included?

服務費有包含在內嗎?

正解 A. Yes, it is. 是的,有包含。

B. I got a flu. 我得了流行性感冒。

C. We have good service. 我們的服務很好。

主題 **14** 　　　　　**個人好惡**

Q1 How's that song?

那首歌如何?

正解 A. Not so good. 不怎麼好聽。

B. The record store is having a sale. 那間唱片行正在舉辦特賣。

C. I can't sing. 我不會唱。

※〔註〕How's...? 的句型是詢問對某事物的看法,像是好或不好、喜歡不喜歡等,只有選項 A. 是合理的回應。

Q2 What kind of juice do you want?
你想要哪種果汁？

A. I'd rather wear jeans than a dress.

我比較想穿牛仔褲而不是裙子。

正解 B. What choices do we have? 我們有什麼選擇？

C. It's on me. 我請客。

※〔註〕選項 A. 答非所問，且企圖利用發音相似的 juice/jeans 來造成混淆，因此是錯誤選項。C. 則是從「提議者」角度出發的應對方式，答非所問。詢問有什麼選擇的選項 B. 才是合理的回答。

Q3 How do you like the university?
你覺得這間大學如何？

正解 A. I love it very much. 我非常喜歡。

B. This university is famous. 這間大學很有名。

C. You're unlike me. 你不像我。

※〔註〕題目詢問對大學的喜歡程度，也就是詢問聽者對大學的感覺，因此只有選項 A. 是合理回答。請注意選項 C. 中的 unlike 是表達「不相像的」的形容詞，相反詞是 like（相像的），題目中出現的 like 則是動詞「喜歡」的意思。

Q4 How would you like it cut?
你想要怎麼剪？

A. Just a haircut. 只要剪頭髮就好。

正解 B. Cut it short all over. 整個剪短。

C. I'd like a shampoo. 我想洗頭。

※〔註〕發問者可能是美髮師，已經知道顧客是要剪髮，A.、C. 的回答方式應該都是在發問者問這句話之前所說的話，時間點上錯誤，故選 B.。

Q5 Don't you want to visit New York sometime?
你不會想要找個時間去參觀紐約嗎？

正解 A. Yes, I do. I'll go there one day. 會，我想。我未來有一天會去。

B. I'll be there in a second. 我馬上要到那裡了。

C. I visited the city several times. 我去過那座城市幾次。

※〔註〕發問者問 Don't you want to... sometime? 問的是「未來的某個時間點」想不想做某事，選項 C. 回答的時間點是「過去」，因此是錯誤選項。選項 B. 回答的時間點雖是未來，但 in a second（馬上）所表達的時間距離太近了，因此不是合理的回應。正確答案是選項 A.，one day 是「未來的某一天」的意思。

第 四 類 數字

主題 15 　　　　　　　　　　**詢 價**

Q1 How much is the room rate?
房間費用多少？

正解 A. It's about $1,200 for one night. 一晚大約 1200 元。

B. We'll stay for 3 nights. 我們會住 3 個晚上。

C. This is for rent. 這是要出租的。

※〔註〕費用 rate [ret] ／出租 rent [rɛnt]。

Q2 Are the meals included in the rent?

這房租裡包括膳食費嗎？

A. Three meals a day. 一天三餐。

B. $100 a meal. 一餐 100 元。

正解 C. No, they aren't. 不，不包括。

Q3 What do you charge?

你們要收多少錢？

A. Can I change to another room? 我可以換到別的房間嗎？

B. I have a 25-cent coin. 我有一個 25 分的硬幣。

正解 C. US$25.00 a week. 一個星期美金 25 元。

※〔註〕要詢問某些服務的收費方式時，就可以用 What do you charge?，例如詢問住宿、乾洗店、修車廠等的收費方式，一般都會回答如：一天（星期）多少錢、一件襯衫多少錢或換一個零件多少錢等等，故選項 C. 為正確答案。

Q4 How much should I pay you?

我要付你多少錢？

正解 A. Oh, it's free. 哦，這是免費的。

B. Oh, you have to pay in cash. 喔，你必須付現金。

C. Should I? 我應該要嗎？

※〔註〕How much...? 是問該付「多少」錢，而不是問「如何」付錢，因此選項 B. 是錯的。選項 C. 是發話者才會說出的話，因此是錯誤選項。特別要注意的是，如果選項內容只單純重複了題目中出現的某個片語或慣用表達，則通常都是錯誤選項。

Q5 It must have cost you a lot.
這一定花了你很多錢。

正解 A. You're worth it. 你值得。

B. I have a lot of it. 這我有很多。

C. Yes, I bought you a coat. 對，我買了一件大衣給你。

※〔註〕這段對話應該是發話者收到了一份禮物，因而客氣地對送禮者表示感謝，因此選項 A. 是最合理的回應。選項 B. 中的 a lot 是形容詞，題目中的 a lot 則是副詞，且語意答非所問，因此是錯誤選項。選項 C. 是送禮者才會說的內容，且是透過發音相似的 cost/coat 企圖造成混淆的陷阱選項，小心不要選錯囉！

主題 16　例行時間

Q1 What time do you get up?
你幾點起床？

A. Why did you get up so early? 你為什麼這麼早起床？

B. It's time to go to bed. 睡覺時間到了。

正解 C. I usually get up at six thirty. 我通常都六點半起床。

Q2 At what time does the store open?
這間店幾點開？

A. At the store. 在店裡。

正解 B. At ten o'clock, sir. 十點，先生。

C. The store is open. 這間店開著。

Q3 What are your working hours?

你的上班時間是什麼時候？

A. Keep early hours. 早睡早起。

正解 ▶ B. It is 9:00 a.m. to 5:30 p.m. 早上九點到下午五點半。

C. I worked from 9:00 a.m. to 5:30 p.m. yesterday.

我昨天從早上九點工作到下午五點半。

Q4 When does the train for Los Angeles leave?

往洛杉磯的火車什麼時候開？

正解 ▶ A. 9:25 on Platform 2. 9 點 25 分，在二號月台。

B. It takes 9 hours by train. 坐火車要 9 個小時。

C. We will leave Los Angeles by 9 o'clock.

我們會在 9 點前離開洛杉磯。

Q5 How long is the ride?

車程多久？

正解 ▶ A. About ten minutes. 大約十分鐘。

B. About ten meters. 大約十公尺。

C. About ten long ropes. 大約十條長繩。

※〔註〕the ride 的意思是一段車程，題目關鍵字是 How long...? 在此是問「多久」的時間，故選 A.。

主題 17 時間約定

Q1 Would 9:00 tomorrow be all right?
明天 9 點可以嗎？

A. At 9:00 last night. 昨晚 9 點。

B. Nothing is right. 沒有一件事是對的。

正解 C. I'm afraid not. 恐怕不行。

Q2 How would 12:45 be?
12 點 45 分如何？

A. The house is made out of wood. 這房子是木造的。

正解 B. Just a second. I'll have to check. 等等，我得確認一下。

C. OK. I'll check the house. 好，我會去檢查房子。

※〔註〕發話者提出了一個會面時間，所以只有 B. 為合理回答。

Q3 Will you be here at nine o'clock tomorrow?
你明天九點鐘會在這裡嗎？

正解 A. Yeah, I will be here. 會啊，我會在這裡。

B. Will you come tonight? 今晚你會來嗎？

C. Yes, I can hear. 是，我聽得到。

※〔註〕同音異字的 "here [hɪr] / hear [hɪr]"；發音相似的 "nine [naɪn] / tonight [tə`naɪt]" 都會造成混淆，務必特別注意。

Q4 See you in the evening at home.
晚上家裡見。

正解 ▸ A. OK, bye. 好，再見。

B. I come back home at 5:00 in the evening. 我傍晚 5 點回家。

C. Did you see? 你有看到嗎？

※〔註〕B.、C. 語意皆無法對應題目句意，故選 A.。這段對話應該是早上要出門時，對家人常說的道別語。

Q5 What time?
什麼時候？

正解 ▸ A. You name the time. 時間你決定。

B. Ten times. 十次。

C. In old times. 古時候。

※〔註〕三個選項所出現的 time 的意思都不相同，依序為「時間」、「次數」、「時代」，因此 A. 為正確答案。name 在此是動詞用法，表示「指定」之意。

主題 **18**　　　　　　　　　　**詢問時間**

Q1 Can you tell me what time it is?
你可以告訴我現在幾點嗎？

正解 ▸ A. It's one o'clock sharp. 現在是一點整。

B. Don't touch. It's sharp. 別摸。這很銳利。

C. Don't ask. 別問。

※〔註〕選項 A. 中的 sharp 是指「～點整」。

Q2 Can you tell me the time, please?
可以請你告訴我現在幾點嗎？

A. Can't you? 你不行嗎？

B. Are you sure? 你確定嗎？

正解 C. Sure. It's twenty to nine. 當然。現在是八點四十分。

Q3 Excuse me, sir. Do you have the time?
不好意思，先生。你知道現在幾點嗎？

A. It's two hundred and twenty. 兩百二十。

正解 B. It's two twenty. 兩點二十分。

C. Two times twenty is forty. 二乘二十等於四十。

※〔註〕time 的另一個意思是數學裡的「乘法」，這裡動詞 time 的字尾一定要加 "-s"；方程式裡的「等於」可以用 is 或 equals 等單數動詞表示。
〔例〕2 × 20 = 40 → Two times twenty equals forty.

Q4 I wonder what time it is.
不知道現在幾點了。

正解 A. I don't think it is five o'clock yet. 我想現在還不到五點。

B. I don't think so. 我不這麼認為。

C. No wonder. 難怪。

※〔註〕這題的背景情境應該是對話雙方都沒戴手錶，也找不到方法可以確認正確時間，所以兩人會使用 I wonder... 與 I don't think... 來表示自己不確定真正的時間。

Q5 What time do you have?
你的錶幾點了？

正解 A. My watch says two o'clock. 我的錶是兩點。

B. Watch what you say. 小心你說的話。

C. Watch out. 小心。

※〔註〕B.、C. 當中的 watch 當動詞有「小心」的意思，與詢問時間的題目問句完全不符。注意！正確答案 A. My watch says... 的動詞 says 為一固定用法，中文通常無法直接翻譯出來。

第 五 類 慣用句型

主題 19　詢問地點

Q1 What city do you live in?
你住在哪個城市裡？

正解 A. I'm in Hualian. 我在花蓮。

B. I live in Korea. 我住在韓國。

C. I live in school housing. 我住校。

※〔註〕題目關鍵字是 What city...?，問的是城市，故選選項 A.。

Q2 Have you decided where to go?
你決定要去哪裡了嗎？

A. Not me. 不是我。

正解 B. Not yet. 還沒。

C. I can't. 我不行。

※〔註〕Have you...? 問的是做了某事沒有，故選 B.。

Q3 Where are we on this map?
我們在這張地圖的哪裡？

A. We're on the bus. 我們在巴士上。

B. You're right. 你是對的。

正解 C. We're right here. 我們就在這裡。

※〔註〕題目問句中的 on this map 表示對話雙方都在看同一張地圖，因此回應時必須指出在地圖上的位置並說 "We're right here."，故選 C.。

Q4 Can you tell me a good place to eat?
你能告訴我哪裡有好吃的嗎？

正解 A. Do you like spaghetti? 你喜歡義大利麵嗎？

B. I know that place. 我知道那個地方。

C. How pretty! 好美！

Q5 What country has the most people in the world?
世界上哪個國家的人最多？

A. People around the world know about it. 全世界的人都知道。

B. Indonesia has the most islands in the world.

　　印尼擁有全世界最多的島嶼。

正解 C. Is it China? 是中國嗎？

主題 **19** 慣用句型 v 詢問地點

主題 20　詢問方法

Q1 How do you go to school?
你怎麼到學校的？

A. Just take a chance. 就碰碰運氣。

正解 B. My father drives me to school. 我父親開車載我去學校。

C. Take it easy. 放輕鬆。

Q2 How can I get there?
我要怎麼到那裡？

A. Go ahead. 去做吧。

B. I'll take it. 我要這個〔這件〕。

正解 C. Take bus 202. 搭 202 號公車。

※〔註〕從題目問句中的 How 與 get there 可以知道，發問者想要知道的是一種「交通方式」，故選 C.。

Q3 What is the easiest way to the zoo?
到動物園最簡單的方法是什麼？

正解 A. By MRT. 搭捷運。

B. It's by the zoo. 它在動物園旁邊。

C. By heart. 憑記憶。

※〔註〕由 What...way...? 可知這也是詢問交通方式的題目，故答案為 A.。

Q4 By which way would you like to pay?
你想要如何付款呢？

正解 A. Here is $2,000 cash. 這是 2000 元的現金。

B. Here you come! 你來啦！

C. Here we are! 我們到了！

Q5 What can I do for you?
我能為你做什麼？〔我能為您服務嗎？〕

A. You can leave now. 你現在可以走了。

B. I'm doing housework. 我正在做家事。

正解 C. I'd like to see the ties. 我想看看領帶。

主題 21 詢問原因

Q1 I have a fever.
我發燒了。

A. Excuse me. 不好意思。

B. You'll be sorry. 你會後悔的。

正解 C. Did you catch a cold? 你感冒了嗎？

※〔註〕這題一定要先聽懂 fever（發燒）的意思，才能選出合理的回應。當你聽到對方說自己發燒了，當然就會先關心他是不是感冒生病了，因此答案是選項 C.

Q2 What's up? You don't look yourself today.
怎麼了？你今天看起來不太對勁。

A. I did it myself. 我自己做的。

B. That sounds great. 那聽起來很不錯。

正解 C. Nothing. 沒事。

Q3 How come you didn't call me last night?
你昨晚怎麼沒打電話給我？

A. I was ... um ... busy. 我在……嗯……忙。

B. I came by a taxi. 我搭計程車來的。

C. Yeah, sure. 是啊，當然。

Q4 Cathy, can you help me with this?
凱西，你可以幫我弄一下這個嗎？

正解 A. Why me again? 為什麼又是我？

B. That's right. 沒錯。

C. Don't mention it. 別客氣。

Q5 I can't come tonight.
我今晚沒辦法過來。

A. It's cool! 太酷了！

B. Why not use a comb? 要不要用梳子？

正解 C. Why not? 為什麼不行？

※〔註〕這段對話的情境應該是雙方已約定要一起前往某處，但發話者卻臨時無法前往。A. 的回應不合常理；B. 則是利用發音相似的 come/comb 企圖造成混淆；選項 C. 追問對方原因，要求取得更多資訊，是合理的正確答案。

主題 22　感官動詞

Q1 Can you hear me?

你聽得到我嗎？

A. OK. I'm here. 好。我在這裡。

正解 ▶ B. Yes, very well. 可以，非常清楚。

C. I'm pretty well, thank you. 我很好，謝謝你。

※〔註〕選項 A. 利用發音相似的 hear/here 來造成混淆；選項 C. 中出現了與正確答案選項 B. 中的 very well 聽起來很相似的 pretty well，不過 I'm pretty well 其實是 I'm fine. 的意思，小心不要搞錯囉！

Q2 What's the smell?

這什麼味道？

A. I can't hear it. 我聽不到。

B. It smells good. 它聞起來不錯。

正解 ▶ C. It smells like garbage. 聞起來像垃圾。

※〔註〕發問者是「聞到」某種味道，而不是「聽到」或「嚐到」，也不是詢問對方對這個味道的感覺，所以正確答案為 C.。

Q3 Why do you sound unhappy to see me?

為什麼你聽起來好像不高興見到我？

正解 ▶ A. Never. You just surprised me. 絕對不是，只是你嚇了我一跳。

B. I'll never see you again. 我不想再見到你。

C. I have a sore throat. 我的喉嚨痛。

※〔註〕這段對話的情境是對話者雙方已經見面了，所以 B. 這句話所表達的時間點不對；選 C. 的人則可能是把題目中的 sound unhappy 聽成了 sound unhealthy（聽起來不健康）。

Q4 This place feels like home.
這地方感覺就像家一樣。

A. How does it feel? 你覺得它怎麼樣？

正解 ▶ B. Then why not stay longer? 那麼何不待久一點呢？

C. How do you feel? 你覺得如何？

※〔註〕發話者已經發表了自己的感覺，覺得這個地方讓他覺得像在家一樣，因此主人就可能會用 B. 來回應，希望對方可以留下來。選項 A.、C. 的時間點不對，這兩句的內容都應該是在發話者說出題目句子之前，而不是用來回應發話者。

Q5 It's freezing out here.
外面這裡很冷。

A. Yeah, I can't feel my feet anymore.
　　是啊，我的腳都沒感覺了。

B. It's not good for you. 這對你來說不好。

C. I'm not feeling well. 我覺得不舒服。

※〔註〕B.、C. 都是利用發音相似的 freezing/feel/feet 來造成混淆的錯誤選項。正確答案是選項 A.，附和發話者的說法，表示外頭的確很冷，並提供自己冷到連腳都失去知覺的更多資訊。

第六類 強調短句

主題 23　驚訝與驚喜

Q1 This is for you.
這是給你的。

正解 ▸ A. What a surprise! 真是太意外了！

B. You can't do this. 你不能這麼做。

C. It's mine. 這是我的。

Q2 Oh, no! I don't believe it.
噢，不！我不相信。

正解 ▸ A. What's the matter? 怎麼了？

B. Do you believe it? 你相信嗎？

C. How can you do this? 你怎麼可以這麼做？

※〔註〕說話者已經明白的表現出震驚、不可置信的情緒，A. 表示出關心之情，為最佳答案。B. 故意唱反調；C.完全答非所問，因此都不是正確答案。

Q3 Mark is late.
馬克遲到了。

正解 ▸ A. That's surprising. He's never late. 真意外。他從不遲到的。

B. Why were you late? 你為什麼遲到了？

C. Give me one second. 等我一下。

※〔註〕題目談論的對象是 Mark，選項 B. 及 C. 的主詞皆不符。選項 A. 表示自己很意外 Mark 竟然會遲到，是最合理的回應方式。

Q4 No, she's not my sister. She's my mother.
不，她不是我姐姐。她是我媽媽。

正解 A. Are you joking? She looks so young.

你在開玩笑嗎？她看起來這麼年輕。

B. No kidding? She's your sister? 沒開玩笑？她是你姐姐？

C. Wow. What a good kid! 哇，好棒的孩子！

※〔註〕kid 的名詞用法是「孩子」的意思，動詞用法則是「開玩笑」的意思，就等於 joke [dʒok]，這個字當名詞就是「笑話」的意思，例如：It's a joke.（這是個笑話（開玩笑的））。

Q5 It can't be true.
這不可能是真的。

正解 A. I'm afraid it is. 恐怕是真的。

B. Yes, it's real. 是，這是真的〔東西〕。

C. For real this time? 這次是真的？

※〔註〕true 是「真相、事實」，real 是「真實的」，兩者意義完全不同，故 B.、C. 皆錯。答案 A. 則是告訴對方很不幸的真相就是如此。

主題24　命令與警告

Q1 Now listen to me carefully.
現在仔細聽我說。

A. You're too careful. 你太過小心了。

B. I do care. 我真的在乎。

正解 C. Yes. What is it? 好。什麼事？

Q2 Just leave me alone, will you?
你就別管我了，好嗎？

正解 A. OK. OK. 好，好。

B. Come on. Let's leave. 來，我們走吧！

C. Go away. 走開。

※〔註〕基本上這是一個委婉的命令句，句子前半段明確說出要對方做的事，後半段的附加問句則使口氣稍微緩和了一些。

Q3 Don't touch! Keep your hands off that vase.
別碰！別碰那個花瓶。

A. Would you hand me that vase? 你可以把那個花瓶拿給我嗎？

正解 B. Hey, take it easy. 嘿，別緊張。

C. It's as easy as pie. 這簡單得很〔小事一樁〕。

※〔註〕It's easy. = It's as easy as pie. = It's a piece of cake.

Q4 Don't forget to brush your teeth.
別忘了刷牙。

正解 A. I won't. 我不會忘的。

B. I'm sorry. 我很抱歉。

C. I forgot. 我忘了。

※〔註〕這裡要特別注意，雖然發話者用的表達方式是 Don't...，但在回應時必須使用未來式，絕對不可用 I don't... 來回答，選項 A. 是最合理的回應方式。

Q5 Watch your step!
小心腳下！

正解 A. Oh, thank you. 噢，謝謝你。

B. Better safe than sorry! 小心為上！

C. How are you? 你好嗎？

※〔註〕題目的這個命令句，實際上是針對受話者提出的貼心提醒，而受話者等於是接受了對方的幫助，因此正確答案會是選項 A.。

主題 **25**　　　　　　　　**催促與延緩**

Q1 Hurry! We are late.
快一點！我們遲到了。

正解 A. OK, coming. 好，來了。

B. Good luck! 祝好運！

C. Take your time. 你慢慢來。

Q2 Will you wait for just one moment, please?
可以請你稍等嗎？

正解 A. Sure. What is it? 當然。怎麼了？

B. Slow down. 慢一點。

C. Don't push me. 別逼我。

Q3 Could you slow down, please?
可以請你慢一點嗎？

正解 A. Oh, I'm sorry. 哦，抱歉。

B. How could you? 你怎麼可以這樣？

C. Wait a minute. 等一下。

Q4 Don't rush. The game begins at 6:30.
別急。比賽是 6 點 30 分開始。

正解 A. Oh, good. We still have time. 哦，好，我們還有時間。

B. The game is over now. 比賽現在結束了。

C. Where are we going? 我們要去哪裡？

※〔註〕說話者表示即將和受話者一起去參加或觀看一場比賽，因此選項 B.、C. 不合常理；正確答案是選項 A.。

Q5 Why all this hurry?
怎麼這麼趕？

A. Don't worry. 別擔心。

B. Don't take too long. 不要花太久時間。

正解 C. I'm late for the bus. 我要趕不上巴士了。

※〔註〕選項 A. 是透過發音相似的 hurry/worry 來造成混淆的錯誤選項，且與選項 B. 一樣都沒有回答到題目的 Why...? 問題，因此正確答案是 C.。

主題 26　　　　　　　拒　絕

Q1 Can I borrow your dress for tonight's party?
我可以借妳的洋裝去參加今晚的派對嗎？

正解 A. No way. 不可能。

　　　B. That's nothing. 那沒什麼。

　　　C. That's not true. 那不是真的。

Q2 Can I help you?
需要幫忙嗎？〔我能協助你嗎？〕

　　　A. We need to get help. 我們必須找人幫忙。

　　　B. No way. 不可能。

正解 C. No, but thank you anyway. 不用，不過還是謝謝你。

Q3 Thanks, but I can't eat seafood.
謝謝，可是我不能吃海鮮。

正解 A. That's too bad! 真可惜！

　　　B. Do you need a hand? 你需要幫忙嗎？

　　　C. Any questions? 有任何問題嗎？

Q4 We have to finish it today.
我們今天必須做完它。

正解 A. That's not possible. 那是不可能的。

　　　B. See you tomorrow. 明天見。

　　　C. I haven't finished it. 我還沒把它做完。

Q5 Do you want me to check the tires?
需要我為您檢查輪胎嗎？

正解 A. No, that's all for now. 不用，現在先這樣就好。

B. I'm tired now. 我現在累了。

C. Excuse me. 不好意思〔打擾了〕。

※〔註〕選項 B. 是利用發音相似的 tires/tired 來造成混淆的錯誤選項；選項 C. 則完全答非所問。選項 A. 是正確答案，表示發話者在說出題目句子之前，已先為受話者提供過一些服務了，而受話者覺得不需要再追加檢查輪胎的這項服務。

主題 27 道謝

Q1 OK, I'll take it. Thank you for your help.
好，我要買這個。謝謝你的幫忙。

正解 A. Anytime. 不客氣。

B. I'm glad to hear that. 我很高興聽到這件事。

C. No, I didn't do anything. 沒有，我什麼都沒做。

※〔註〕這段對話最可能是發生在顧客與店員之間，最合理的回應是選項 A.，這裡的 Anytime. 就是 Anytime you need help, just come to me.（隨時需要幫忙就來找我）的意思。

Q2 Thank you for coming to my birthday party.
謝謝你來參加我的生日派對。

正解 A. It's my pleasure. 這是我的榮幸。

B. As you pleased. 請隨意〔照你喜歡的方式做〕。

C. You are wonderful. 你好棒。

Q3 Thank you. I had a lot of fun.
謝謝你。我玩得很開心。

A. What do you like to play? 你喜歡玩什麼？

正解 — B. I'm glad to hear that. 我很高興聽你這麼說。

C. I'm so glad for you. 我真為你高興。

Q4 Here's your birthday present. I hope you like this.
這是你的生日禮物。希望你會喜歡。

正解 — A. It's just what I want. Thank you. 這就是我想要的。謝謝你。

B. I will do what I can. 我會盡我所能。

C. It was nothing like that. 根本不是這麼回事。

※〔註〕當你收到一份禮物時，當然要謝謝對方，A. 除了表示感謝之外，更以 It's just what I want. 這句話來表示自己「強烈」地喜歡對方所選的禮物。

Q5 Are you all right? Let me help you stand up.
你還好嗎？讓我來扶你站起來。

A. Don't worry. I will help you. 別擔心。我會幫你。

B. Sit down, please. 請坐下。

正解 — C. Thanks. You're very kind. 謝謝。你人真好。

主題 **28** 　　　　　　　　　**讚 美**

Q1 This is my new dress. I bought it yesterday.
這是我的新洋裝。我昨天買的。

正解 A. That's nice. 很不錯。

B. You're nice. 你真好。

C. It's a nice boat. 這是一艘好船。

※〔註〕讚美別人的穿著是一種提升人際關係的好方法,而選項 A. 的 That's nice. 是日常生活中很常用到的讚美表達。選項 B. 的主詞與題目句子不符;C. 則是利用發音相似的 bought/boat 來造成混淆的錯誤選項。

Q2 I still can't believe I made this all by myself.
我還是不敢相信這全是我自己做的。

正解 A. Good for you! 真棒!

B. Great. Let's do together. 太棒了。我們一起做。

C. OK, that's all. 好,就這樣。

Q3 Dinner's ready!
晚餐好啦!

正解 A. Um, it smells good. 嗯,聞起來好香。

B. I'm dying for a drink. 我超想喝杯飲料的。

C. What would you like for dinner? 你晚餐想吃什麼?

※〔註〕晚餐一定是剛準備好,還熱騰騰的,正散發出引人食欲的香味,所以回應者說 "It smells good."。

Q4 How do you like the cake?
你覺得蛋糕怎麼樣？〔喜歡嗎？〕

A. Just look at what you've done. 你就看看自己做了什麼。

B. Take it or leave it. 要不要隨便你。

正解 C. It's delicious! 很好吃！

Q5 I'm proud of you.
我以你為榮。

正解 A. Really? You are? 真的？你真的這麼認為嗎？

B. Well done. 做得好。

C. Cheer up! 開心一點〔加油〕！

※〔註〕當對方做了一件令人佩服的事，例如成績特別突出、英勇救人等等，這時候就可以對他說 "I'm proud of you."。這裡的回應者可能沒預期會受到讚美，所以才會不可置信地說 "Really? You are?"。

主題 29　　　　　　**道 歉**

Q1 Hey, Benny. Sorry, I'm late.
嘿，班尼。對不起，我遲到了。

A. You'll be sorry. 你會後悔的。

正解 B. What kept you so long? 你怎麼這麼久才來？

C. What for? 為什麼？

Q2 Sorry, I have to go now.
抱歉，我現在得走了。

正解 A. OK, see you tomorrow. 好，明天見。

B. I had better go by myself. 我最好親自去。

C. I'm out of here. 我要離開這裡了。

Q3 Excuse me. There's a call for you.
不好意思，有您的電話。

A. I'll give you a call. 我會打電話給你。

B. What do you call it? 牠叫什麼名字？

正解 C. OK, put it through. 好，接過來。

Q4 Pardon me. Can you say it again?
不好意思，您可以再說一次嗎？

A. Let me think about it. 讓我考慮一下。

正解 B. Forget it. 算了。

C. Never. 絕不。

※〔註〕發話者可能在和對方說話時分心了，所以想請對方再說一次，但是對方因為不想再重述一次，所以回答 Forget it.。

Q5 Well, you finally got here.
嗯，你終於到了。

A. I will do my best. 我會盡我的全力。

正解 B. Sorry. Let me treat you a coffee. 抱歉。讓我請你喝杯咖啡吧。

C. You got it. 沒錯。

主題 **30**　　　　　　　　　安撫與鼓勵

Q1 David's OK now. He'll come to school tomorrow.

大衛現在沒事了。他明天會來上學。

正解 A. That's good news. 這是個好消息。

B. Did he agree? 他答應了嗎？

C. I'm fine. 我很好。

※〔註〕聽得出來討論的對象 David 應該是生病或受傷了，但現在好了，那真的是好消息，因此答案為 A.。注意！ news 字形看似可屬名詞的複數（字尾加上了 -s），但其實是個不可數名詞，前面不可加任何冠詞。

Q2 Sorry, I broke your cup.

對不起，我打破了你的杯子。

正解 A. That's OK. Did you get hurt? 沒關係。你有受傷嗎？

B. Please don't hurt me! 請不要傷害我！

C. The cup is broken. 這杯子破了。

Q3 I'm not sure I can do it.

我不確定我做得到。

A. Surely you will. 你一定會〔去做〕。

B. Come on this way. 走這裡。

正解 C. Come on. Give it a try. 別這樣。試試看吧。

※〔註〕當對方不確定自己有能力可以完成某事，需要的就是別人的鼓勵，選項 C. 的意思就是要對方至少試一試，也許就成功了。A. 的助動詞錯了，應改成 "Surely you can."。選項 B. 則與題目句意完全不符。

Q4 I don't think I can make it.
我不認為我做得到。

A. Go ahead. Don't worry about me. 去吧，不用擔心我。

B. Sure. Take a chance. 當然，碰碰運氣嘛。

正解 C. You'll never know until you do it. 你得做了才知道。

※〔註〕A. 錯在討論的話題主旨從一件事情變成了一個人，因此選項 C. 才是正確答案。

Q5 It's too late to prepare for the exam.
現在準備考試太晚了。

正解 A. Better late than never. 遲做總比不做好。

〔【喻】亡羊補牢猶未晚也。〕

B. Hurry up. 快一點。

C. What's this for? 這是做什麼用的？

主題 **31** 表示不介意

Q1 I'm sorry that Sally can't come.
抱歉，莎莉不能來。

正解 A. It's okay. 沒關係

B. Please say it again. 請再說一遍。

C. You're welcome. 不客氣。

Q2 I'm sorry for the trouble.
我很抱歉造成了困擾。

正解 A. Never mind. 別在意。

B. What would you like? 你想要什麼？

C. Don't talk to me. 別跟我說話。

Q3 What happened to you?
你發生了什麼事？

A. It happens. 常有的事。

B. I'm doing fine. 我很好。

正解 C. It's nothing important, really. 沒什麼事，真的。

Q4 Do you mind if I open the window?
你介意我把窗戶打開嗎？

A. Don't talk too much. 別說太多話。

B. It's not important. 這不重要。

正解 C. No, go ahead. 不，去開吧。

Q5 Sorry, I can't help with dinner.
抱歉，我沒辦法幫忙做晚餐。

正解 A. Oh, that's no problem. 噢，這沒關係。

B. I just want to help. 我只是想要幫忙。

C. I have no idea. 我不知道。

主題 **32** 猜 測

Q1 Is it all right?
這樣沒關係嗎？

A. It's all done. 都做好了。

正解 ▶ B. I guess so. 我想是吧。

C. I'll write it down. 我會把它寫下來。

Q2 You will help me out, right?
你會幫我的，對嗎？

正解 ▶ A. That all depends on what it is. 那要看是什麼事。

B. You're welcome. 不客氣。

C. I'm fine. 我很好。

※〔註〕help out ～ 幫助～擺脫困難。

Q3 How long will Jimmy be out of school?
吉米會離開學校多久？

A. There's only half an hour left. 只剩半小時了。

B. Sooner or later. 遲早會發生。

正解 ▶ C. I guess "forever". 我猜是「永遠」。

※〔註〕因為題目詢問的是 How long...?（多久～？），所以回應內容應該是「一段時間」，而非一個時間點，因此最合理的答案是選項 C.。

Q4 I bet you were the best in the class.
我敢說你是班上最優秀的。

A. I just want to help people. 我只是想要幫助人們。

正解 B. Well, I did get an A. 這個嘛，我的確是拿到了個 A。

C. I will cheer for you! 我會為你加油的！

※〔註〕bet [bɛt] 與某人打賭。

Q5 Have you got your work done for today?
你今天的作業做完了嗎？

A. We should work hard everyday. 我們每天都應該要努力。

B. I don't go to work on weekends. 我週末不上班。

正解 C. No, but maybe the teacher won't ask for it.
沒有，但是老師可能不會要收。

※〔註〕題目問句的時態是現在完成式，因此問的是「到目前為止，作業是否已經做完了」。選項 A.、B. 是現在式，因此表達的是事實或固定會發生的事，因此不是正確答案；選項 C. 先以 No 表示作業還沒做完，再隨後補充自己的猜想，提供更多資訊，是最恰當的回應方式。

主題 **33** 　　　　　　　**尋求認同**

Q1 I don't believe you.
我不相信你。

A. I can't believe it, either. 我也不相信〔這件事〕。

正解 B. But it's true. 但這是真的。

C. But we are leaving. 但是我們要離開了。

Q2 Take a look at this picture. How is it?
看看這張照片。你覺得怎麼樣?

正解 ► A. You did a great job. 你拍得很棒。

B. May I take a picture of you? 我可以拍一張你的照片嗎?

C. I'd like some more, please. 我還想要一些,謝謝。

Q3 Should I go?
我應該去嗎?

正解 ► A. Yes, go ahead. 是的,去吧。

B. Do you play golf? 你有打高爾夫球嗎?

C. It's better than nothing. 總好過什麼都沒有。

Q4 Shall we tell him?
我們要告訴他嗎?

正解 ► A. Sure. He's our friend. 當然。他是我們的朋友。

B. I'm sorry. 我很抱歉。

C. It's terrible. 真糟糕。

Q5 I can't do this.
這我辦不到。〔我不能這麼做〕

A. Do you think I'm stupid? 你覺得我很笨嗎?

B. Why are you doing this? 你為什麼要這麼做?

正解 ► C. Of course you can. 你當然辦得到。

主題 34　表達認同

Q1 It's a good book.
這是一本好書。

A. I want some cookies. 我想要一些餅乾。

B. I like to read a book on weekends. 週末時我喜歡看書。

正解 C. You're right. 沒錯。

Q2 Let's go to a party.
我們去參加派對吧。

A. It was great. 派對很棒。→ [過去式]

B. Yeah, I went. 是啊，我去了。→ [過去式]

正解 C. What a great idea. 真是個好主意。

Q3 It's hard work to plant trees in the desert.
要在沙漠裡種樹很困難。

A. Yeah, it's my plan. 是啊，這是我的計畫。

B. It seems great! 這看起來很棒！

正解 C. I agree. 我同意。

Q4 Do you really like it?
你真的喜歡它嗎?

正解 A. Yes, very much. 對,非常喜歡。

B. Yes, it's very noisy. 對,它非常吵。

C. Yes, we're alike. 對,我們很像。

※〔註〕like 除了有動詞「喜歡」的意思之外,形容詞的意思是「相像的」,alike 也是「相像的」的意思,但是兩者的用法不盡相同。請見以下例句:

Ex: Are you *like* your brother? 你像你哥哥嗎?
Ex: Are you and your brother *alike*? 你和你哥哥像嗎?

Q5 It looks like a warm place.
那看來像是個溫暖的地方。

A. Yes, Luke won the first place in the game.
是啊,路克在比賽贏中得了第一名。

B. Yes, she has a warm heart. 是啊,她很熱心。

正解 C. Yes, I think so too. 是啊,我也這麼認為。

※〔註 1〕warm 除了表「溫暖」之外,還有「熱心」的意思。place 除了表示「地方」之外,也可以用來表達「名次」:the first place 第一名、the second place 第二名……等。

※〔註 2〕選項中的類音字組有 "look [lʊk] / Luke [luk]","warm [wɔrm] / won [wʌn]"。

主題 35　不完全肯定

Q1 She has a good voice and sings beautifully.
她的聲音很好聽，而且歌唱得很好。

A. I don't know she's divorced. 我不知道她離婚了。

B. Is she getting better? 她好多了嗎？

正解 C. Is that true? 真的嗎？

※〔註〕利用發音相似的 "voice [vɔɪs] / divorced [dəˋvɔrst]" 來造成混亂。

Q2 That's a nice dress. It looks good on you.
那件洋裝很美。妳穿起來很好看。

A. Thanks. Don't bother. 謝謝。不用麻煩了。

B. I'm not myself today. 我今天不太對勁。

正解 C. Do you think so? 你這麼認為嗎？

Q3 Will we make it on time?
我們可以準時趕到嗎？

A. Yes, we'll be there. 是，我們會到那裡。

正解 B. I hope so. 我希望可以。

C. Are you sure? 你確定嗎？

Q4 Of the countries you've been to, which do you like best?
在你曾去過的國家之中，你最喜歡哪一個？

A. I like Seattle best. 我最喜歡西雅圖〔城市名〕。

B. Oh, I've been to lots of countries. 噢，我去過了很多國家。

正解 C. It's hard to say. Each country is different.
這很難說。每個國家都不一樣。

Q5 Chinese is pretty difficult, isn't it?
中文滿難的，不是嗎？

正解 A. It seemed that way at first. 一開始似乎是那樣。

B. Are they? 他們有嗎？

C. I'm not Chinese. 我不是中國人。

※〔註〕Chinese 有「中文」和「中國人」的意思。

主題 **36**　　　　**不認同**

Q1 I don't think we can trust him.
我不認為我們可以信任他。

正解 A. Of course we can. 我們當然可以。

B. Trust me, you can make it. 相信我，你做得到。

C. Believe it or not. 信不信由你。

※〔註〕題目發話者的意思是否定的口吻，A. 的回答卻是正面的，否定了發話者的負面意見。B.、C. 分別出現了 trust「信任」和 believe「相信」，中文意思相似，但英文意義卻是不同的，因此在使用時要特別小心。

Q2 I'm going to ask him to quit smoking.
我要去要求他戒菸。

A. No, you may not. 不，你不可以。

正解 ▸ B. It's no use. He won't listen to you. 沒用的。他不會聽你的。

C. He kept on smoking all the time. 他總是一直在抽菸。

Q3 She said she would lend me her car.
她說過會借我她的車。

A. Now is the right time. 現在是時候了。

B. She will never sell her car. 她絕對不會把她的車賣掉的。

正解 ▸ C. It's impossible. 這不可能。

Q4 You can fix the machine, can't you?
你可以把機器修好，不是嗎？

正解 ▸ A. Sorry to let you down. 對不起讓你失望了。

B. No, I don't have a fax machine. 不，我沒有傳真機。

C. I believe in you. 我相信你。

※〔註〕這題中出現的類音字組有 fix the machine [fɪks ðə məˋʃɪn] / fax machine [fæks məˋʃɪn]。

Q5 Why don't we give it up?
我們為什麼不放棄呢？

正解 ▸ A. Never think about it. 想都別想。

B. OK, I'll give it a try. 好，我會試試看。

C. I can't forgive you. 我無法原諒你。

主題 37　提供或尋求協助

Q1 Can you help me do this ?
你可以幫我做這個嗎？

正解 A. No, do it yourself. 不行，你自己做。

B. This will help. 這會有幫助。

C. There's no hope for me. 我沒希望了。

※〔註〕選項 B. 的主詞從人（you）變成了事物（this）且答非所問；選項 C. 則是利用發音相似的 help/hope 來造成混淆的錯誤選項。選項 A. 堅決拒絕了對方的請求，因此是合理的回應方式。

Q2 Pardon me, Sir. Can you tell me what time it is?
不好意思，先生。你可以告訴我現在幾點嗎？

A. Let me think it over. 讓我仔細考慮一下。

正解 B. Sorry, I don't have a watch. 抱歉，我沒有手錶。

C. I've got plenty of time. 我不趕時間。

※〔註〕think it over = think about it 仔細想想；考慮

Q3 I'll turn on the light.
我來把燈打開。

正解 A. No, don't bother. 不，不用麻煩了。

B. Turn right here. 這裡右轉。

C. You have no right to do this. 你沒有權利這樣做。

※〔註〕這題裡的類音字組是 "light [laɪt] / right [raɪt]"。

Q4 Shall I open the window for you?
要我幫你把窗戶打開嗎？

正解→ A. Yes, please. That would be very kind of you.

好，謝謝。你人真的非常好。

B. We need to get help. 我們得去找人幫忙。

C. This is difficult. 這很難。

Q5 Would you like me to answer the phone?
你要我來接這通電話嗎？

A. It's not the answer. 這不是答案。

B. I'll help you. 我會幫你。

正解→ C. If you wouldn't mind. 如果你不介意的話。

※〔註〕選項 A. 中的 answer 是名詞「答案」的意思，而不是題目中的動詞意義「接聽（電話）」。選項 B. 答非所問。選項 C. 則是客氣地接受對方的提議，是三個選項中最合理的回應方式。

主題 38 **請求許可與允諾**

Q1 Can we buy this teapot?
我們可以買這個茶壺嗎？

A. It's tea time. 下午茶時間到了。

正解→ B. It depends on you. 由你決定。

C. The tea is really hot. 這茶真的很燙。

Q2 May I eat some cake?
我可以吃些蛋糕嗎？

A. Get me some, please. 請幫我拿一些。

B. I'd love some. Thanks. 我想來一點。謝謝。

正解 C. Please help yourself. 請自行取用。

※〔註〕選項 A.、B. 表示自己也想要吃蛋糕，答非所問。選項 C. 是正確答案，回應者可能是某個餐會的主辦人等會提供蛋糕的人。

Q3 Could I see the room?
我可以看一下房間嗎？

正解 A. Sure. Come follow me. 當然，請隨我來。

B. Oh, I can't believe you're saying this.
噢，我不敢相信你會說這種話。

C. We don't have enough money. 我們沒有足夠的錢。

※〔註〕這段對話應該是房屋出售或房間出租的情境，回應者應是屋主，B.、C. 的回答不合理。A. 為正確答案。

Q4 Do you mind if I take one away?
你介意我拿一個走嗎？

正解 A. No, go ahead. 不會，你拿吧。

B. Save it! 省省吧！

C. I didn't mean to do it. 我不是故意那樣做的。

※〔註〕選項 B. 的這種的回應很無禮，非最佳選項；C. 則是答非所問。A. 是同意對方的要求或舉動時會使用的表達方式，因此是正確答案。

主題
38
強調短句 V 請求許可與允諾

Q5 Can I try?
我可以試試嗎？

A. Try me. 試試看〔我的忍耐度〕。

B. It fitted you very well. 這個非常適合你。

正解 C. Why not? 有何不可？

※〔註〕Can I try? 這句話指的是 Can I try to do ~?，和選項 A. Try me. 意義上完全無關；會說出選項 B. 這個回應，則可能是把題目中的 try 聽成了「試穿（衣服等）」的 try on，因此是錯誤選項。選項 C. 意在鼓勵對方放手一試，是最適合的回應方式。

主題 **39** 建 議

Q1 What should we do for dinner tonight?
我們今天晚上的晚餐該怎麼辦？

A. We'll have dinner at 7:00. 我們會在 7 點吃晚餐。

B. How about watching a movie? 看部電影如何？

正解 C. How about eating out? 出去吃如何？

Q2 Let's go for a drive somewhere this weekend.
這個週末我們開車去兜風吧。

A. Come out and play! 出來玩嘛！

B. I'll buy the tickets. 我會買票。

正解 C. That's a good idea. 這是個好主意。

※〔註〕提議者已經說出了提議的具體內容，也就是 go for a drive，選項 A. 卻反倒只說要出去，所以不是最好的回應方式。既然是開車兜風，就不需要買票，故 B. 錯誤。C. 為正確答案，表示回應者十分贊成對方的提議。

Q3 I wish I knew about painting.
真希望我會畫畫。

正解 ► A. Why don't you learn? 你為何不學呢？

B. You knew it. 你知道的。

C. How did you know? 你怎麼知道的？

Q4 I'd like something for a sunburn.
我想找曬傷用的東西。

A. Bring an umbrella. 帶把傘。

B. I don't like this. 我不喜歡這個。

正解 ► C. You might want to try this. 你可能會想試試這個。

※〔註〕透過發話者所說的內容，可以知道他已經曬傷了，因此選項 A. 不合理，選項 B. 中的 like 是動詞「喜歡」的意思，和題目中的 I'd like... = I would like... 用法不同。選項 C. 提出了具體的建議，是最恰當的回應方式。

Q5 Should I take the bus?
我應該搭公車嗎？

A. Yes, I'll go. 是，我會去。

正解 ► B. No. It's only a three-minute walk. 不用。走路只要三分鐘。

C. You should take the chance. 你應該要冒險試試看。

※〔註〕選項 A.、C. 答非所問；選項 B. 表示要去的地方走路三分鐘就到了，因此不需要搭公車，是最適合的回應方式。

主題 40　　　　　　　確　認

Q1 Did he say when he would be home?
他有說他什麼時候會在家嗎？

正解 ► A. He didn't say. 他沒說。

B. He'll be back. 他會回來的。

C. I happened to overhear what he said.
我剛好不小心聽到了他說的話。

Q2 Have you made the sandwiches yet?
你已經做好三明治了嗎？

正解 ► A. I'll start right away. 我會馬上開始做。

B. No chance at all. 毫無機會。

C. How many? 有多少個？

Q3 We have your size, but not in that color.
我們有你的尺寸，但不是那個顏色。

A. This shirt is very colorful. 這件襯衫非常色彩繽紛。

正解 ► B. Can you order one for me? 你可以幫我訂一件嗎？

C. No more excuses. 別再找藉口了。

Q4 What do you mean by that?
你那樣說是什麼意思？

正解 A. I mean it's expensive. 我的意思是這很貴。

B. I know what you mean. 我知道你的意思。

C. I really mean it. 我真的是認真的。

Q5 I saw that magic show.
我看了那場魔術表演。

A. How was your show? 你的表演怎麼樣了？

B. Can't you see me? 你看不到我嗎？

正解 C. Yeah? Tell me more about it.
是嗎？再多告訴我一點和這場表演有關的事。

※〔註〕選項 A.、B. 皆答非所問。正確答案是選項 C.，顯然回應者對這場 magic show（魔術表演）十分感興趣，而且沒有去觀賞過這場表演。

問 > 什麼地方

Conversation 1.

W: Where are you going, Steven?

M: I'm going to Taipei Train Station.

W: Are you going by taxi?

M: No, I'm going to take a bus.

Q1: Where is Steven going?

A. Taipei Train Station.

B. The taxi stand.

C. The bus stop. ——正解

中文翻譯

| 簡短對話 **1** | 女人：你要去哪裡，史蒂芬？
男人：我要去台北火車站。
女人：你要搭計程車去嗎？
男人：不，我要搭公車。 | >>> | 問：史蒂芬要去哪裡？
A. 台北火車站。
B. 計程車招呼站。
C. 公車站牌。 |

※〔註〕對話第二句中提到的「台北火車站（Taipei Train Station）」是最終目的地，但 Steven 必須先搭上交通工具，也就是他選擇搭乘的「公車（bus）」，才能到達台北火車站，因此正確答案是選項 C. 的公車站牌。

Conversation 2.

W: Hi, Sam. I phoned you yesterday, but you were out.

M: I was with Cindy. We had a good time at the park.

Q2: Where was Sam yesterday?

A. At Cindy's home.

B. At his home.

C. At the park. ——正解

中文翻譯

| 簡短對話 **2** | 女人：嗨，山姆。我昨天打了電話給你，可是你出去了。
男人：我那時和辛蒂在一起。我們在公園很愉快。 | >>> | 問：昨天山姆在哪裡？
A. 在辛蒂家。
B. 在自己家。
C. 在公園。 |

※〔註〕直到最後一句話才真的說出所在地 "at the park"，故選 C.。

Conversation 3.

W: Kyle. Are you going to Paris or Beijing?

M: I've decided to go to Paris. What about you, Mary?

W: I can't make up my mind right now.

Q3: Where has Mary decided to go?

A. Paris.

B. Beijing.

C. She hasn't decided where to go yet. ◄ 正解

中文翻譯

| 簡短
對話
3 | 女人：凱爾，你要去巴黎還是北京？
男人：我決定要去巴黎了。那妳呢，瑪莉？
女人：我目前無法下定決心。 | ≫ | 問：瑪莉決定了要去哪裡？
A. 巴黎。
B. 北京。
C. 她還沒決定要去哪裡。 |

※〔註〕對話中談到的地點都是「男子」Kyle 的選擇。問題卻是問「女子」Mary 要去哪裡，本題型要注意的是人稱問題。

Conversation 4.

W: Peter, did you ever live in America?

M: No, I studied in London for two years. Now I'm working in Taipei.

Q4: Where is Peter now?

A. In Taiwan. ◄ 正解

B. In London.

C. In America.

中文翻譯

| 簡短
對話
4 | 女人：彼得，你住過美國嗎？
男人：沒有，我在倫敦讀過兩年
書。現在我在台北工作。 | ≫ | 問：彼得現在在哪裡？
A. 在台灣。
B. 在倫敦。
C. 在美國。 |

※〔註〕Taipei 是 Taiwan 的首都；London 是 England 的首都；Washington D.C. 是 America 的首都。

※〔註〕這題要注意的是「時態」問題，過去住過 London，在那裡念書（studied），但題目是問現在彼得人在哪裡。

主題
1
問
ｖ
什
麼
地
方

主題 **2**　　　　　　　　　　問 > 什麼人

Conversation 1.

M: Where is Ted? Jenny, do you know?

W: He's in the library, Mike.

Q1: Who is Mike looking for?

A. Jenny.
B. The library.
C. Ted.　→ 正解

中文翻譯

簡短對話 1	男人：泰德在哪裡？珍妮，妳知道嗎？ 女人：他在圖書館，麥克。	>>>	問：麥克在找誰？ A. 珍妮。 B. 圖書館。 C. 泰德。

※〔註〕這一題問的是 Who「人」的問題，對話中出現了三個人名，內容是 Mike 在問 Jenny 知不知道某個人（Ted）在哪裡，故選 C.。

Conversation 2.

W: I come to work by MRT, so I'm always on time.

M: The buses are always late, so I usually ride a motorbike.

Q2: Who usually goes to work by bus?

A. The man.
B. The woman.
C. Neither of them.　→ 正解

中文翻譯

簡短對話 2	女人：我搭捷運來上班，所以我總是準時到。 男人：公車總是遲到，所以我通常會騎機車。	>>>	問：誰通常搭公車上班？ A. 男人。 B. 女人。 C. 兩人都不是。

※〔註〕雖然男子提到了 bus 這個字，但其實他是在抱怨公車不準時。對話中的兩人，都不是搭公車上班，所以答案為 C.。

Conversation 3.

W: Let's eat out tonight.
M: I don't feel like going out.
W: I'll treat you.
M: No. I'll pay for myself.

主題

2

問
∨
什
麼
人

Q3: Who will pay for the dinner?

A. The woman.
B. The man.
C. Both of them. ← 正解

中文翻譯

簡短 對話 **3**	女人：我們今天晚上出去吃吧。 男人：我不想出去。 女人：我會請你。 男人：不，我要自己付。	>>>	問：誰會付晚餐的錢？ A. 女人。 B. 男人。 C. 兩人都會。

※〔註〕雖然女子說她會請客 "I'll treat you."，但是男子說了 "No, I'll pay for myself." 來拒絕女子的提議，這表示兩人會各付各的，答案選 C.。

Conversation 4.

W: What did your parents think of the show?
M: My father disliked it, but my mother liked it.

Q4: Did the man's parents like the show?

A. Both of them like it.
B. Neither of them liked it.
C. His mother liked it, but his father didn't. ← 正解

中文翻譯

簡短 對話 **4**	女人：你父母覺得那場秀怎麼 樣？ 男人：我父親不喜歡，可是我母 親喜歡。	>>>	問：男子的父母喜歡那場秀嗎？ A. 兩個人都喜歡。 B. 兩個人都不喜歡。 C. 他母親喜歡但父親不喜歡。

※〔註〕對話中提到兩個人去看 show，其中一人（the man's father）不喜歡，另一人（the man's mother）卻喜歡，故選 C.。

主題 3　　問 > 什麼種類

Conversation 1.

M: Hi, Diana. What are you reading?

W: Oh hi, Bill. I'm catching up on my math. There is a test tomorrow.

Q1: What is Diana studying?

A. Math. ——正解
B. A novel.
C. A test paper.

中文翻譯

簡短對話 1	男人：嗨，戴安娜。妳在看什麼？ 女人：喔，嗨，比爾。我在惡補數學。明天有一場考試。	>>>	問：戴安娜在念什麼？ A. 數學。 B. 小說。 C. 考卷。

※〔註〕catch up on ~（努力趕上～）

※〔註〕Diana 並沒有直接回答她在 reading 或 studying 什麼，她用了一個動詞片語 catch up on my math，表示她在努力趕上數學的進度，也就是在惡補數學的意思。

Conversation 2.

Boy: Mom, I want some soda.

W: Sorry. We've got no soda. We only have some milk and a bottle of fruit juice.

Q2: What does the boy want?

A. Soda. ——正解
B. Milk.
C. Fruit juice.

中文翻譯

簡短對話 2	男孩：媽，我想喝一些汽水。 女人：抱歉。我們沒有汽水了。我們只有一些牛奶和一罐水果果汁。	>>>	問：男孩想要什麼？ A. 汽水。 B. 牛奶。 C. 水果果汁。

Conversation 3.

M: Betty, why are you so nervous?

W: I have an English spelling contest in 10 minutes.

Q3: What is Betty going to take part in?

A. She is good at English spelling.

B. The spelling contest. ── 正解

C. Betty is nervous.

中文翻譯

簡短對話 3	男人：貝蒂，妳為什麼這麼緊張？ 女人：10 分鐘後我有一場英文拼字比賽。	>>>	問：貝蒂要參加什麼？ A. 她很擅長英文拼字。 B. 拼字比賽。 C. 貝蒂很緊張。

※〔註〕題目問的是貝蒂要 "take part in"「參加」的是什麼，故答案為 B.。

Conversation 4.

M: I want to grab something to eat. Do you want to come with me?

W: No, I'm really full now.

Q4: What does the man want to do?

A. Find a bookstore.

B. Write homework.

C. Get some food. ── 正解

中文翻譯

簡短對話 4	男人：我想要去找點東西吃。妳要和我一起去嗎？ 女人：不要，我現在真的很飽。	>>>	問：這個男人想要做什麼？ A. 找一家書店。 B. 寫回家作業。 C. 取得一些食物。

※〔註〕這一題的關鍵在於要聽到題目中的 something to eat（可以吃的東西），選項中與吃相關的就是選項 C. 了。

主題 **4**　　問 > 做什麼

Conversation 1.

M: Are you going to the movie tonight?

W: No, I'm going to watch a volleyball game at home.

Q1: What is the woman going to do tonight?

A. Go to the movie theater.

B. Watch TV.　←正解

C. Play volleyball.

中文翻譯

簡短對話 **1**	男人：妳今晚要去看那場電影嗎？ 女人：不，我要在家看排球比賽。	>>>	問：這名女子今晚要做什麼？ A. 去電影院。 B. 看電視。 C. 打排球。

※〔註〕What ... the woman... do...?，問的是「女子」要做的事，女子回答 "watch a volleyball game at home"，也就是打算在家「看電視」的意思。

Conversation 2.

W: Jim, did you go to Ann's birthday party yesterday?

M: Yes, I did.

W: What about the food?

M: It was delicious.

Q2: Where did Jim go yesterday?

A. He had dinner with Ann.

B. He went to Ann's party.　←正解

C. He threw a birthday party.

中文翻譯

簡短對話 **2**	女人：吉姆，你昨天去了安的生日派對嗎？ 男人：是，我去了。 女人：食物怎麼樣？ 男人：很美味。	>>>	問：吉姆昨天去了哪裡？ A. 他和安共進晚餐。 B. 他去了安的派對。 C. 他辦了一場生日派對。

※〔註〕對話一開始就說出答案了 "go to Ann's birthday party"，故選 B.。注意：Jim 是去參加別人的 party，不是自己 "throw"「舉辦」了一個 party，因此不可選 C.。

Conversation 3.

M: I'm going to the supermarket, Mom.
W: Please get some fruit. We don't have much of it.

Q3: What does the mother want the son to do?

A. To go shopping with her.
B. To get more money.
C. To buy some fruit. ← 正解

中文翻譯

簡短對話 3	男人：媽，我要去超級市場。 女人：麻煩買一些水果。我們沒什麼水果了。	>>>	問：這位母親想要兒子做什麼？ A. 和她一起去購物。 B. 拿到更多錢。 C. 買一些水果。

※〔註〕女子（媽媽）要男子（兒子）去超級市場時順便 "get some fruit"，故選 C.。

Conversation 4.

M: Help yourself to more food, Melody.
W: Oh no, thanks. Can I have some tea, please?

Q4: What did the man ask Melody to do?

A. To help him get some food.
B. To have some more food. ← 正解
C. To drink some tea.

中文翻譯

簡短對話 4	男人：自己再拿點吃的吧，美樂蒂。 女人：喔不，謝謝。可以請你給我一點茶嗎？	>>>	問：這名男子要美樂蒂做什麼？ A. 幫他拿些食物。 B. 再多吃點。 C. 喝點茶。

※〔註〕從這段對話可以知道男子是主人，女子是客人，主人常會客氣地請客人多吃一些 "have more food"，並表示不要客氣，自己動手 "Help yourself..."，故選 B.。

主題 **5**　　　　　　　問 > 點鐘 · 時間

Conversation 1.

M: It's already 5:45. Why isn't your sister here yet?
W: I told her to be here at 5:30. What happened?

Q1: What time did the woman tell her sister to come?

A. At 5:45.
B. At 5:35.
C. At 5:30. ──正解

中文翻譯

簡短對話 1	男人：已經 5 點 45 分了。妳妹妹怎麼還沒來？ 女人：我告訴過她 5 點半在這裡。發生了什麼事？	>>>	問：女子告訴她妹妹幾點來？ A. 5 點 45 分。 B. 5 點 35 分。 C. 5 點 30 分。

※〔註〕對話中出現了兩個時間，而女子的回答正是答案 I told her (= my sister) to be here (=come here) at 5:30，答案為 C.。

Conversation 2.

M: Oh, it's ten o'clock.
W: Don't worry. The clock is fast. You still have 15 minutes.

Q2: What time is it now?

A. It's ten o'clock.
B. It's a quarter past ten.
C. It's a quarter to ten. ──正解

中文翻譯

簡短對話 2	男人：噢，十點了。 女人：別擔心。這個時鐘快了，你還有 15 分鐘。	>>>	問：現在幾點？ A. 十點。 B. 十點十五分。 C. 九點四十五分。

※〔註〕時鐘雖然指十點，但實際上這個鐘卻快了十五分鐘，表示現在是九點四十五分 nine forty-five，另一種說法就是選項 C. 的說法 "a quarter to ten"。

Conversation 3.

W: What time does the store open?

M: It opens at 10:00 a.m.

W: How late does it stay open?

M: It stays open until 9:00 p.m.

Q3: What time is the store closed?

A. At 10:00 p.m.
B. At 9:00 a.m.
C. At 9:00 p.m. ← 正解

中文翻譯

簡短對話 3	女人：這家店什麼時候開？ 男人：早上 10 點開始營業。 女人：它會開到多晚？ 男人：一直開到晚上 9 點。	>>>	問：這家店幾點打烊？ A. 晚上 10 點。 B. 早上 9 點。 C. 晚上 9 點。

※〔註〕男子最後一句話說 "It (= the store) stays open until 9:00 p.m."，意思等於 "The store closes at 9:00 p.m."，所以答案為 C.。

Conversation 4.

M: It's Monday today. I hope the science museum is open.

W: Don't worry. It's open 9:00 a.m. to 6:00 p.m. weekdays, and 9:00 a.m. to 12:00 a.m. Saturdays, closed Sundays.

Q4: When is the science museum open on Sunday?

A. 9:00 a.m. to 6:00 p.m.
B. 9:00 a.m. to 12:00 a.m.
C. It is closed. ← 正解

中文翻譯

簡短對話 4	男人：今天是星期一。我希望科學博物館有開。 女人：別擔心。它平日從早上 9 點開到晚上 6 點，星期六是早上 9 點到中午 12 點，星期天則沒開。	>>>	問：科學博物館星期天什麼時候開？ A. 早上 9 點到晚上 6 點。 B. 早上 9 點到中午 12 點。 C. 它沒開。

※〔註〕science 科學；museum 博物館；science museum 科（學）博（物）館
※〔註〕這題中出現的時間點很多，但其實女子所說的最後一句話 "It's ... closed Sundays" 就是答案。

主題 6   問 > 日期

Conversation 1.

W: How time flies! Tomorrow is Monday.

M: I have to spend the whole day doing my homework today.

Q1: What day is today?

A. It's Monday.
B. It's Sunday. ←正解
C. It's Saturday.

中文翻譯

| 簡短對話 1 | 女人：時間過得真快！明天是星期一了。
男人：我今天得花一整天做功課。 | >>> | 問：今天星期幾？
A. 星期一。
B. 星期天。
C. 星期六。 |

※〔註〕女子說 "Tomorrow is Monday."，表示 "Today is Sunday."，故答案為 B.。

Conversation 2.

W: Jack. Would you like to go swimming?

M: Not today, Tina. My family is going picnicking.

W: Well .... How about Friday then?

M: That sounds fine.

Q2: When will Jack go swimming?

A. Today.
B. Not Friday.
C. On Friday. ←正解

中文翻譯

| 簡短對話 2 | 女人：傑克，你想去游泳嗎？
男人：今天不行，蒂娜。我們家要去野餐。
女人：嗯……那星期五呢？
男人：聽起來可以。 | >>> | 問：傑克什麼時候會去游泳？
A. 今天。
B. 不是星期五。
C. 在星期五。 |

※〔註〕picnic 野餐； go picnicking = go on a picnic 去野餐

※〔註〕Jack 回答 "That sounds fine"，表示 go swimming 的時間在 Friday，答案為 C.。

Conversation 3.

M: When can I come to see the doctor?

W: The doctor will be busy this week. Wait... Wednesday is OK.

Q3: When can the man come to see the doctor this week?

A. On Wednesday. 　正解

B. Any day.

C. Next week.

中文翻譯

簡短對話 3	男人：我什麼時候可以來看醫生？ 女人：醫生這星期都會很忙。等一下……星期三可以。	>>>	問：本週男子何時可以去看醫生？ A. 在星期三。 B. 任何一天。 C. 下星期。

※〔註〕女子可能是診所的 receptionist，也就是負責接聽電話和招呼病患的接待員，她最後說 "...Wednesday is OK."，故男子可在星期三看診，答案為 A.。

Conversation 4.

M: When is your son's birthday?

W: On March 4. Mine, too.

M: No kidding! So is mine.

Q4: What date is the man's birthday?

A. In March.

B. In April.

C. On March 4. 　正解

中文翻譯

簡短對話 1	男人：妳兒子的生日是什麼時候？ 女人：在三月四日。我也是。 男人：真的？我也是。	>>>	問：男子的生日在幾月幾日？ A. 在三月。 B. 在四月。 C. 在三月四日。

※〔註〕When... 的問法可以只回答月分；但如果是問 What date...，那麼除了月分之外，還要回答出確切的日期。

※〔註〕女子說 "Mine, too."，男子說 "So is mine."，表示他們的生日都在 March 4，而且 What date 的回答一定要是確切的日期，所以答案是 C.。

主題 7 　　問 > 季節 · 月份 · 氣候

Conversation 1.

W: What's your favorite season?

M: I like summer best. I like water sports. How about you?

W: I like spring more. Too much sun bothers me.

Q1: What season does the man like best?

A. Spring and summer.

B. Spring.

C. Summer. ━正解

中文翻譯

簡短對話 1	女人：你最喜歡的季節是什麼？ 男人：我最喜歡夏天，我喜歡水上運動。妳呢？ 女人：我比較喜歡春天，太陽太大會讓我很煩。	>>>	問：男子最喜歡什麼季節？ A. 春天和夏天。 B. 春天。 C. 夏天。

※〔註〕bother 使困擾。Ex: Stop bothering me! 別再煩我了！

※〔註〕男子與女子在對話中各自說了自己喜歡的 season（季節），因此在聽題目時，必須特別注意問的對象是誰。這題是問 the man，因此答案是選項 C.。

Conversation 2.

W: It's freezing today, isn't it?

M: The radio says the sun will come out later.

W: The temperature will stay above 10 in the day-time, but at night it will fall below 7.

Q2: What's the weather like?

A. It's freezing and rainy.

B. It's sunny and hot.

C. It's freezing but sunny. ━正解

中文翻譯

| 簡短對話 **2** | 女人：今天超冷，不是嗎？
男人：聽收音機說等一下太陽會出來。
女人：白天氣溫會一直維持在 10 度以上，但晚上會掉到 7 度以下。 | >>> | 問：天氣如何？
A. 超冷又下雨。
B. 晴朗炎熱。
C. 超冷但晴朗。 |

※〔註〕女子說的第一句話 "It's freezing."，加上男子的回應 "... the sun will come out..."，所以答案為 C。

Conversation 3.

W: Was it cold here last winter?

M: Yes, it was. And December is much colder than January and February.

Q3: Which month was the coldest month last winter?

A. December. ——正解

B. January.

C. February.

中文翻譯

| 簡短對話 **3** | 女人：去年冬天這裡冷嗎？
男人：冷啊，而且十二月比一月和二月冷多了。 | >>> | 問：去年冬天哪個月分最冷？
A. 十二月。
B. 一月。
C. 二月。 |

※〔註〕男子說 "December is much colder..."，所以答案為 A。

Conversation 4.

W: It's very cold now.

M: Yes, it is. November and December were cold enough. I don't think the cold weather will be over before February.

Q4: In which month are they talking?

A. January. ——正解

B. February.

C. November.

中文翻譯

| 簡短對話 **4** | 女人：現在非常冷。
男人：是啊。11 月和 12 月已經
　　　夠冷了。我想冷天氣在二
　　　月前是不會結束的。 | >>> | 問：他們是在哪個月分進行對話的？
A. 一月。
B. 二月。
C. 十一月。 |

※〔註〕這題必須特別注意時態的表達方式，男子說 "November and December were cold...." 又說 "...over before February."，介於十二月和二月中間的月份，那當然就是 January，故選 A.。

談論天氣的開場白

1. What bad/good weather!
   多糟（好）的天氣！
2. Lovely day, isn't it?
   天氣真好，不是嗎？
3. It looks like rain, don't you think so?
   看來像要下雨了，你不覺得嗎？
4. It's too hot for this time of year, don't you think so?
   對於每年的這個時候來說太熱了，你不認為嗎？

主題 8 　問 > 數字與計算問題

Conversation 1.

W: What's your telephone number? Is it 3281-6547?
M: No, it's 3218-6574.

Q1: What is the man's phone number?

A. 3218-5467.
B. 3218-6574. ◀ 正解
C. 3281-6547.

中文翻譯

| 簡短對話 1 | 女人：你的電話號碼幾號？ 是 3281-6547 嗎？ 男人：不，是 3218-6574。 | >>> | 問：男子的電話號碼是幾號？ A. 3218-5467。 B. 3218-6574。 C. 3281-6547。 |

Conversation 2.

W: Tim, are you eighteen?

M: No, my sister is eighteen. I'm only fifteen.

W: You're so young.

Q2: How old is Tim's sister?

A. She is fifteen years old.

B. She is 3 years younger than Tim.

C. She is 3 years older than Tim. ——正解

中文翻譯

| 簡短對話 2 | 女人：提姆，你是 18 歲嗎？ 男人：不，我姐姐是 18 歲。我只 有 15 歲。 女人：你好小啊。 | >>> | 問：提姆的姐姐幾歲？ A. 她是 15 歲。 B. 她比提姆小三歲。 C. 她比提姆大三歲。 |

※〔註〕題目問的是 "Tim's sister"，Tim 的回答 "my sister is eighteen."，接著他又說 "I'm only fifteen."，表示他的姐姐「大」他三歲，答案為 C.。

Conversation 3.

W: How much are these coffee cups?

M: $200 each, or $300 for the two.

Q3: How much does one coffee cup cost if you buy two?

A. $200.

B. $300.

C. $150. ——正解

中文翻譯

簡短
對話
3

女人：這些咖啡杯多少錢？
男人：每個 200 元，兩個 300 元。

>>>

問：如果你買兩個咖啡杯，一個多少錢？
A. 200 元。
B. 300 元。
C. 150 元。

※〔註〕這題比較難，無法直接在對話裡找到數字，必須做一點算術。前提是你如果一次買兩個杯子，就會比較便宜，" $300 for the two"，所以平均一個杯子只要 "$150"，故答案為 C.。

Conversation 4.

W: What's the time by your watch, Peter?

M: It's half past seven, but my watch is seven minutes slow.

Q4: **What is the correct time?**

A. Seven thirty.
B. Seven twenty-three.
C. Seven thirty-seven.　正解

中文翻譯

簡短
對話
4

女人：彼得，你的手錶幾點了？
男人：七點半，但是我的手錶慢了七分鐘。

>>>

問：正確時間為何？
A. 七點三十分。
B. 七點二十三分。
C. 七點三十七分。

※〔註〕這題同樣要做一點算術，Peter 手錶上的時間是 "half past seven" = 7:30，但是彼得的錶慢了七分鐘，所以這個時間要再加 7 分鐘才對，故正確時間是 7:37，答案選 C.。

主題 9　　　比 較

Conversation 1.

W: I'm Mary. I'm thirty.

M: I'm Ben. I'm ten years older than you.

W: Really? You look younger than me.

Q1: Who is younger?

A. Ben is younger.

B. Mary is younger. ◀ 正解

C. They're of the same age.

中文翻譯

簡短對話 1	女人：我是瑪莉，我 30 歲。 男人：我是班，我比妳大 10 歲。 女人：真的嗎？你看起來比我年輕。	>>>	問：誰比較年輕？ A. 班比較年輕。 B. 瑪莉比較年輕。 C. 他們兩個同年。

※〔註〕age 年齡； What's your age? ＝ How old are you? 你幾歲？

※〔註〕因為 Ben 說 "I'm ten years older..."，所以答案就會選 B. Mary is younger.

Conversation 2.

M: Who is the tallest girl in your class, Alice?

W: Let me see. Mary is tall, but Jane is taller than Mary, and Rebecca is taller than Jane.

Q2: Who is the tallest girl?

A. Jane.

B. Mary.

C. Rebecca. ◀ 正解

中文翻譯

| 簡短對話 2 | 男人：艾莉絲，誰是妳班上最高的女生？
女人：我想想。瑪莉很高，可是珍比瑪莉高，然後莉貝卡又比珍高。 | 問：誰是最高的女生？
A. 珍。
B. 瑪莉。
C. 莉貝卡。 |

※〔註〕Alice 的回應很有邏輯，出現的人名是一個比一個高（tall--> taller--> tallest），所以最後出現的人名 "Rebecca" 就是最高的人，正確答案是 C.。

Conversation 3.

M: Excuse me. May I have a sheet of paper, please?
W: Certainly. Here you are.
M: Thank you. Oh, this is too small.

Q3: What does the man want?

A. He wants a sheep.
B. He wants a bigger sheet of paper. ← 正解
C. He wants a smaller sheet of paper.

中文翻譯

| 簡短對話 3 | 男人：不好意思。可以請妳給我一張紙嗎？
女人：當然。這給你。
男人：謝謝妳。噢，這張太小了。 | 問：男子想要什麼？
A. 他想要一隻羊。
B. 他想要一張比較大的紙。
C. 他想要一張比較小的紙。 |

※〔註〕類音字 sheet [ʃit] 一張 / sheep [ʃip] 羊；綿羊

※〔註〕相似發音 sheet（一張）/sheep（羊），男子要的是 a "sheet" of paper，與 sheep 一點關係也沒有。至於是要什麼樣的紙張？他最後說 "This is too small." 那就表示要 "bigger" 的，故答案選 B.。

Conversation 4.

M: This dress is not as expensive as the blouse. Isn't it?
W: No. Neither is the handbag.

Q4: What is the most expensive?

A. The dress.
B. The blouse. ← 正解
C. The handbag.

中文翻譯

| 簡短對話 4 | 男人：這件洋裝沒有這件上衣貴。不是嗎？
女人：是啊。這個手提包也是。 | >>> | 問：最貴的是什麼？
A. 洋裝。
B. 上衣。
C. 手提包。 |

※〔註〕not as expensive as = cheaper than

※〔註〕要聽懂這段對話有三個重點：

    1) "X" is not as expensive as "Y" = "Y" is more expensive

    2) ... is not... Isn't it? 回答 "No" 表示對方說的「沒錯」。

    3) Neither is "Z" = "Z" is not as expensive as "Y" = "Y" is more expensive

        結論就是：最貴的（the most expensive）東西是 "Y"，答案為 B.。

主題 10　　　　Yes-No 問題

Conversation 1.

W: Did you get the letter, Jack?

M: What letter?

W: Well, no news is good news.

Q1: Did Jack get the letter?

    A. Yes, he did.

    B. No, he didn't.　← 正解

    C. We don't know.

中文翻譯

| 簡短對話 1 | 女人：傑克，你有收到信嗎？
男人：什麼信？
女人：嗯，沒消息就是好消息。 | >>> | 問：傑克有收到信嗎？
A. 有，他收到了。
B. 不，他沒收到。
C. 我們不知道。 |

※〔註〕news 的意思是「新聞；消息」。

※〔註〕Jack 的回應 "What letter?"，表示他根本不知道有信，也就是說他並沒有收到信，故答案為 B.。

Conversation 2.

M: Where do you work, Susan?

W: I worked in a museum near a library before, but I began to work in a school three months ago.

Q2: Did Susan ever work in a library?

    A. No, she didn't.　　正解

    B. Yes, she did.

    C. Yes, she worked in a library for three months.

中文翻譯

簡短對話 2	男人：蘇珊，妳在哪裡工作？ 女人：我以前在靠近圖書館的博物館工作，可是我三個月前開始在學校裡工作了。	>>>	問：蘇珊曾在圖書館裡工作嗎？ A. 不，她沒有。 B. 有，她有。 C. 有，她在圖書館工作過三個月。

※〔註〕Susan 在回答男子的問題時提到了三個地點 museum、library、school，但是仔細聽她說的是 "a museum near a library"，提到圖書館只是為了讓男子了解她以前工作的那個博物館的確切位置而已，並非她工作的地方，所以答案為 A.。

Conversation 3.

M: Lucy, you should rest for a while. Even ten minutes would be fine.

W: No way. There's so much work to do.

Q3: Is Lucy going to take a rest?

    A. No, she doesn't like working.

    B. Yes, she has to work.

    C. No, she has to work.　　正解

中文翻譯

簡短對話 3	男人：露西，妳應該休息一下。即使十分鐘也好。 女人：不要。有這麼多工作要做。	>>>	問：露西會去休息嗎？ A. 不，她不喜歡工作。 B. 是，她必須工作。 C. 不，她必須工作。

※〔註〕rest（休息）當動詞時，等於名詞用法的 take a rest。

※〔註〕Lucy 回應的很明白 "No way."，表示自己不要休息，答案為 C.。

Conversation 4.

W: What's the matter?

Boy: I can't find my mother. I don't know the way home.

Q4: Can the boy go back home by himself?

A. He can't find his mother.
B. Yes, he can.
C. No, he can't. ← 正解

中文翻譯

簡短對話 4

女人：怎麼了？
男孩：我找不到媽媽。我不知道回家的路。

>>>

問：男孩可以自己回到家嗎？
A. 他找不到媽媽。
B. 是，他可以。
C. 不，他不行。

※〔註〕這個對話應該是小男孩迷路時，女子熱心詢問他發生了什麼事。男孩表示自己找不到媽媽，且不知道回家的路，即 "He can't go back home by himself."，答案為 C.。

主題 11 混淆音

Conversation 1.

W: Have you seen Ms. Smith recently, Stephen?

M: No, Sandy. I heard that she has gone back to New York.

Q1: Who has gone back to America?

A. Stephen.
B. Ms. Smith. ← 正解
C. Sandy.

中文翻譯

簡短對話 1

女人：史蒂芬，你最近有看到史密斯女士嗎？
男人：沒有耶，珊蒂。我聽說她已經回去紐約了。

>>>

問：誰已經回美國了？
A. 史蒂芬。
B. 史密斯女士。
C. 珊蒂。

※〔註〕Smith/Stephen/Sandy 三個名字的字首發音都是 [s]，易造成混淆，對話者提到的是 Ms. Smith 回紐約（美國的城市）的消息，答案為 B.。

Conversation 2.

M: Don't you think Blake runs the fastest?

W: He's faster than Frank, but slower than Eric.

Q2: Who runs the slowest?

    A. Blake.

    B. Frank. ⟶ 正解

    C. Eric.

中文翻譯

簡短對話 2	男人：你不認為布萊克跑得最快嗎？ 女人：他比法蘭克快，但是比艾瑞克慢。	≫≫	問：誰跑得最慢？ A. 布萊克。 B. 法蘭克。 C. 艾瑞克。

※〔註〕Mike, Frank, Eric 三個名字的字尾都是 [k]，易造成混淆。這一題除了要聽懂三個人名之外，還必須馬上反應出相反詞 fast/slow 間的關係，最後還得知道比較詞的用法，跑步速度快慢依序為 Frank is fast; Blake is faster; Eric is the fastest，答案為 B.。

Conversation 3.

M: What can I do for you, ma'am?

W: I'm looking for a coat for my daughter.

Q3: What does the woman want to buy?

    A. A dog.

    B. A coat. ⟶ 正解

    C. A cat.

中文翻譯

簡短對話 3	男人：夫人，我能為妳服務嗎？ 女人：我在為我女兒找件大衣。	≫≫	問：這名女子想買什麼？ A. 一隻狗。 B. 一件大衣。 C. 一隻貓。

※〔註〕dog/daughter 發音相似，只相差在字尾； coat/cat 則只相差在中間的母音，所以容易混淆，但女子要買的其實是 a coat，答案為 B.。

Conversation 4.

M: Could you wrap it up for me?

W: Sure. Is there anything else I can get for you?

M: That should be it. Thank you.

Q4: What did the man buy?

A. A cellphone.

B. A pair of shoes.

C. We don't know. 正解

中文翻譯

| 簡短 對話 4 | 男人：妳可以幫我把它包起來嗎？
女人：當然。還有什麼其他東西需要我幫你拿嗎？
男人：這樣應該就可以了。謝謝妳。 | >>> | 問：這名男子買了什麼？
A. 一支手機。
B. 一雙鞋子。
C. 我們不知道。 |

※〔註〕題目中出現了發音相似的單字組合 should/shoes，但對話內容中根本沒提到男子買了什麼東西，因此答案要選 C.。

主題 12　推　測

Conversation 1.

W: I hope you like this place.

M: I love it. Do they have sushi?

W: Sure!

M: Great. I'd like to try it.

Q1: Where are they?

A. In a restaurant. 正解

B. In a toy shop.

C. In a shoe store.

中文翻譯

| 簡短對話 1 | 女人：我希望你喜歡這個地方。
男人：我很喜歡。他們有壽司嗎？
女人：當然！
男人：太好了。我想吃吃看。 | ≫≫ | 問：他們在哪裡？
A. 在餐廳。
B. 在玩具店。
C. 在鞋店。 |

※〔註〕題目並沒有直接說出對話者所在地點是哪裡，但由 sushi（壽司）可知，對話進行地點與「吃」有關，三個選項裡只有 A.「餐廳」與對話情境相符，故選 A.。

Conversation 2.

W: The wind is blowing through the door. Don't you feel the cold, Vincent?

M: Oh, sorry. I didn't notice that.

Q2: What will Vincent do?

A. He will open the door.
B. He will answer the door.
C. He will close the door. ──正解

中文翻譯

| 簡短對話 2 | 女人：風從門口吹進來了。文生，你沒有感覺到冷嗎？
男人：噢，抱歉。我沒注意到這件事。 | ≫≫ | 問：文生會做什麼？
A. 他會打開門。
B. 他會去應門。
C. 他會關上門。 |

※〔註〕男子因為風從門吹進了屋裡造成女子不適而向她道歉，因此可以推測，唯有 close the door（關上門）風才不會吹進來，因此男子接下來應該會把門關上，答案是 C.。

Conversation 3.

M:　How was everything at school today?

Girl: I got 100 on my math test.

M:　I'm so proud of you!

Q3: What does the girl do?

A. She's a student. ──正解
B. She's a teacher.
C. She studies English.

中文翻譯

| 簡短對話 3 | 女人：妳今天在學校過得如何？
女孩：我數學考了 100 分。
女人：我好為妳驕傲！ | >>> | 問：女孩是做什麼（工作）的？
A. 她是一個學生。
B. 她是一個老師。
C. 她研究英文。 |

※〔註〕從對話裡的關鍵字 school、math test 來推測，唯有「學生」是可能的身分，另外兩種身分都無法透過對話內容來判斷出來，因此選項 A. 是正確答案。

主題
12
推測

Conversation 4.

M: Ms. Patrick, when do you usually go to work?

W: I work at home because I'm a writer. And I go to bed about seven o'clock in the morning.

Q4: When does Ms. Patrick usually work?

A. She works at midnight. ◀ 正解
B. She works at home.
C. She works as a writer.

中文翻譯

| 簡短對話 4 | 男人：派翠克小姐，妳通常什麼時候去上班？
女人：我在家工作，因為我是個作家，而且我大概早上七點上床睡覺。 | >>> | 問：派翠克小姐通常在什麼時候工作？
A. 她在半夜工作。
B. 她在家工作。
C. 她的工作是作家。 |

※〔註〕因為女子最後說自己大概在早上七點上床睡覺，因此可以推測她都在半夜工作，正確答案是選項 A.。

主題13　　　健　康

Conversation 1.

M: I have a stomachache.

W: Oh, that's too bad. Have you seen a doctor?

M: I'm on my way to the clinic.

W: Take care. Bye.

Q1: **What's wrong with the man?**

A. He's bad.

B. He's a doctor.

C. He got a stomachache. ←正解

中文翻譯

簡短對話 1	男人：我胃痛。 女人：噢，這真糟糕。你去看過醫生了嗎？ 男人：我正在去診所的路上。 女人：保重，再見。	>>>	問：這名男子怎麼了？ A. 他很壞。 B. 他是個醫生。 C. 他胃痛。

※〔註〕"What's wrong with+（某人）?" 所指的是某人正在為某事困擾，大部分的情況是身體上出現了病痛問題，中文意思接近「（某人）怎麼了？」、「（某人）有什麼不對勁？」，在對話的開頭，男子就表示自己胃痛，因此 C. 是最合理的答案。

Conversation 2.

M: Sara has been absent for a few days. What's wrong with her?

W: She's got the flu and is home in bed now.

Q2: **Why is Sara absent?**

A. She is sick. ←正解

B. She is wrong.

C. She is not home.

中文翻譯

| 簡短 對話 **2** | 男人：莎拉已經缺席好幾天了。 她怎麼了？
女人：她得了流感，所以現在在 家裡休息。 | >>> | 問：莎拉為什麼缺席？
A. 她病了。
B. 她錯了。
C. 她不在家。 |

※〔註〕女子說 She's got flu.，表示 Sara 得了流感，也就是她生病了，因此正確答案是選項 A.。

Conversation 3.

M: I have to go to the hospital after school.

W: Are you sick?

M: No, I'm not. My mother is in the hospital.

W: I hope she will get well soon.

Q3: Who's in the hospital?

A. The man.
B. The woman.
C. The man's mother. 正解

中文翻譯

| 簡短 對話 **3** | 男人：下課後我必須到醫院去。
女人：你生病了嗎？
男人：不，我沒有。我母親住院 了。
女人：我希望她能早日康復。 | >>> | 問：誰在住院？
A. 這名男子。
B. 這名女子。
C. 這名男子的母親。 |

Conversation 4.

M: Good afternoon, Ms. Stone. Do you feel better?

W: Yes, thank you. But I've still got pains in my back.

Q4: What is the relationship of the man and the woman?

A. Father and daughter.
B. Doctor and patient. 正解
C. Teacher and student.

中文翻譯

| 簡短對話 4 | 男人：午安，史東小姐。妳有覺得比較好嗎？
女人：有，謝謝你。但我的背還是會痛。 | >>> | 問：這一對男女是什麼關係？
A. 父親與女兒。
B. 醫生和病患。
C. 老師和學生。 |

※〔註〕在講 relationship（關係）的時候，所有名詞的前面都不加任何冠詞（a, an, the），就像選項所呈現的那樣。

※〔註〕由男子對女子的稱謂 "Ms. Stone" 來看，兩人的關係應該不是非常親密，故 A. 不對；再由女子的回應中出現的 "pains in my back" 看出 B. 應該是較合理的答案。

醫生為病患檢查的表達方式

1. Open your mouth and say "Ah ~".
   張開你的嘴巴說：「啊～」。

2. I want to take your temperature.
   我想量一下你的體溫。

3. Let me listen to your heart.
   讓我聽一下你的心臟。

主題 14　　會面與道別

Conversation 1.

M: Clair, I just saw Lisa.

W: Really? where?

M: On the other side of the room.

W: Let's go say hello.

Q1: Whom did the man see?

A. Clair.

B. Lisa.　← 正解

C. Holly.

中文翻譯

| 簡短對話 1 | 男人：克萊兒，我剛剛看到麗莎了。
女人：真的嗎？在哪裡？
男人：在這房間的另一頭。
女人：我們去打個招呼吧。 | ⟫⟫⟫ | 問：這名男子看到誰了？
A. 克萊兒。
B. 麗莎。
C. 荷莉。 |

※〔註〕男子在對話中說 I just saw Lisa.，因此正確答案是選項 B.。這裡利用在同一句話中提及兩個人名來造成混淆。在進行對話時，常會以人名開啟對話，但這個名字並不是對話主題，作答時要特別小心。

Conversation 2.

（門鈴聲）

M: Hey Julie, you look great.

W: Thanks. You're handsome, too.

M: So are you ready to go to the party?

W: Sure, Joe. Where's your car?

Q2: Where are they talking?

A. At Julie's home. ◀ 正解
B. At the party.
C. In Joe's car.

中文翻譯

| 簡短對話 2 | 男人：嘿，茱莉，妳看起來好美。
女人：謝謝。你也很帥。
男人：那妳準備好去派對了嗎？
女人：當然，喬。你的車在哪裡？ | ⟫⟫⟫ | 問：他們在哪裡講話？
A. 在茱莉家。
B. 在派對上。
C. 在喬的車裡。 |

※〔註〕男子說 "... ready to go to the party?"，也就是說他們還沒抵達派對現場，女子說 "Joe. Where's your car?" 則表示他們還沒進到 Joe 的車內，因此正確答案為 A.。

Conversation 3.

M: I really must be going now.
W: Can't you stay a little longer?
M: I really can't.
W: OK. Drive carefully. Bye.

Q3: What is the man doing?

A. He's saying goodbye. ── 正解
B. He's driving.
C. He is going to stay longer.

中文翻譯

| 簡短對話 3 | 男人：我現在真的得走了。
女人：你不能再待久一點嗎？
男人：真的不行。
女人：好吧。開車小心。再見。 | >>> | 問：這名男子在做什麼？
A. 他在道別。
B. 他在開車。
C. 他會再待久一點。 |

※〔註〕選項 B.、C. 都重複了對話中的部分內容，但內容卻都剛好與對話內容相反，也就是說 He's NOT driving. 而且 He's NOT going to stay longer.。可由男子說 I really must be going now. 判斷出正確答案為 A.。

Conversation 4.

W: Sorry, I've got to go now.
M: So soon?
W: Yes, I have to be home by 3 o'clock. I have a piano class.
M: OK. See you later.

Q4: Why is the woman leaving?

A. She will be leaving by 3 o'clock.
B. She has a piano class. ── 正解
C. She has a piano.

中文翻譯

簡短對話 **4**	女人：抱歉，我現在必須走了。 男人：這麼快？ 女人：是啊，我必須在三點以前 　　　　到家。我要上鋼琴課。 男人：好吧，再見。	>>>	問：為什麼這名女子要離開？ A. 她會在三點前離開。 B. 她有鋼琴課。 C. 她有鋼琴。

※〔註〕女子說 "I have a piano class."，表示自己因為有鋼琴課，所以必須先離開，因此答案選 B.。這題的選項同樣是利用對話中的部分內容來刻意設下陷阱，如果沒有仔細聽，那就可能因此誤選到陷阱選項。

主題 **15**	用 餐

Conversation 1.

W: Bill, what would you like to drink?

M: I'd like some water, please.

W: Anything else?

M: Well. Some cake, please.

Q1: What would Bill like to eat and drink?

　　A. Some bread and water.

　　B. Some cake and coffee.

　　C. Some cake and water. ← 正解

中文翻譯

簡短對話 **1**	女人：比爾，你想喝什麼？ 男人：我想喝點水，謝謝。 女人：還要其他的嗎？ 男人：這個嘛，來點蛋糕，謝謝。	>>>	問：比爾想要吃和喝什麼？ A. 一些麵包和水。 B. 一些蛋糕和咖啡。 C. 一些蛋糕和水。

※〔註〕男子一開始就說 "I'd like some water."，後來又說 "Some cake, please."，故正確答案為 C.。

Conversation 2.

W: I am so full. The duck was excellent.

M: I hope you saved room for dessert.

W: Oh no, dessert?

Q2: How does the woman feel?

    A. She feels hungry.

    B. She feels like eating some dessert.

    C. She feels full.   正解

中文翻譯			
簡短 對話 **2**	女人：我好飽。這道鴨肉真棒。 男人：我希望妳有留肚子吃甜 點。 女人：哦，不，甜點？	>>>	問：這名女子覺得如何？ A. 她覺得餓。 B. 她想吃些甜點。 C. 她覺得很飽。

※〔註〕room（空間）；save room（留下空間）意指留下肚子（stomach）的空間來吃其他東西。

Conversation 3.

W: There's a new restaurant open nearby.

M: What kind of food do they have?

W: Italian. Would you like to try?

M: Certainly. Let's go.

Q3: What will they probably have?

    A. Pizza and spaghetti.   正解

    B. Fried chicken and soda.

    C. Rice and fish.

中文翻譯			
簡短 對話 **3**	女人：附近有一家新餐廳開了。 男人：他們賣哪種食物？ 女人：義大利菜。你想試試看嗎？ 男人：當然。我們走吧。	>>>	問：他們可能會吃什麼？ A. 披薩和義大利麵。 B. 炸雞和汽水。 C. 米飯和魚。

※〔註〕因為他們要前往的是一家「義大利」餐廳，A. 是義式餐廳中最可能提供的餐點。B. 則可能是 fast food restaurant（速食餐廳）裡的菜色，C. 則可能是亞洲餐廳裡的菜色，例如 Chinese/Japanese/Korean/Thai restaurant（中國／日本／韓國／泰國餐廳）。

Conversation 4.

M: Good morning. What would you like?

W: A cola for me and a coffee for my friend.

M: Would you like anything to eat with that? A pancake or a sandwich?

W: No, thank you.

主題
15
用餐

Q4: What does the customer want?

A. Cola and coffee. 正解
B. Coffee and cake.
C. Pancake and sandwiches.

中文翻譯

簡短對話 4	
男人：早安。您想點什麼？ 女人：我要一杯可樂，我朋友要一杯咖啡。 男人：妳想點些什麼搭配著吃嗎？鬆餅或三明治？ 女人：不用，謝謝你。	問：這名顧客想要什麼？ A. 可樂和咖啡。 B. 咖啡和蛋糕。 C. 鬆餅和三明治。

※〔註〕顧客一開始點了飲料，她說 "A cola... and a coffee...."，接下來雖然店員提供了食物的選項，但她拒絕了，因此正確答案為 A.。

中式早點

饅頭	steamed bun
蛋餅	egg pancake roll
飯糰	rice ball
豆漿	soy milk
燒餅	clay oven roll
油條	fried bread stick

主題 16　　　購 物

Conversation 1.

W: May I help you?

M: Yes. Do you have this jacket in size 40?

W: I'm not sure. Let me look in the stockroom.

M: Thanks.

Q1: What is the man looking for?

A. A shirt.

B. A jacket. ◀━ 正解

C. A coat.

中文翻譯

簡短對話 1	女人：我能為你服務嗎？ 男人：是的。你們這件夾克有 40 號的嗎？ 女人：我不確定。讓我去倉庫看一下。 男人：謝謝。	≫≫≫	問：男子在找什麼？ A. 襯衫。 B. 夾克。 C. 大衣。

※〔註〕男子問店員 "Do you have this jacket...?"，由此清楚知道他想買一件夾克，答案為 B.。

Conversation 2.

M: Hi, are you being helped?

W: No, I'm not. I'm interested in some scarves.

Q2: What is the man?

A. He's a police officer.

B. He's a shop salesman. ◀━ 正解

C. He's a fashion designer.

中文翻譯

| 簡短
對話
2 | 男人：嗨，有人為您服務嗎？
女人：不，沒有。我想看些圍巾。 | >>> | 問：男子的職業是什麼？
A. 他是警察。
B. 他是店員。
C. 他是時裝設計師。 |

※〔註〕本題對話中出現的 "Are you being helped?" 等同於 "May I help you?（我能為您服務嗎？）"。透過女子的回答 "I'm interested in some scarves." 可知答案為 B.。

Conversation 3.

M: Can I try these pants on?

W: Yes, you can. The fitting room is over there.

M: They don't fit. Please show me bigger ones.

Q3: Do the pants fit the man?

A. He doesn't look good on them.

B. They are too big.

C. They are too small. ◄正解

中文翻譯

| 簡短
對話
3 | 男人：我可以試穿這些褲子嗎？
女人：可以。試衣間在那裡。
男人：這些不合身。請幫我拿大
一點的。 | >>> | 問：褲子對男子而言合身嗎？
A. 他穿起來不好看。
B. 太大了。
C. 太小了。 |

※〔註〕男子試穿（try on）後發現褲子不合自己的尺寸，說 "... show me bigger ones."，要求女子拿尺寸大一點的給自己，也就是說試穿過的這些褲子太小了，答案為 C.。

Conversation 4.

W: Would you like some help?

M: Do you have the book "Harry Potter and the Goblet of Fire"?

W: Yes, it's right here. It's on sale.

Q4: Where is this dialogue taking place?

A. In a book shop. ◄正解

B. In a library.

C. In a record store.

中文翻譯

簡短對話 4	女人：您需要協助嗎？ 男人：你們有《火盃的考驗》這本書嗎？ 女人：有，就在這裡。它現在在特價。	>>>	問：這段對話是在哪裡發生的？ A. 在書店裡。 B. 在圖書館裡。 C. 在唱片行裡。

※〔註〕男子詢問 "Do you have the book...?"，由此判斷對話發生的地點不是 A. 就是 B.；但接下來女子提到 "... It's on sale."，在圖書館不會有書特價，因此正確答案為 A.。

店員讚美顧客的表達方式

1. It suits you well. 這很適合你。
2. You look good in it. 你穿起來很好看。
3. It looks good on you. 穿在你身上很好看。
4. The skirt matches your pink blouse.
   這件裙子很搭妳的粉紅色上衣。
5. The necktie goes with your blue shirt.
   這條領帶和你的藍色襯衫很搭。

主題 17　約定‧預約

Conversation 1.

M: I'm going to miss you.
W: Me too. Let's keep in touch.
M: Yeah. Don't forget to write me.

Q1: Who's the woman?

A. She is Miss Yu.
B. She is the man's Miss Right.
C. We don't know. ──正解

中文翻譯

| 簡短對話 1 | 男人：我會想妳的。
女人：我也是。我們要保持聯絡喔！
男人：是啊，別忘了寫信給我。 | >>> | 問：這名女子是誰？
A. 她是尤小姐。
B. 她是男子的夢中情人。
C. 我們不知道。 |

※〔註〕Write me. 就是「寫信給我」的意思，這是用來提醒對方與自己保持聯絡的慣用表達。

Conversation 2.

M: Excuse me. My name is Adam Ford. I have an appointment with the dentist at 3:30.

W: Yes, Mr. Ford. The dentist will be ready to see you in a minute. Have a seat.

M: Thank you.

Q2: **Who will the man see?**

A. Mr. Ford.
B. No. 4.
C. The dentist. ——正解

中文翻譯

| 簡短對話 2 | 男人：不好意思。我的名字是亞當‧福特。我和牙醫約在 3 點 30 分。
女人：好的，福特先生。牙醫馬上就可以看你了。請坐。
男人：謝謝妳。 | >>> | 問：男子將見到誰？
A. 福特先生。
B. 四號。
C. 牙醫。 |

※〔註〕appointment [ə`pɔɪntmənt] （會面的）約定
dentist [`dɛntɪst] 牙醫
have a seat = take a seat 請坐

Conversation 3.

W: You'll be here for two nights. Is that correct, Mr. Katz?

W: Yes, that's correct.

Q3: When will Mr. Katz leave the place?

A. The day after tomorrow. — 正解

B. Tomorrow.

C. Today.

中文翻譯

| 簡短對話 3 | 女人：你會在這裡待兩個晚上。是這樣嗎？蓋茲先生？ 男人：是，沒錯。 | >>> | 問：蓋茲先生什麼時候會離開這個地方？ A. 後天。 B. 明天。 C. 今天。 |

※〔註〕女子說 "You'll be here for two nights..."，意思就是男子在此地度過兩晚後就會離開，也就是「後天」，答案為 A.。

Conversation 4.

W: I'd like to book a flight to Taipei, please.

M: Surely, ma'am. What date?

W: June 6.

Q4: How will the woman go to Taipei?

A. On June 6.

B. By plane. — 正解

C. Ride a train.

中文翻譯

| 簡短對話 4 | 女人：我要訂往台北的班機，謝謝。 男人：沒問題，女士。日期哪一天呢？ 女人：六月六日。 | >>> | 問：女子將如何到台北？ A. 在六月六日。 B. 搭飛機。 C. 坐火車。 |

※〔註〕flight [flaɪt] 班次；班機，「book a flight to＋地點」是「預訂前往（某地點）的班機」的意思，flight 還可以改成 train（火車）或 bus（巴士）等交通工具。

※〔註〕對話一開始女子就說 "I'd like to book a flight...."，而訂機票是為了要前往台北，因此正確答案為 B.。

主題 18 學校

主題 18　學　校

Conversation 1.

M: The English lesson is so interesting. Don't you think so, Lily?

W: No, I think it's boring. I like math more.

Q1: Which is more interesting for Lily?

A. Neither English nor math is interesting.

B. Math. 正解

C. English.

中文翻譯

| 簡短對話 1 | 男人：英文課真是有趣。莉莉，妳不覺得嗎？
女人：不，我覺得它很無聊，我比較喜歡數學。 | >>> | 問：對莉莉而言，哪個比較有趣？
A. 英文和數學都無趣。
B. 數學。
C. 英文。 |

※〔註〕女子（Lily）說 "I like math more."，換句話說就是 "Math is more interesting."，答案為 B.。

Conversation 2.

M: Your Japanese is good. When did you begin to learn Japanese?

W: Two years ago. I met a very good teacher.

Q2: How long has the woman learned Japanese?

A. She begins to learn Japanese.

B. She has learned Japanese for two years. 正解

C. She met a very good Japanese teacher.

中文翻譯

| 簡短對話 2 | 男人：妳的日文很好。妳是從什麼時候開始學日文的？
女人：兩年前。我遇到了一位非常好的老師。 | >>> | 問：女子已經學了多久的日文？
A. 她開始學日文了。
B. 她已經學了兩年的日文。
C. 她遇到了一位非常好的日文老師。 |

※〔註〕以 How long...? 開頭的疑問句，問的是「一段時間」，對話中女子提到自己 Two years ago 開始學日文，因此答案是選項 B.。

Conversation 3.

M: Excuse me. Where can I find the English teachers' office?
W: It's on the second floor, between the math teachers' office and the Chinese teachers' office.
M: Thank you.

Q3: Where does the man want to go?

A. To the English teachers' office.　→ 正解
B. To the third floor.
C. To the Chinese teachers' office.

中文翻譯

| 簡短對話 3 | 男人：不好意思。英文老師的辦公室在哪裡呢？
女人：它在二樓，在數學和國文老師辦公室的中間。
男人：謝謝妳。 | >>> | 問：男子想要去哪裡？
A. 去英文老師的辦公室。
B. 去三樓。
C. 去國文老師的辦公室。 |

※〔註〕男子一開始就問 "Where can I find the English teacher's office"，表示自己想去的是英文老師的辦公室，所以答案為 A.。

Conversation 4.

W: What score did you get in French, John?
M: I got 98 at first, but the teacher found a mistake and changed it into 95.

Q4: What was the man's score?

A. It was 95.　→ 正解
B. It was less than 95.
C. It was 98.

中文翻譯

| 簡短對話 4 | 女人：約翰，你的法文拿到幾分？
男人：原本是 98 分，可是老師發現了一個錯誤，就把它改成 95 分了。 | >>> | 問：男子的分數是多少？
A. 95 分。
B. 低於 95 分。
C. 98 分。 |

※〔註〕對話中提到老師一開始給錯分數，後來才把分數改成 95 分，也就是男子真正該得的分數，所以答案為 A.。

主題 19   工 作

Conversation 1.

W: What does your wife do, Ian?

M: Lillian used to be a nurse, but she quit the job three months ago. Now she looks after our new baby.

Q1: What is Lillian's job now?

A. She is a nurse.
B. She is looking for a job.
C. She is a housewife. ──正解

中文翻譯

| 簡短對話 1 | 女人：伊安，你太太的工作是什麼？ 男人：莉莉安曾經是護士，可是三個月前她辭職了。現在她在照顧我們剛出生的孩子。 | ≫≫ | 問：莉莉安現在的工作為何？ A. 她是一名護士。 B. 她正在找工作。 C. 她是一位家庭主婦。 |

※〔註〕對話內容中說 Now she looks after our new baby.，表示莉莉安目前在家照顧小孩，因此正確答案是選項 C.。

Conversation 2.

W: Something must have bothered you.

M: I'm having a meeting with the manager. She is unhappy with me.

W: What's wrong?

M: I was absent for the Tuesday meeting.

Q2: What is bothering the man?

A. He has a meeting on Tuesday.
B. He is unhappy with the meeting.
C. The manager is angry. ──正解

中文翻譯

簡短
對話
2

女人：一定有什麼事在困擾著
　　　你。
男人：我要和經理開會。她對我
　　　很不高興。
女人：怎麼了？
男人：我缺席了星期二的會議。

>>>

問：什麼事正困擾著這名男子？
A. 他在星期二有場會議。
B. 他對會議不高興。
C. 經理在生氣。

※〔註〕男子說 ".... the manager. She is unhappy...."，換句話說就是經理對自己生氣（angry）了，答案為 C.。

Conversation 3.

W: How was your interview with the company?

M: It's tomorrow. I'm worried.

W: Don't worry. You should do fine.

M: I hope so.

Q3: What are they talking about?

A. About finding a job. ←─ 正解
B. About hopes.
C. About running a company.

中文翻譯

簡短
對話
3

女人：你那間公司的面試怎麼
　　　樣？
男人：是在明天。我很擔心。
女人：別擔心。你應該沒問題
　　　的。
男人：我希望是這樣。

>>>

問：他們在談論什麼？
A. 找工作。
B. 希望。
C. 經營公司。

※〔註〕女子一開始就提到了「那間公司的面試」，因此可以知道他們是在說與找工作有關的事情，正確答案是選項 A.。

Conversation 4.

W: I'm going to quit my job, Jeff.
M: Why?
W: I'm going to Paris to study. I want to become an artist.

Q4: What does the woman do?

　　　　A. An artist.
　　　　B. A pianist.
　　　　C. We don't know. ◀━ 正解

中文翻譯

簡短對話 4	女人：傑夫，我打算要辭職了。 男人：為什麼？ 女人：我要到巴黎念書。我想當藝術家。	⟫⟫⟫	問：女子的工作為何？ A. 藝術家。 B. 鋼琴家。 C. 我們不知道。

※〔註〕這裡必須注意到題目問句的時態 "What does... do?" 是現在式，問的是女子「現在」的工作是什麼，但對話中女子只提到要辭職，以及未來想成為藝術家，並沒有說出目前的工作為何，所以答案為 C.

主題 **20**　　　　　**社 交**

Conversation 1.

W: Would you like some cookies or cake?
M: I like both, but I'd just like something to drink now.

Q1: What does the man want now?

　　　　A. Cookies and cake.
　　　　B. Some drinks. ◀━ 正解
　　　　C. Bread.

中文翻譯

| 簡短對話 **1** | 女人：你要來點餅乾或蛋糕嗎？
男人：我兩樣都喜歡，可是我現在只想要來點喝的。 | >>> | 問：這名男子現在想要什麼？
A. 餅乾和蛋糕。
B. 一些飲料。
C. 麵包。 |

※〔註〕男子雖然說自己餅乾和蛋糕都喜歡，但後面卻說他現在（now）只想要來點喝的（would like something to drink），因此正確答案是選項 B.。

Conversation 2.

M: Jane. Help yourself to more food, please.

W: No, thanks. I'm full.

Q2: What did the man ask Jane to do?

A. To help him get some food.

B. To have some more food. ◀ 正解

C. To leave some food.

中文翻譯

| 簡短對話 **2** | 男人：珍，請自己再去多拿點食物吧。
女人：不用了，謝謝。我飽了。 | >>> | 問：男子要珍做什麼？
A. 幫他拿點食物。
B. 再多吃點食物。
C. 留一點食物。 |

※〔註〕Help yourself to more food 是「自己再去多拿點食物」的意思，因此正確答案是選項 B.。

Conversation 3.

M: Anna. Everybody is singing and dancing. Why are you here?

W: I'd rather stay out for a while. Why do people smoke at all? It's so smoky in there.

Q3: Why is Anna staying out?

A. She doesn't like dancing.

B. She doesn't like people in there.

C. She doesn't like people smoking in there. ◀ 正解

中文翻譯

| 簡短 對話 **3** | 男人：安娜，大家都在唱歌跳舞。妳怎麼在這裡？ 女人：我比較想在外面待一會。大家到底為什麼要抽菸啊？裡面真的菸味好重。 | >>> | 問：為什麼安娜待在外面？ A. 她不喜歡跳舞。 B. 她不喜歡裡面的人。 C. 她不喜歡大家在裡面抽菸。 |

主題 **20** 社交

※〔註〕對話中出現的 I'd rather ~ 是「我比較想~」的意思。Anna 用疑問句 Why do people smoke 來說明自己待在外面（stay out）的理由。

Conversation 4.

W: I think it's about time we got going.

M: Already? Won't you have more coffee?

W: I'd love to, but I have to get up early tomorrow.

Q4: What is the relationship between the man and the woman?

    A. Singer and audience.

    B. Shop owner and customer.

    C. Host and guest. 正解

中文翻譯

| 簡短 對話 **4** | 女人：我覺得我們差不多該走了。 男人：已經要走了嗎？你們不再多喝點咖啡嗎？ 女人：我很想，可是我明天必須早起。 | >>> | 問：男子和女子間的關係為何？ A. 歌手和觀眾。 B. 商店老闆和顧客。 C. 主人和客人。 |

※〔註〕audience [`ɔdɪəns] 觀眾；受眾
     owner [`onɚ] 物主；擁有者
     host [host] 主人

 短文聽解

第一類 廣播

主題 1 交通工具上

Q1 Please look at the following three pictures.
Listen to the following announcement. Where does it take place?
This is Captain Josh. We are now flying at a height of about 2000m. As the weather condition turns bad, we are expecting turbulence during the flight. Please stay in your seat and have your seat belt fastened. Meals will be served in 15 minutes. Thank you for your cooperation.

解答 C

 請看以下三張圖。
請聽以下公告。這段公告發生在哪裡?
我是機長喬許。我們現在的飛行高度約為兩千公尺。由於天氣轉壞,我們預期飛行過程中將會有亂流。請坐在您的位子上並扣上安全帶。餐點將在 15 分鐘後供應。謝謝您的合作。

※〔註〕在飛機上聽到的廣播內容是常考的題目,大概分為「起飛前」、「飛行途中」及「即將降落」三種階段的題型,本題考的是在飛行途中的廣播,關鍵字是 flying,「坐遊覽車/高鐵」,我們會說 take/ride on a coach or High Speed Rail,廣播中出現的 turbulence 是另一關鍵字,是「亂流」的意思,故正確答案為 C。

Q2 Please look at the following three pictures.

Listen to the following announcement. Where does it probably take place?

Good morning passengers. The next train to Yilan is arriving in two minutes. Please stay behind the yellow line until the train makes a complete stop. Thank you and have a nice journey.

解答 C

請看以下三張圖。

請聽以下公告。這段公告可能發生在哪裡？

各位乘客早安。下一班到宜蘭的火車將在兩分鐘後進站。請在黃線後等候直到列車完全停妥。感謝您的搭乘並祝您旅途愉快。

※〔註〕仔細看過三張圖後，考生必須要有這三張圖分別是MRT（捷運）、City（市）及train station（火車站）或train platform（火車月台）的概念，本廣播內容的關鍵字為train，且出現了兩次，正確答案為C。

Q3　Please look at the following three pictures.
Listen to the following talk. Where might you hear this?
Good morning everyone! Welcome to Japan. I am your tour guide, Diana. And Mark, our handsome driver, who's now driving us to the hotel, is going to take us safely to those well-known scenic spots in Tokyo for the following five days. Let's give him a big hand.

解答　A

請看以下三張圖。
請聽以下這段話。你可能會在哪裡聽到這段話？
大家早！歡迎來到日本。我是你們的導遊戴安娜，還有正在載我們去飯店的帥氣司機馬克，接下來的五天他會安全地帶我們到那些東京的著名景點遊覽。讓我們給他一個熱烈的掌聲。

※〔註〕本題考這段話發生的地點所在何處，破題點是 ...driver is now driving...to the hotel 這一句，透過這句話，可以知道「司機正開往飯店」，代表旅客跟導遊正在遊覽車上，所以正確答案為 A。

主題 2 電台

Q1
Please look at the following three pictures.
Listen to the following talk. Where can you hear this talk?
This is FM 92.6, Taipei Music. I am Christine sharing lovely music with you from 2 to 4 every weekday. Next is the last song for today. Do join me on air tomorrow at the same time.

解答 B

 請看以下三張圖。
請聽以下這段話。你可以在哪裡聽到這段話？
這裡是 FM 92.6 台北音樂台。我是克莉絲汀，每週一到週五下午兩點到四點與你分享美妙的音樂。接下來是今天最後一首歌曲，明天同一時間繼續和我一起在空中相遇吧。

※〔註〕電台廣播類型的考題，考生只要聽到音檔開頭出現 FM 或 Radio 這兩個字，就能百分百確定正確答案是什麼，本題一開始就清楚說明 this is FM 92.6，故本題正確答案為 B。

Q2　Please look at the following three pictures.
Listen to the following talk. What might be the background?
Good evening dear audience. I'm your night host Ben. Thank you for tuning in to FM 99.9, your best LOHAS broadcast. Today I would like to talk about how to choose a good bike. And you are welcome to call in to share your own buying and biking experiences.

解答　A

請看以下三張圖。
請聽以下這段話。這段話的背景可能是什麼？
親愛的聽眾們晚安。我是你們的晚間主持人班。謝謝你們收聽你最棒的樂活電台 FM 99.9。今天我想要討論的是，要如何選購一台好的腳踏車，歡迎打電話進來分享你們自己購買和騎腳踏車的經驗。

※〔註〕本題問的是說這段話的「背景 background」為何？關鍵字在 FM 99.9，聽到 FM 考生就一定知道這段話是電台廣播的內容，另外 audience（聽眾）、tune in（收聽）、broadcast（廣播）也都是答題關鍵字，且是「電台廣播」類題型常出現的字，本題正確答案為 A。

Q3 Please look at the following three pictures.
Listen to the following talk. Who is the speaker?
Welcome back to Love Radio. I'm Jenny, your weekend DJ. The song you just listened to is from Jay. Jay released his new album last week and I am glad to have him in the studio in the second hour. Stay tuned in for more Jay.

解答 B

請看以下三張圖。
請聽以下這段話。說話者是誰？

歡迎回到愛戀電台，我是你的週末 DJ 珍妮。剛剛聽到的歌曲來自傑爾。傑爾在上星期推出了他的新專輯，而我很高興能在第二個小時請到他來錄音室。想知道更多的傑爾，別轉台。

※〔註〕本考題屬變化型，考 Who（誰）而不是常出現的 Where、What place（在什麼地點），答題關鍵在 I'm Jenny, your...DJ「我是你的 DJ」，當然 radio（這裡指電台）、stay tuned（別轉台）都有助於確認正確答案是什麼，本題正確答案為 B。

主題 3　百貨公司・賣場

Q1 Please look at the following three pictures.
Listen to the following announcement. Where will you most probably hear this announcement?
Welcome to Love Mall. We would like your attention, please. A customer is looking for her 6-year-old daughter, who is wearing a purple dress and white shoes. If you happened to see her around, please accompany her to our information counter on the 1st floor. Your help is much appreciated. Thank you and wish you a wonderful shopping day.

解答 A

請看以下三張圖。
請聽以下公告。你最有可能會在哪裡聽到這段公告？
歡迎來到愛戀購物中心。我們想要請您留意。有一位客人在找她的 6 歲女兒，她身穿紫色洋裝跟白鞋子。如果您碰巧看到她在附近，請陪同她到我們一樓的服務台。非常感謝您的幫忙。謝謝您並祝您購物愉快。

※〔註〕先仔細看完三張圖，考生應該知道 shopping center/mall（購物中心）、police station（警察局）以及 restroom（洗手間）等單字，所以當聽到第一句 Welcome to Love Mall，答案就已經揭曉，最後的 ...wish you a wonderful shopping day，shopping 一字讓答案更為明確，故本題正確答案為 A。

Q2 Please look at the following three pictures.
Listen to the following announcement. At what place might you hear this announcement?
Good day customers, thank you for shopping at SMART Super. To celebrate the 20th birthday of SMART, customers are offered a lucky draw coupon for every $300 purchase. The biggest prize is $200,000 in cash. Try your luck at your nearest SMART supermarket.

解答 B

請看以下三張圖。
請聽以下公告。你可能會在哪裡聽到這段公告？

 顧客好，感謝您惠顧 SMART 超市。為慶祝 SMART 的 20 歲生日，顧客單筆滿 300 元即可獲得摸彩券一張。最大獎是現金 20 萬元。到離您最近的 SMART 超市試試手氣吧。

※〔註〕「超級市場」的英文是 supermarket；「傳統市場」則是 market，本題的關鍵字當然是 super 及 market，出題者故意把 supermarket 的 super 拆出來擺在前面出現，是希望讓題目更符合國外的文化與習慣，考生也可從中學習。本題正確答案為 B。

Q3　Please look at the following three pictures.
Listen to the following announcement. Where might you hear this?
Sale! Sale! Sale! We are offering a summer offer on every item
from July 1st to July 8th. Women's clothes are up to 50% off.
Gentlemen are able to buy one tie and get one free. Kids under ten
years old are free to enjoy their time in our toy land while you
shop.

解答　C

請看以下三張圖。
請聽以下公告。你可能會在哪裡聽到這段公告？

降！降！降！我們所有產品從 7 月 1 日到 8 日都有夏日優惠。女
性服飾五折起，男仕領帶買一送一。在你購物的時候，10 歲以下
的孩童可以在我們遊戲區內玩樂。

※〔註〕這三張圖分別是咖啡店
coffee shop/café；夜 市 night
market；百 貨 公 司 department
store。考生在聽到 sale 時，馬上
就可以知道這段公告跟「打折，
優惠」有關，圖中三個地方都有
可能會聽到這樣的公告，但接下
來出現的 women's clothes、ties
都不可能出現在咖啡店，而夜市
也不會有 toy land（遊戲區），
因此正確答案為 C。

第二類 留言

主題 4 親友間

Q1
Please look at the following three pictures.
Listen to the following message. What are the parents going to do?
Hey sweetheart, your mom and I are taking the afternoon train to your place. Don't bother to pick us up. We will meet you at the Grand Hotel at 6, OK? Can't wait to see your birthday present, right? See you later. Love you.

解答 C

請看以下三張圖。
請聽以下訊息。這對爸媽打算要做什麼？

嘿，甜心，妳媽媽跟我正要搭下午的火車到妳那裡。不用麻煩來接我們。我們 6 點在格蘭飯店見，好嗎？妳等不及要看妳的生日禮物了，對吧？待會見。愛妳。

※〔註〕本題考「爸媽打算做什麼」，答題關鍵在 We will meet you at the Grand Hotel...，代表爸媽即將要跟女兒碰面，接著爸爸提到生日禮物的事，所以可推知應該是要為女兒慶祝生日，正確答案為 C。

Q2 Please look at the following three pictures.
George left a message to Sam. Where might Sam probably go after hearing the message?
Sam, I'm George. I've been calling for the past few hours. Brad was hit this morning and is now in the operation room. Please call back as soon as you hear my message. This is not something funny.

解答 B

請看以下三張圖。
喬治留了一則訊息給山姆。山姆在聽到這則訊息之後，可能會去哪裡？

山姆，我是喬治。我已經打了好幾個小時的電話了。布萊德今天早上被撞了，現在人在手術室裡。聽到我的訊息請馬上回電。這不是開玩笑。

※〔註〕本題考「聽完留言後，Sam 可能會去哪裡」，答題關鍵字是 was hit（被撞／打）以及 operation room（手術室），Sam 的朋友 Brad 人在醫院，而根據 George 在留言中緊張憂心的語氣，可推知 Sam 在聽完留言後會趕往醫院，故本題正確答案為 B。

Q3 Please look at the following three pictures.
Listen to the following message. Where is Carol?
Time to get out of your bed, Carol. It's bright and sunny outside, just perfectly fit for a walk or ride. You're not going to waste your life in bed. I'm on the way to your place. See you in a minute.

解答 A

請看以下三張圖。
請聽以下訊息。凱蘿在哪裡？

是時候起床了，凱蘿。外面陽光普照，很適合去散散步或騎車。妳不要在床上浪費生命了。我現在在去妳家的路上。馬上見。

※〔註〕本題考「Carol 現在在哪裡？」，詢問聽訊息的人的所在地點，答題關鍵字是 bed，訊息中也出現了 get out of bed（離開床／起床）、waste your life in bed（在床上浪費生命），所以本題正確答案為 A。

| 主題 **5** | **公事** |

Q1 Please look at the following three pictures.
Listen to the following message. How is Peter going to deliver the report?
Peter, this is Ryan. I need you to do me a favor. I'm out with my client. Could you kindly bring me the annual report which is left on my desk? I need that by one and please meet me at 12:30 at the café around the corner. A million thanks.

解答 A

請看以下三張圖。
請聽以下訊息。彼得會如何送達報告？

彼得，我是雷恩，我需要你幫我一個忙。我現在人在外面見客戶。可以麻煩你幫我把我忘在桌上的年度報告送過來嗎？我下午一點時需要這份報告，拜託你十二點半在轉角的咖啡店跟我碰面。萬分感謝。

※〔註〕本題考「Peter 會如何送達報告？」，首先考生聽到 I'm now with my client，就可知 Ryan 不在公司，所以 C 不對。而解題關鍵是 meet me at...the café...，故本題正確答案為 A。

Q2 Please look at the following three pictures.
Kate's boss left her a message. What might she probably do after listening to the message?
Morning Kate, I got an emergency call from Mr. Jackson early this morning. As you might guess, I am now heading to the airport. Please cancel all the meetings and appointments originally scheduled. Please keep your cell phone on and stay alert to my emails.

解答 B

請看以下三張圖。
凱特的老闆留了一則訊息給她。她在聽完這則訊息之後,可能會做什麼?

 早安,凱特。我今天一大早接到了傑克森先生的緊急電話。就像妳可能猜到的那樣,我現在正在去機場。麻煩妳取消所有原定的會議及會面。請把手機開著,並注意我的電子郵件。

※〔註〕本題考「女人在聽完老闆的訊息後可能會做什麼」,答題關鍵是 cancel all meetings and appointments... 老闆因為有急事而臨時不在,請他的祕書或助理取消所有會議及會面,所以女人接下來最有可能會做的是忙著打電話(或 email)通知取消事宜,故本題正確答案為 B。

Q3 Please look at the following three pictures.
Judy was sick and she left a message to her supervisor. Where might Judy be?
Good morning, Mrs. White. This is Judy. I'm afraid I need to ask for a sick leave today. I had a fever and diarrhea. My doctor kept me here in the clinic for further check-up. Sorry for the absence and I'll be back to the office as soon as I can.

解答　B

請看以下三張圖。
茱蒂生病了,她留了一則訊息給她的主管。茱蒂可能在哪裡?

 早安,懷特太太。我是茱蒂。我今天恐怕要請病假。我發燒又拉肚子。醫生要求我留在診所做進一步檢查。很抱歉要請假,我會盡快回去上班的。

※〔註〕本題詢問「Judy 生病了,且留言給她的主管,她現在人在哪裡?」,首先聽到 ask for a sick leave(請病假),就代表 Judy 不可能在辦公室,所以 C 不對。剩下醫院跟診所,答題關鍵就是 clinic,是「診所」的意思,而 Judy 說 doctor kept me in the clinic,所以本題正確答案為 B。

主題 6　提醒

Q1
Please look at the following three pictures.
Listen to the following message. What is suggested?
Dear customer, your account at City Telecom shows a balance of $2500. Please cover the balance within 72 hours or your communication service will be suspended. Thank you for using City Telecom.

解答 A

請看以下三張圖。
請聽以下訊息。建議了什麼？

親愛的用戶，您在城市電信的帳戶尚有餘款 $2500 未付。請於 72 小時內繳納，否則您的通話服務將被中止。感謝您使用城市電信服務。

※〔註〕本題詢問「建議事項」，答題關鍵是 balance、cover the balance。balance 在此是「餘款」的意思，雖然它本身有「餘額」之意，但因為 Telecom（電信公司）提到 cover the balance（補繳餘額），因此這是一通提醒繳費的留言，而最後的 ...or your communication service will be suspended 就是提醒用戶要補繳費用，故本題正確答案為 A。

Q2 Please look at the following three pictures.
Listen to the following message. On what kind of product might you hear this?
Good day, you have five new messages. Listen to messages, please press 1. Delete messages, please press 2. Main menu, please press 9. To leave, press 0 or hang up.

解答 B

請看以下三張圖。
請聽以下訊息。你可能會在什麼類型的產品上聽到這則訊息？
您好，您有五則新訊息。聆聽訊息請按 1，刪除訊息請按 2，回到主選單請按 9，離開請按 0 或掛斷。

※〔註〕本題考「你會在哪一種產品中聽到這則訊息？」，一般來說不會用筆記型電腦來聽訊息，所以 A 不對。本題答題關鍵為 hang up，指「掛斷」，能「掛斷」的只有手機跟室內電話，所以本題正確答案為 B。

Q3 Please look at the following three pictures.

A credit card company left a message to a customer. What can be told from the message?

Dear customer, thank you for shopping with Metro Credit card. Your latest purchase amount is $10,000 at Mountain Restaurant. Please confirm or check with our staff at 080-565-656.

解答 B

請看以下三張圖。

信用卡公司留了一則訊息給顧客。從這則訊息中可以得知什麼？

 親愛的用戶，感謝您使用大都會信用卡消費。您最新的消費金額為 10,000 元於山頂餐廳。請確認或來電 080-565-656 與我們員工查詢。

※〔註〕本題考「一間信用卡公司留言給一名用戶，我們從訊息中可以得知什麼？」，A 是兩個人在餐廳用餐，雖然留言提到了 Restaurant，但我們無法確定這個用戶跟幾個人在用餐，所以 A 不對。而 C 描繪用戶在購物，也許真是用戶做過的事，但訊息中完全沒有提到。本題關鍵在於 thank you for shopping with Metro Credit，代表用戶才剛剛用 Metro 信用卡刷卡消費，所以本題正確答案為 B。

第三類 簡短談話

主題 7 問「什麼地方」

Q1 Please look at the following three pictures.
Listen to the following short talk. What might be the place?
Good evening guys. This should be the biggest live concert you have ever seen. Thank you to all the fans from Taiwan, Japan, Hong Kong and Singapore. Are you ready to rock? Let's do it!

解答 A

請看以下三張圖。
請聽以下簡短談話。這裡可能是什麼地方？
大家晚安。這應該是你們看過最大的現場演唱會了。謝謝從台灣、日本、香港還有新加坡來的所有粉絲。你們準備好要搖滾了嗎？我們開始吧！

※〔註〕演唱會是 concert；電影院是 movie theater 或 cinema；舞台劇是 play，當考生聽到 the biggest live concert 時就可確定答案是什麼了，本題正確答案為 A。

Q2

Please look at the following three pictures.

Listen to the following short talk. What place is probably mentioned?

Hello everyone. You might be amazed by the spectacular appearance of this building. It's no different to a palace. Truth is this highly protected building had been a palace since 1900 and was only renovated into a historical museum in 2002.

解答 C

請看以下三張圖。

請聽以下簡短談話。提到的地方可能是哪裡？

 大家好。這座建築物宏偉的外觀或許讓你驚豔。它跟皇宮沒兩樣（它就像是一座宮殿）。其實這座受到高度保護的建築物，自 1900 年起就一直是一座宮殿，且要到 2002 年才被改建為歷史博物館。

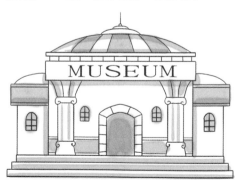

※〔註〕本題有一定難度，考生必須仔細聽取細節，首先看完三張圖後，要有這些單字概念：城堡是 castle；宮殿是 palace；博物館是 museum。palace 一字雖然出現兩次，但在談話中是指「（美得跟）宮殿一樣 no different to a palace」、「自 1900 年（到 2002 年）它一直是一座宮殿 ...had been a palace since 1900...」，所以這座 building（建築物）不是宮殿更不是城堡，它現在已被 renovated（改建）成了一座 museum（博物館），所以本題正確答案為 C。

Q3 Please look at the following three pictures.
Listen to the following short talk. Which place suits the description best?
Thank you, Mr. Lee, for your statements. Next, the opposition will be given three minutes to deliver their arguments. Captain of the opposition, please proceed to the front. You may start when you hear the ring.

解答 A

請看以下三張圖。
請聽以下簡短談話。哪一個地方最符合這段描述？
謝謝李先生的陳述。接下來，反方將有三分鐘的時間提出他們的論點。反方隊長，請上前。聽到鈴聲後請開始。

※〔註〕本題詢問「哪一個地方最符合描述？」，the opposition 是考生必須要理解的字，在辯論比賽中是指「反方」，不過就算考生不懂 the opposition 的意思，簡短對話中出現的 arguments（論點）、captain of the opposition（反方隊長）都是答題關鍵，所以本題正確答案為 A。

主題 8	問「做什麼」

Q1

Please look at the following three pictures.

Listen to the following short talk. What will Sarah do on Friday?

Sarah has a busy week. On Monday and Wednesday morning, she has to teach a new English class. She can't wait to meet her new students. On Tuesday, she's going to have dinner with a friend. Yet Sarah put off a date with Chris on Friday night because the next day is a big day. She is having a huge party at home in the afternoon and there's so much to prepare before that.

解答 B

請看以下三張圖。

請聽以下簡短談話。莎拉在星期五會做什麼？

莎拉這星期很忙。星期一和三的早上，她得去上新開的英文課。她等不及要見到她的新學生了。星期二的時候，她要去和朋友吃晚餐。不過莎拉推遲了星期五晚上和克里斯的約會，因為隔天是個重要的日子。她那天下午要在家裡辦一場盛大的派對，而在那場派對之前有非常多事情要準備。

※〔註〕本題考「Sarah 星期五會做什麼？」，因此考生必須注意聽關鍵字 Friday（星期五）前後的內容，對話中提到 put off a date with...on Friday，指「推遲與……的約會」，所以 A 不對。接下來說 because the next day is a big day...having a huge party，這裡的 next day 是指隔天，星期六 Saturday 才會在家裡辦派對，所以 C 不符。而最後一句 ...ther's so much to prepare before that 則表示在辦派對之前要好好準備，因此本題正確答案為 B。

Q2
Please look at the following three pictures.
Listen to the following short talk. What might Mr. Henson plan to do?

Christmas is around the corner. This year, Mr. Henson wants to give his family a surprise. He's going to buy a toy car for his two kids and decorate the house with a Christmas tree and ribbons for his wife.

解答　C

請看以下三張圖。
請聽以下簡短談話。漢森先生可能計畫要做什麼？

中文
翻譯
聖誕節將至。今年，漢森先生想要給他的家人一個驚喜。他打算替他的兩個小孩買一台玩具汽車，並為太太用聖誕樹和緞帶布置家裡。

※〔註〕本題考「Mr. Henson 可能計畫要做什麼？」，從這段話的內容來看，Mr. Henson 計畫在 Christmas 給家人一個 surprise，所以他「打算」，也就是這段話裡出現的「he's going to...」，因此 buy a toy car 跟 decorate the house with a Christmas tree... 都是答案，故本題正確答案為 C。

Q3 Please look at the following three pictures.
Listen to the following short talk. What might Wendy probably do next?
Wendy came home to find the door unlocked. Her living room was a mess, the drawers were opened and her favorite bottles of wine were gone. Worst of all, the cash and jewelry kept under her pillow were all stolen.

解答 B

中文翻譯 請看以下三張圖。
請聽以下簡短談話。溫蒂接下來可能會做什麼?
溫蒂回到家發現門沒有鎖。她的客廳一團亂,抽屜被打開了,而且她最愛的酒沒了。最糟糕的是,她放在枕頭底下的現金跟珠寶全都被偷走了。

※〔註〕本題考「Wendy 接下來可能會做什麼?」,本題考生只要聽懂 find the door unlocked(發現門沒有鎖)還有最後一個字 stolen(被偷),就能順利解題。溫蒂回到家發現客廳一片混亂 a mess、酒沒了 wine were gone、現金跟珠寶被偷了 cash and jewelry were stolen,因為她回到家發現門沒有鎖,且遭小偷光顧,所以接著她一定是去報案,故本題正確答案為 B。

主題 **9**　　　　　　　　　　**推測**

Q1　Please look at the following three pictures.
Listen to the following short talk. What can be expected from Lucy?
Lucy is worried about Pitt. Since he was taken for a walk yesterday, he has looked pale and hasn't eaten much. Pitt used to bark loudly but now he is real quiet. Lucy is going to take Pitt to a place.

解答 C

中文翻譯

請看以下三張圖。
請聽以下簡短談話。透過露西可以預期會發生什麼事？
露西很擔心彼特。從他昨天散步回來後，他就一直看起來很蒼白又吃得不多。彼特之前會大聲吠叫，但他現在真的很安靜。露西打算帶彼特去一個地方。

※〔註〕本題考「透過 Lucy 可以預期會發生什麼事？」，單就題目提供的三張圖，無法判斷 Pitt 到底是人還是狗，本題的答題關鍵字為 bark（吠叫），會吠叫的只有狗，而不是人，所以本題正確答案為 C。

Q2

Please look at the following three pictures.
Listen to the following short talk. What might Marie buy?
Marie is moving to her new apartment next month. Her friend Ann promised to buy her a set of furniture which includes a couch and two armchairs. So Marie is looking for an item to go with the sofas, something she can put coffee or tea on.

解答 A

請看以下三張圖。
請聽以下簡短談話。瑪麗可能會買什麼？
瑪麗下個月要搬到新公寓。她的朋友安答應送她一組家具，包括一張沙發以及兩張扶手椅。所以瑪麗在找一件可以搭配沙發，且可以讓她把咖啡或茶放在上面的物件。

※〔註〕本題考「Marie 可能會買什麼？」，這段話中提到 Marie 的朋友 Ann「答應買一張沙發跟兩張扶手椅給她」promised to buy her a couch and two armchairs，所以選項 B 不對。本題的答題關鍵為 ...looking for ...something she can put coffee or tea on，表示她想買的是「她可以把咖啡或茶放在上面 put on 的東西」，所以不會是 coffee maker（咖啡機），而是會買一張 tea table/coffee table（茶几），故本題正確答案為 A。

Q3
Please look at the following three pictures.
Listen to the following short talk. What can be told about Mark's girlfriend?
Mark had a date with his girlfriend. He booked a nice restaurant and had some lovely roses ready. On the way to the restaurant, he passed by a candy shop. His girlfriend has a sweet tooth, so he went in.

解答 A

請看以下三張圖。
請聽以下簡短談話。關於馬克的女朋友，可以得知什麼？
馬克跟女朋友約會，他訂了一家很棒的餐廳，也準備了一些漂亮的玫瑰花。在去餐廳的路上，他經過了一家糖果店。他的女朋友很愛吃甜食，所以他走了進去。

※〔註〕本題考「從簡短對話中可得知有關馬克女朋友的什麼？」，從這段話中可以知道，馬克為了這次約會準備了花，可見他女朋友應該是喜歡花的，所以 C 不對。馬克 pass by（經過）一家 candy shop（糖果店），他就 went in（走進去）到糖果店裡，可見他是要買東西給女朋友，本題答題關鍵是 sweet tooth，如果說某人 has a sweet tooth，那就是指「他／她很愛吃甜食」，故本題正確答案為 A。

第四類 其他

主題 10 綜合問題

Q1 Please look at the following three pictures.
Listen to the following short talk. Which is Lena?
Lena is my best friend. We have known each other for ten years.
She has small eyes and has short hair. We both like sports and love
to put on jeans and T-shirts. We seldom go shopping.

解答 C

請看以下三張圖。
請聽以下簡短談話。哪一位是麗娜？

 中文翻譯 麗娜是我最好的朋友。我們已經認識彼此十年了。她眼睛小小的，留著短髮。我們兩個都喜歡運動，愛穿牛仔褲跟 T 恤。我們很少去逛街。

※〔註〕Lena has short hair（Lena 留著短髮），所以 A 不符。兩個女生喜歡運動 like sports 而很少去逛街 seldom go shopping，因此本題正確答案為 C。

Q2　Please look at the following three pictures.
Listen to the following short talk. Which picture matches the talk?
Little Angel Kindergarten is one of the most beautiful schools in
the city. There is a huge fountain at the center of the square, and a
playground is on the left. Classrooms and office buildings are on
the right hand side, surrounded by a lovely garden.

解答　C

請看以下三張圖。
請聽以下簡短談話。哪一張圖符合這段話？

小天使幼兒園是本市最漂亮的學校之一。廣場中央有一座大型噴水
池，左邊則是操場。右手邊是被美麗花園圍繞的教室及辦公大樓。

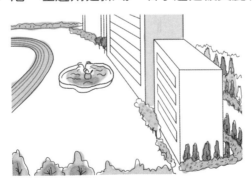

※〔註〕看完三張圖後，考生如
果知道 playground（操場）、
building（大樓）、fountain（噴
水池）這幾個重要的單字，就一
定能答對。不過其實只要知道其
中的 playground 是什麼意思，還
是可以順利拿分。因為這段話中
只出現了 a playground（一個操
場），所以 A 不符。而且對話中
提到 a playground on the left「在
左邊的操場」，所以 B 不對，因
此本題正確答案為 C。

Q3 Please look at the following three pictures.
Listen to the following short talk. Which picture is the best match?
Jane bought a gift for her sister's baby. It was baby pajamas with
adorable strawberry prints on it. And it goes with a pair of socks.

解答 A

請看以下三張圖。
請聽以下簡短談話。哪一張圖最符合？
珍買了一個禮物給她姊姊的寶寶。禮物是上面有可愛草莓圖案的寶
寶睡衣。而且還搭配了一雙襪子。

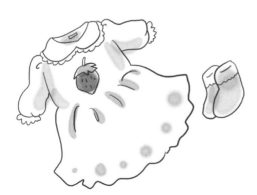

※〔註〕pajamas 是睡衣，baby
pajamas 當然就是寶寶穿的睡衣，
所以 C 不符。本題的答題關鍵有
兩個，一是 strawberry prints（草
莓圖案），另一個是 goes with a
pair of socks（搭配了一雙襪
子），因此本題正確答案是 A。

全民英檢初級聽力測驗

模擬測驗

作答提示

▶ 請善用前面所學，聆聽音
檔並進行作答。

全民英檢初級聽力測驗　🎧 Test.mp3

　　本測驗分四個部分，全部都是單選題，共 30 題，作答時間約 20 分鐘。作答說明為中文，印在試題冊上並經由光碟放音機播出。

第一部分：看圖辨義
　　　　共 5 題，每題請聽光碟放音機播出題目和三個英文句子之後，選出與所看到的圖畫最相符的答案。每題只播出一遍。

例：（看）

（聽）

Look at the picture. What happened?
A.　A man is driving a car.
B.　The cars bumped into each other.
C.　Both of the cars are going really fast.

正確答案為 B.。

聽力測驗第一部分試題自本頁開始。

A.　Question 1

B.　Question 2 and 3

C.   <u>Question 4 and 5</u>

共 10 題，每題請聽光碟放音機播出的英文句子，再從試題冊上三個回答中，選出一個最適合的答案。每題只播出一遍。

例： （聽） How was your trip to Taitung?

（看） A. My mom is really angry about me.
B. I actually stayed at home.
C. The dog is barking at him.

正確答案為 B.。

6. A. I would like to have a cup of coffee, please.
B. I'm sorry, too.
C. I'm very excited.

7. A. No, I don't have any plan.
B. Yes, I plan to visit a farm.
C. I am going mountain climbing.

8. A. It is a beautiful day. Do you want to go for a walk?
B. It is Friday. We have Science.
C. It's Halloween. Did you get your costume ready?

9. A. Yes, she is walking her dog.
B. No, she is very humble.
C. Yes, she is taking a shower.

10. A. I'm currently not available.
B. Good morning, I am pretty busy at work.
C. It is a lovely morning, isn't it?

11. A. Are you sick?
B. I'm feeling good.
C. Have a nice day.

12. A. I know. How have you been recently?
B. I'm 10 years old, and you?
C. You look very young in this dress.

13. A. It is far away from my hometown.
B. It is way too long.
C. It is about an hour.

14. A. I enjoy window shopping very much.
B. I go to the department store.
C. I hate shopping at the shopping mall.

15. A. Subway might be the choice.
B. It's enjoyable to walk around downtown.
C. Walk for two blocks and you will be there.

第三部分：簡短對話
共 10 題，每題請聽光碟放音機播出的一段對話和一個相關的問題後，再從試題冊上三個選項中，選出一個最適合的答案。每段對話和問題只播出一遍。

例： （聽） （女） I asked Sarah to help me with the birthday party.
（男） I thought she would be busy on this Saturday.
（女） She said she could help me prepare the food.
（男） That's really nice of her!
（女） Yeah, I'm glad to have a friend like her.

Question: When will the birthday party be held?

（看） A. Last Saturday
B. Next Saturday
C. This Saturday

正確答案為 C.。

16. A. The woman is always late.
   B. The woman is always on time.
   C. The woman is making a mistake.

17. A. He asks Jenny to bite something.
   B. He asks Jenny to get something to eat.
   C. He asks Jenny to be home soon.

18. A. The man is talking about something near the corner.
   B. The woman is talking about how to study for the midterm exam.
   C. They are talking about the coming test.

19. A. She wants to make some money.
   B. She wants to quit her job.
   C. She wants to make a pair of jeans with pockets.

20. A. They work for the same company.
   B. They are both getting married.
   C. They have never met each other before.

21. A. He wants to have a lot of fun.
   B. He wants to eat a lot of bananas.
   C. He wants to make a fruit tart.

22. A. The woman is definitely going to Spain as an exchange student.
    B. The woman didn't get accepted by the program.
    C. The woman filled out the correct document.

23. A. The man asks the woman to turn the cooked eggs upside down.
    B. The man is asking the woman if the weather is nice or not.
    C. The man doesn't like his beef well-done.

24. A. The passport doesn't belong to the woman.
    B. The woman has a good hairstyle.
    C. The woman is someone he knows.

25. A. The woman wants to bargain with the clerk.
    B. The woman has a check book in her purse.
    C. The woman doesn't have cash at the moment.

第四部分：短文聽解

共 5 題，每題有三個圖片選項。請聽光碟放音機播出的題目，並選出一個最適當的圖片。每題只播出一遍。

例： （看）

A.

B.

C.
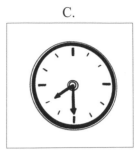

（聽）

Listen to the following telephone message. What time will Julie and Lisa meet?

    Julie, this is Lisa. I know we are supposed to meet on eight o'clock, but my alarm clock didn't go off this morning, and I didn't get up on time. Therefore, I will be 30 minutes late. I'm sorry to keep you waiting.

正確答案為 C.。

Question 26

A.

B.

C.

Question 27

A.

B.

C.

Question 28

A.

B.

C.

Question 29

A.

B.

C.

Question 30

A.

B.

C.

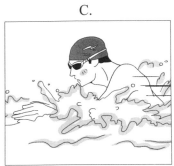

- 結束 -

模擬測驗

第一部分：看圖辨義

A. Question 1

Question number 1: What does this sign tell us?

這個標誌告訴我們什麼？

A. Keep the fire away from you. 遠離火源。

B. You are not allowed to smoke here. 這裡禁止吸菸。

C. Smoking is not healthy. 抽菸不健康。

答題解說

答案：B.。這個標誌常常會在公共場所看到，提醒一般民眾「此處禁止吸菸」，因此正確答案是 B.。

答題關鍵

keep...away 這個片語，意指「（使）遠離」；動詞 allow 意指「允許」，not allowed 就是「不被允許」的意思；healthy 是形容詞「健康的」，與題目所示圖畫的內容不符。

字詞解釋

fire n. 火　　**smoke** v. 抽菸　　**healthy** adj. 健康的

相關文法或用法補充

在生活中常會用到「keep sth. away from」這個片語，意思是「讓（某人）遠離（某事物）」。例如，當你想提醒朋友在爬山時不要靠近懸崖邊，可以說："Keep away from the edge of the cliff."，提醒對方「遠離懸崖邊」。

B. **Question 2 and 3**

Question number 2: Where might these two men be?

這兩個男人可能在哪裡？

A. They are at a movie theater. 他們在電影院。

B. They are at a museum. 他們在博物館。

C. They are at an amusement park. 他們在遊樂園。

答題解說

答案：A.。本題從日常休閒生活場景中取材，只要聽懂並理解各選項中的關鍵字：movie theater（電影院）、museum（博物館）、amusement park（遊樂園），即可選出正確答案。題目詢問「這兩個男人可能在哪裡」，透過圖片可以看出他們兩人是在電影院裡，所以正確答案是 A.。

答題關鍵

透過圖片內容，可以看到屬於電影院的座位與配置。

字詞解釋

movie n. 電影　　**museum** n. 博物館　　**amusement park** n. 遊樂園

相關文法或用法補充

美式英文中的電影院 movie theater，在英式英文中則多半稱為 cinema；所以「我們打算去電影院」可以說 "We are going to the movie theater." 或 "We are going to the cinema."。

B. Question 2 and 3

What is the man sitting on the right doing?

坐在右邊的男人正在做什麼？

A. He is asking the other man to apologize.

他正在要求另一個男人道歉。

B. He is waving goodbye to the other man.

他正在向另一個男人揮手道別。

C. He is telling the other man to be quiet.

他正在告訴另一個男人保持安靜。

答題解說

答案：C.。本題詢問「坐在右邊的男人正在做什麼」，因此必須仔細觀察圖片右方男人的動作及神情，從圖片中可清楚看見右邊的男人把手指放在嘴前、比出請對方保持安靜的手勢，因此正確答案是 C.。

答題關鍵

動詞 apologize 的意思是「向（某人）道歉」，從圖片中可看出右邊的男人正在請對方停止講電話，但無法確認他是否有要求對方道歉；動詞 wave 意指「揮（手等）」，而 wave goodbye 則是「揮手道別」，圖中並無人揮手；選項 C. 中的形容詞 quiet 是「安靜的」，從圖片可看出兩人身在電影院中，而左方男子在電影院中講電話，勢必會影響到他人看電影，因此右邊的男人告訴對方要保持安靜，正確答案是選項 C.。

字詞解釋

apologize v. 向（某人）道歉　　**wave** v. 揮（手等）　　**quiet** adj. 安靜的

相關文法或用法補充

apologize 是美式英文的拼法，如果是英式英文，則拼字要改成 apologise。若是想表達「向（某人）道歉」，後面要加上介系詞 to，例如，當你想對好朋友 Judy

道歉時，可以說 "I want to apologize to Judy."；若是想表達對某件事物感到抱歉，則要用 for，例如，當你想為自己遲到的行為道歉時，就可以說 "I want to apologize for being late."。

C. **Question 4 and 5**

Questions number 4: Where is the woman?

這個女人在哪裡？

A. She is in the kitchen. 她在廚房裡。

B. She is in the living room. 她在客廳裡。

C. She is in the bedroom. 她在臥室裡。

答題解說

答案：B.。本題詢問「這個女人在哪裡」，從題目圖片可清楚看見沙發椅、抱枕、落地窗等會出現在一般人家中客廳的家具及空間配置，因此可以判斷正確答案是 B.。

答題關鍵

kitchen 是「廚房」，圖中並無任何廚房用品及擺設；bedroom 是「臥室」，圖中並無任何床具或寢具，因此正確答案是 B.。

字詞解釋

kitchen n. 廚房　　**living room** n. 客廳　　**bedroom** n. 臥室

相關文法或用法補充

living room 是「客廳」的意思，在題目提供的這張圖片中，還出現了其他生活中的常用單字，圖片中央的「長沙發」是 couch；沙發上的「抱枕」是 cushion；但如果是放在床上的「枕頭」則是 pillow，牆上掛著的「畫」是 painting，這些單字經常出現在各種測驗中，一定要把它們記住喔！

C. **Question 4 and 5**

Questions number 5: What is happening in the picture?
圖中正在進行什麼？

A. The woman is mopping the floor. 女人正在拖地。

B. The woman is cleaning the window. 女人正在清理窗戶。

C. The woman is sweeping the floor. 女人正在掃地。

答題解說

答案：C.。題目詢問「圖中正在進行什麼」，因此必須仔細觀察圖片中的人物動作及事物狀態。從圖片中可清楚看見女人手上握著掃把，且正在清理地上的垃圾，一旁則擺放著畚箕，女人明顯正在掃地，因此正確答案是 C.。

答題關鍵

mop 是「拖擦（地板等）」的意思，但圖中沒有出現拖把或水桶等拖地必備工具；clean 是「清理」的意思，window 則是「窗戶」，與圖片中女人的動作不符；sweep 的意思是「掃除」，準確描述了女人的動作，因此正確答案是 C.。

字詞解釋

mop v. 拖擦　　**clean** v. 清潔，清理　　**window** n. 窗戶　　**sweep** v. 掃除

相關文法或用法補充

sweep the floor 描述的動作是「用掃把掃地」；如果是用吸塵器打掃的話，則會說 vacuum the floor（用吸塵器吸地板），現在非常流行的「掃地機器人」的英文則是 robot vacuum。

第二部分：問答

6. **I beg your pardon?** 可以請您再說一次嗎？

A. I would like to have a cup of coffee, please. 我想要一杯咖啡，謝謝。
B. I'm sorry, too. 我也很抱歉。
C. I'm very excited. 我覺得非常興奮。

答題解說

答案：A.。當你沒有聽清楚對方說了什麼，希望他（她）再說一次時，就可以禮貌地說 "I beg your pardon?"。選項 B. 和選項 C. 均答非所問，且根據題目對話內容來判斷，這段對話的背景情境可能是在餐廳點餐。當服務人員沒有聽清楚你想要點什麼，而希望你可以再說一次時，就會說 "I beg your pardon?"，因此正確答案是 A.。

答題關鍵

B. I'm sorry, too. 是「我也很抱歉」的意思，與題目問句無關。C. I'm very excited. 是「我覺得非常興奮」，與題目問句無關。

字詞解釋

pardon n. 原諒　　**coffee** n. 咖啡　　**excited** adj. 感到興奮的；情緒激動的

相關文法或用法補充

在想為某些行為請求原諒時，可以說「I beg your pardon for V-ing.」。舉例來說，當你想為自己的遲到道歉時，可以說 "I beg your pardon for being late."。

7. **What is your plan for the coming weekend?** 你這週末有什麼計畫？

A. No, I don't have any plan. 不，我沒有任何計畫。
B. Yes, I plan to visit a farm. 沒錯，我計畫去參觀農場。
C. I am going mountain climbing. 我要去爬山。

答題解說

答案：C.。題目問句是以 Wh- 疑問詞開頭的疑問詞疑問句，因此必須回答具體資訊，而不能以 Yes 或 No 來回答，因此以 Yes 或 No 開頭的選項都不會是正確答案。題目詢問這個週末的具體計畫，正確答案是選項 C.。

答題關鍵

聽到題目問句開頭的 What，就知道不能以 Yes 或 No 來回答，因此可以快速排除選項 A. 和 B.。

coming adj. 即將到來的　**weekend** n. 週末　**farm** n. 農場

相關文法或用法補充

the coming weekend 也就是 this weekend（即將到來的這個週末）的意思。「go＋V-ing」是「從事某種活動」的意思。例如 We are going fishing.（我們要去釣魚）；如果句中要加上名詞，名詞則會放在 go 和 V-ing 的中間，寫成「go＋n.＋V-ing」，例如 We are going mountain climbing.（我們要去爬山）。

8. **What day is it? What classes do we have today?**
   今天星期幾？我們今天要上什麼課？

   A. It is a beautiful day. Do you want to go for a walk?
      今天天氣很好。你想要去散步嗎？
   B. It is Friday. We have Science. 今天是星期五。我們有自然課。
   C. It's Halloween. Did you get your costume ready?
      今天是萬聖節。你的服裝準備好了嗎？

答題解說

答案：B.。題目問句是以 Wh- 疑問詞開頭的疑問詞疑問句，因此必須回答具體資訊。題目詢問「今天星期幾？我們要上什麼課？」，在選項中只有選項 B. 中提及星期及課程名稱，因此正確答案是 B.。

答題關鍵

直翻選項 A. 中的 It is a beautiful day. 的話是「這是美好的一天」，不過其實這句話是「今天天氣很好」的意思，與題目問句無關；選項 C. 提及了特定節日，並詢問對方是否準備好了相對應的過節服裝，內容與題目問句無關，因此是錯誤選項。

字詞解釋

beautiful adj. 美好的　**Friday** n. 星期五　**Science** n. 自然
Halloween n. 萬聖節

相關文法或用法補充

- It is a beautiful day. 通常用於形容天氣晴朗；其他用來形容天氣的俗語還有：There's not a cloud in the sky. 意指「晴空萬里」；It's raining cats and dogs. 則是「傾盆大雨」的意思；The sun has got his hat on. 則意指「陰天」。
- 生活中經常聽到的課程名稱還有 Mathematics（數學）、Chemistry（化學）、Physics（物理）、Geography（地理）、History（歷史）、Chinese（國文）、English（英文）、P.E.（＝ Physical Education 體育）。

9. **Is your grandmother home?** 你的奶奶在家嗎？

A. Yes, she is walking her dog. 是，她正在遛狗。
B. No, she is very humble. 不是，她非常謙虛。
C. Yes, she is taking a shower. 是，她正在沖澡。

答題解說

答案：C.。題目問句是以 be 動詞開頭的疑問句，因此回答應以 Yes 或 No 開頭。作答時必須選擇以 Yes 或 No 回答，並按照題目內容提供相關資訊的選項。題目詢問「你的奶奶在家嗎？」，因此最適合的選項是 C.。

答題關鍵

選項 A. 表示「是，她正在遛狗」，但「遛狗」是戶外活動，不會待在家裡，因此不應以 Yes 作答；B. 是「不是，她非常謙虛」，完全答非所問；而選項 C. 中表示「是，她正在沖澡」，「沖澡」一般是在家中進行的室內活動，因此可以知道奶奶的確在家，選項 C. 是正確答案。

字詞解釋

grandmother n. 奶奶   **humble** adj. 謙虛的   **shower** n. 淋浴

相關文法或用法補充

雖然都是洗澡，但是 take a bath 與 take a shower 所做的動作並不相同；bath 是「澡盆；浴缸」的意思，因此 take a bath 是「泡澡」，而 shower 則是「淋浴」，因此 take a shower 是「沖澡」的意思，不過不論是 bath 還是 shower 都只能與動詞 take 搭配。

10. **Good morning! How have you been recently?** 早安！你最近過得如何？

A. I'm currently not available. 我目前沒空。
B. Good morning, I am pretty busy at work. 早安，我工作滿忙的。
C. It is a lovely morning, isn't it? 真是個美好的早晨，不是嗎？

答題解說

答案：B.。當別人詢問「早安！最近過得如何？」時，通常回答會先重複「早安」，向對方打招呼，再提供更多與自己近況有關的資訊。

答題關鍵

選項 A. 中的 available 是「有空閒的」，所以這句話就是「我目前沒空」的意思，完全答非所問；選項 C. 說「真是個美好的早晨，不是嗎？」，與題目的詢問內容完全無關；選項 B. 則在重複「早安」之後，繼續說 I am pretty busy at work.（我工作滿忙的），以這句話回答題目詢問的 How have you been recently?，因此選項 B. 是正確答案。

字詞解釋

currently adv. 目前地　　**available** adj. 有空閒的　　**pretty** adv. 相當地
lovely adj. 美好的

相關文法或用法補充

「早安、午安、晚安」用英文表達分別是 good morning、good afternoon、good night，但 good night 也會在晚上與人道別時用，這時就是「再見」的意思；另外，good evening 也是「晚安」的意思，不過通常是在晚上與人見面打招呼時使用。

11. **I'm not feeling good today. 我今天覺得不太舒服。**

A. Are you sick? 你生病了嗎？
B. I'm feeling good. 我覺得很好。
C. Have a nice day. 祝你有愉快的一天。

答題解說

答案：A.。當別人跟你說「我今天覺得不太舒服」時，正常情況下，應該會先關心對方是否是生病了，因此這裡會選擇反問 Are you sick?（你生病了嗎？）的選項 A.。

答題關鍵

選項 B. 是「我覺得很好」的意思，表示自己當下處於舒適的狀態，與題目內容完全相反且無關；選項 C. 的 Have a nice day. 是用在與對方分別前，祝福對方順利的慣用表達，與題目問句完全無關，因此正確答案是 C.。

字詞解釋

sick adj. 生病的　　**good** adj. 好的　　**have a nice day** phr. 祝你有愉快的一天

相關文法或用法補充

當覺得自己的狀態不佳或生病時，除了題目中的 I'm not feeling good. 之外，還可以說 I'm feeling unwell. 或 I'm feeling sick/ill.。
一起看看身體不舒服時會出現的各種症狀要怎麼說吧！
headache（頭痛）、running nose（流鼻水）、bleeding nose（流鼻血）、
sore throat（喉嚨痛）、toothache（牙痛）、stomachache（胃痛；肚子痛）、
diarrhea（腹瀉）、allergy（過敏）。

12. I haven't seen you in ages! 好久不見！

A. I know. How have you been recently? 真的。你最近過得怎麼樣？
B. I'm 10 years old, and you? 我 10 歲，你呢？
C. You look very young in this dress. 你穿這件洋裝看起來非常年輕。

答題解說

答案：A.。當別人跟你說「好久不見」時，一般來說會先附和對方，再接著問候對方最近過得如何；I know 原本是「我知道」的意思；但這裡是口語的表達方式，意思是「真的，對呀」；之後才回問對方近況 "How have you been recently?"，因此正確答案是選項 A.。

答題關鍵

選項 B. 的意思是「我 10 歲，你呢？」，與題目問句內容完全無關；題目問句中的 in ages，是用來形容「很久」的表達方式，與年齡無關；選項 C. 說「你穿這件洋裝看起來非常年輕」，答非所問，因此選項 A. 是正確答案。

字詞解釋

recently adv. 最近地　　**young** adj. 年輕的　　**dress** n. 洋裝　　**in ages** phr. 很久

相關文法或用法補充

"I haven't seen you in ages." 這句話，裡面用到了「現在完成式」，現在完成式有以下的常見用法：

❶ 一件在過去時間點開始的事件，到目前為止持續進行。〔**持續**〕

句子裡的時間有兩種表達方式：① since＋特定時間　② for＋一段時間
I have lived in Kaohsiung for 10 years.
我已經住在高雄 10 年了。（持續 10 年）
I have lived in Kaohsiung since 2010.
我從 2010 年開始住在高雄。（從 2010 年持續到現在）

❷ 從以前到現在做過這件事情的經驗。〔**經驗**〕

I have read this book for 3 times.
我已經看過這本書 3 次了。

13. How long does it take to fly from Kaohsiung to Taipei?
從高雄飛到台北要花多久時間？

A. It is far away from my hometown. 它離我的家鄉很遠。
B. It is way too long. 真的太久了。
C. It is about an hour. 大概一小時。

答題解說

答案：C.。當題目問句以 how long 開頭時，詢問的是「時間多長」，因此作答時必須選擇「一段時間」。題目詢問「從高雄飛到台北要花多久時間？」，因此回答「大概一小時」的選項 C. 是正確答案。

答題關鍵

選項 A. 的意思是「它離我的家鄉很遠」，答非所問；B. 是「太久了」的意思，這裡的 way too（太～）是用來強調 long（久的）的副詞片語，當等待或耗費的時間太長時，常常會用這句話來表達，但在這裡不適合用來回應題目問句，因此選項 C. 是正確答案。

字詞解釋

fly v. 飛行，飛翔　　**far** adj. 遙遠的　　**hometown** n. 家鄉

相關文法或用法補充

「way too＋形容詞／副詞」是一個很常用到的口語慣用表達方式，意思是「太～」，例如 It is way too expensive to buy a house in Taipei.（在台北買房子真的太貴了）。

14. Where do you usually go shopping? 你通常會去哪裡購物？

A. I enjoy window shopping very much. 我非常喜歡櫥窗購物。
B. I go to the department store. 我會去百貨公司。
C. I hate shopping at the shopping mall. 我討厭在購物中心購物。

答題解說

答案：B.。當題目問句以 where 開頭時，詢問的是「地點」，因此作答時可直接排除不是回答地點的選項。題目詢問「你通常會去哪裡購物？」，因此直接回答地點「department store（百貨公司）」的 B. 是正確答案。

答題關鍵

選項 A. 表示「我喜歡櫥窗購物」，window shopping（櫥窗購物）的意思不是購買櫥窗裡的東西，而是「只逛不買」，並未提及任何地點，答非所問；選項 C. 是「我討厭在購物中心購物」的意思，表達對於「在購物中心購物」這件事的好

惡而非題目詢問的地點，答非所問，因此只有選項 B. 是適合的答案。

enjoy v. 享受；喜愛做　**department store** n. 百貨公司　**mall** n. 購物中心

除了 window shopping（櫥窗購物，只逛不買），目前最流行的「網路購物」的說法是 online shopping，在網路上「訂購」的這個動作，和去餐廳點餐一樣都是用 order，「下一筆訂單」的說法則是 place an order。

15. **What's the best way to get downtown from the airport?**
從機場到市中心的最佳方法是什麼？

A. Subway might be the choice. 地下鐵可能是你的選擇。
B. It's enjoyable to walk around downtown. 在市中心到處走走很令人愉快。
C. Walk for two blocks and you will be there. 走過兩個街區後，你就會到那裡了。

答案：A.。題目以 what 開頭的疑問詞疑問句詢問「從機場到市中心的最佳方法」，因此作答時必須選擇提供具體交通方式的選項內容，而選項 A. 是適合的正確答案。

選項 B. 表示「在市中心到處走走很令人愉快」，答非所問；這裡利用題目問句中有出現的 downtown 來造成混淆，必須特別留意；選項 C. 是提供路線指引的表達方式，而不是具體的交通方式，答非所問，因此選項 A. 是正確答案。

downtown n. 市中心　**subway** n. 地下鐵　**choice** n. 選擇
enjoyable adj. 令人愉快的　**block** n. 街區

常見的大眾交通運輸工具
- 火車：train
- 捷運：MRT = Metro Rail Transit 或 Mass Rapid Transit
- 地下鐵：subway（美式）、underground 或 tube（英式，tube 是較為口語的說法）
- 輕軌：LRT = Light Rail Transit
- 公車：public bus
- 客運：bus（美式）、coach（英式）

第三部分：簡短對話

16. M: Why are you late today?

    W: I was stuck in traffic.

    M: again?

    W: It wasn't my fault.

    Question: What can be inferred from the conversation?

    A. The woman is always late.

    B. The woman is always on time.

    C. The woman is making a mistake.

    英文翻譯

    男：妳今天為什麼遲到？

    女：我被塞在車陣中了。

    男：又這樣？

    女：這不是我的錯。

    問題：從這段對話中可推論出什麼？

    A. 這個女人總是遲到。

    B. 這個女人總是很準時。

    C. 這個女人正在犯錯。

    答題解說

    答案：A.。題目要求考生根據對話內容進行「推論」，考生作答時必須完整理解對話內容才可做出正確推論。對話中男人詢問女人的遲到原因，當女人表示自己是因為塞車才會遲到時，男人卻說「又這樣？」，從這句話可推論，女人不是第一次遲到，最恰當的答案是選項 A.。

    答題關鍵

    即使無法完全理解對話內容，只要掌握對話中的關鍵字 again（再次），就可推知對話中出現的某個行為或事件不是第一次發生。

    字詞解釋

    traffic n. 車流量；車陣　　**fault** n. 錯誤　　**on time** phr. 準時　　**mistake** n. 錯誤

    相關文法或用法補充

    fault 跟 mistake 都是「錯誤」的意思，但用法卻不一樣喔！

- fault 是「當事者必須為此負責」型的錯誤，且帶有責備當事者的意味，通常會在釐清錯誤責任歸屬時用到這個字，常以「It's sb's fault.」的方式表達。

  It's Lisa's fault. 這是麗莎的錯。

- mistake 是「當事者不一定要為此負責」型的錯誤。在表達犯錯的「犯」時，會使用動詞 make。

  My mother was angry at the mistake I made. 我母親對我犯的錯感到生氣。

17. **M: Hey! Jenny, I'm going to be home late.**
    W: But, dad, I'm starving.
    M: Why don't you grab a bite to eat first?
    W: Ok, I'll have some cereal.

    Question: What does Jenny's father suggest Jenny to do?
    A. He asks Jenny to bite something.
    B. He asks Jenny to get something to eat.
    C. He asks Jenny to be home soon.

    英文翻譯

    男：嘿！珍妮，我會晚一點到家。
    女：可是，爸爸，我超餓的。
    男：妳要不要先吃點東西？
    女：好吧，我會去吃些穀片。

    問題：珍妮的父親建議珍妮做什麼？
    A. 他要珍妮去咬某個東西。
    B. 他要珍妮去拿點東西吃。
    C. 他要珍妮快點回家。

    答題解說

    答案：B.。題目要求考生透過對話內容，理解對話中父親給予女兒的建議內容。對話中女兒表示自己非常餓，父親因此建議她先吃點東西，因此正確答案是 B.。

    答題關鍵

    這題詢問父親建議女兒的內容，因此作答時必須特別注意用來提出建議的表達方式，這段對話中出現的「why don't you...」即是很常見的提議表達，意思是「你要不要～」，因此這題的答案就很有可能出現在 why don't you... 之後的內容，此

外，這段對話中出現了 starving（非常飢餓的）、food（食物）、cereal（穀片）等與食物有關的答題關鍵字，也可推論出這段對話的內容和飲食建議有關。

suggest v. 建議　**starving** adj. 非常飢餓的　**bite** n. 小份量的食物
cereal n. 早餐麥片；穀物

- 特別注意動詞 bite 在不同時態下的形態不同：
  現在式 bite、過去式 bit、過去分詞 bitten。
  bite 可當動詞或名詞。當動詞時，意指「咬」；當名詞時，意指「（一口可吃的）小份量食物」。
- cereal 是常見於英國和美國的早餐或點心，通常會搭配牛奶或豆漿食用。
  常見的中式早餐的英文有：
  - 粥：congee（英式）、porridge（美式）
  - 包子：steamed stuffed bun
  - 蔥油餅：scallion oil pancake
  - 油條：deep-fried dough stick、fried bread stick
  - 豆漿：soy milk
  - 米漿：peanut rice milk

18. M: The midterm exam is around the corner.

W: I haven't studied anything yet.

M: Me either.

W: We should go to the library together this weekend.

Question: What are they talking about?

A. The man is talking about something near the corner.

B. The woman is talking about how to study for the midterm exam.

C. They are talking about the coming test.

男：期中考快到了。

女：我什麼都還沒念。

男：我也還沒。

女：我們這週末應該一起去圖書館。

問題：他們在談論什麼？

A. 這個男人正在談論靠近轉角的某事物。

B. 這個女人正在談論要如何準備期中考。

C. 他們正在談論即將到來的考試。

答題解說

答案：C.。題目要求考生理解對話內容，並歸納出對話主題。這段對話中的兩人正在談論即將到來的期中考相關事項，因此正確答案是 C.。

答題關鍵

這段對話中出現了 midterm exam 和 library 等與考試相關的關鍵字，因此可推論出這段對話與考試相關。而透過男人所說的 The midterm exam is around the corner.（期中考快到了），可知期中考即將到來，因此最恰當的答案是選項 C.。此外，題目詢問的是 they，選項 A. 和 B. 的主詞卻分別是 the man 和 the woman，因此不可能會是正確答案。

字詞解釋

midterm exam phr. 期中考　　**around the corner** phr. 即將到來

library n. 圖書館　　**study** v. 學習

相關文法或用法補充

study 也有名詞用法，意思是「研究；書房」，例如 There are a lot of books in my study.（我的書房裡有很多書）中的 study 就是「書房」的意思。

其他與考試相關的常見字詞還有：final exam（期末考）、pop quiz（（隨堂）小考）、test（測驗）、written exam（筆試）、oral exam（口試）等等。

19. M: What are you going to do this summer vacation?

W: I am going to get a part-time job.

M: Why do you need to work part-time?

W: I want to earn some pocket money.

Question: What is the woman's plan?

A. She wants to make some money.

B. She wants to quit her job.

C. She wants to make a pair of jeans with pockets.

男：妳這個暑假打算做什麼？

女：我要去找份打工。

男：你為什麼需要打工？

女：我想要賺點零用錢。

問題：這個女人的計畫是什麼？

A. 她想賺些錢。

B. 她想辭掉她的工作。

C. 她想做一件有口袋的牛仔褲。

答題解說

答案：A.。題目要求考生理解整體對話內容，並歸納出對話主題。對話中男人詢問女人的暑假計畫，女人則表示自己要找份打工來賺零用錢，因此最恰當的答案是選項 A.。

答題關鍵

這段對話的一開頭，男人先說 What are you going to do this summer vacation?，詢問女人的暑假計畫，也就是題目問句中的 plan，由此可知，女人接下來的回答就是本題的正確答案，女人回答 I am going to get a part-time job.，表示自己要找份打工。然而，選項中卻沒有出現這個答案，因此必須繼續注意聽對話內容，男人接著詢問女人想要打工的原因，女人回答 I want to earn some pocket money.，這裡的解題關鍵字是 earn（賺取），不過就算不知道這個字的意思也沒關係，光看 want some pocket money，也可知道女人是因為想賺零用錢才要去打工，因此答案是選項 A.。

字詞解釋

summer vacation phr. 暑假　　**part-time job** phr. 打工　　**earn** v. 賺取

pocket money phr. 零用錢

相關文法或用法補充

不論是 summer vacation 還是 part-time job 都是所謂的「複合名詞（compound noun）」，這種名詞形態在生活中常常出現，指的是以數個單字組成的名詞，組成方式有很多種，以下為其中四種最常見的複合名詞：

名詞＋名詞 （連在一起）	名詞＋名詞 （分開書寫）	以連字號(-) 相連	名詞＋動詞 （連在一起）
bathroom 浴室 cupboard 碗櫥 software 軟體	middle class 中產階級 plastic bag 塑膠袋 swimming suit 泳裝	check-in 報到 take-off 起飛 make-up 化妝品	haircut 理髮 rainfall 降雨量 waterfall 瀑布

20. W: Hi, Kenny, welcome to my wedding. I'm glad you are here.

M: Hey, Alice, do you know the blonde woman who stands under the tree?

W: Of course, that's Sandra.

M: Have you met her before?

W: Yes, we are co-workers.

Question: What do we know about Alice and Sandra?

A. They work for the same company.

B. They are both getting married.

C. They have never met each other before.

英文翻譯

女：嗨，肯尼，歡迎來我的婚禮。我很開心你來了。

男：嘿，艾莉絲，妳認識那個站在樹下的金髮女人嗎？

女：當然，那是珊卓拉。

男：妳之前有見過她嗎？

女：有啊，我們是同事。

問題：關於艾莉絲與珊卓拉，我們知道什麼？

A. 她們在相同公司工作。

B. 她們兩位都要結婚了。

C. 她們之前從來沒有見過彼此。

答題解說

答案：A.。題目要求考生理解整體對話內容，並鎖定關於特定對象的資訊，音檔內出現多個人名時，題目常會圍繞在特定提問對象（在本題是艾莉絲及珊卓拉）上，聆聽音檔時應特別注意每個人名之間的關係。對話中的兩人在婚禮上相遇並彼此寒暄，肯尼詢問艾莉絲是否認識站在樹下的金髮女人，艾莉絲回答：「當然，那是珊卓拉。」，並進一步表示珊卓拉和自己是同事，由此可知珊卓拉和艾莉絲在同一間公司工作，正確答案是選項 A.。

本題詢問與艾莉絲及珊卓拉有關的資訊，因此必須透過對話內容找出與她們兩人都有關的資訊，在對話的最後一句艾莉絲說 Yes, we are co-workers.，這裡出現了答題關鍵字「co-workers（同事）」，因此正確答案是選項 A.。

字詞解釋

welcome adj. 受歡迎的　　**wedding** n. 婚禮　　**glad** adj. 高興的
co-worker n. 同事

相關文法或用法補充

一起來看看還有哪些與婚禮相關的字彙吧！

- 新娘：bride
- 新郎：groom
- 伴娘（兩位以上）：bridesmaids
- 伴娘（一位）：maid of honor
- 伴郎（一位）：best man
- 伴郎（兩位以上）：groomsmen
- 男花童（負責護送新郎新娘的婚戒）：ring bearer
- 女花童（負責灑花）：flower girl

21. W: Are you ready for the party tonight?

　　M: Of course. I'm ready to go bananas.

　　W: So am I! I'll pick you up at 10 P.M.

　　M: Alright, see you then.

Question: What does the man want to do at the party?

A. He wants to have a lot of fun.

B. He wants to eat a lot of bananas.

C. He wants to make a fruit tart.

英文翻譯

女：你準備好參加今晚的派對了嗎？
男：當然。我準備好要狂歡了。
女：我也是！我晚上 10 點會去接你。
男：好，到時候見。

問題：男人想在派對上做什麼？

A. 他想要盡情玩樂。

B. 他想要吃很多香蕉。

C. 他想要做一份水果塔。

答案：A.。題目要求考生理解整體對話內容，並依對話上下文進行合理推論。對話中的兩人正在討論今晚要去派對的事，男人表示自己準備好要在派對上狂歡了，因此正確答案是 A.。

題目詢問男人想要在派對上做什麼，因此作答時必須根據男人所說的內容來作答。本題的答題關鍵字是 go bananas，考生必須知道 go bananas 的涵義才能順利作答。go bananas 是一個常見的英文俚語，意思是「狂歡」，因此利用 have a lot of fun 來換句話說的 A. 是正確答案。

go bananas phr. 狂歡　　**pick up** phr. 接（某人）

tart n. 果醬餡餅；（水果等）塔類

還有一些常見的有趣英文俚語，一起記下來吧！

- go ape：極度生氣

  My teacher went ape because I was an hour late.
  我的老師因為我遲到一小時而暴怒。

- chicken out：因害怕而退縮、放棄

  I was going to go bungee jumping, but I chickened out.
  我本來想去高空彈跳，但因為害怕而退縮了。

- dogs are barking：腳痛

  After shopping all day, my dogs are barking.
  在逛了一整天街後，我的腳好痛。

- let the cat out of the bag：說溜嘴、洩密

  I had a surprise party planned for my parents, but then my brother let the cat out of the bag.
  我本來幫我爸媽規劃了一個驚喜派對，但後來我哥哥說溜嘴了。

22. **M: Didn't you apply for an exchange student program to Spain?**

   W: Don't talk about it. I was rejected.

   M: I'm sorry to hear that. How come?

   W: Well, I filled the wrong application form.

   Question: What can be inferred from the conversation?

   A. The woman is definitely going to Spain as an exchange student.

   B. The woman didn't get accepted by the program.

   C. The woman filled out the correct document.

男：你不是申請了去西班牙的交換學生計畫嗎？

女：別提了。我被拒絕了。

男：真遺憾。怎麼會這樣？

女：這個嘛，我填到錯誤的申請表了。

問題：從對話中可推論出什麼？

A. 女人絕對會去西班牙當交換學生。

B. 女人沒有錄取這個計畫。

C. 女人填寫了正確的文件。

答案：B.。題目要求考生依對話整體內容進行推論，對話中的兩人就女人是否有成功申請到西班牙當交換學生進行討論，女人在對話中提及自己因為填到錯誤的表格而未被錄取，因此正確答案是 B.。

本題的答題關鍵字在於女人所說的 rejected（遭到拒絕），如果知道 reject 是「拒絕」的意思，那就可以輕鬆選出正確答案的選項 B.，但若不知道 reject 的意思，也可透過男子接下來說的 I'm sorry to hear that.，知道女人未被交換學生計畫錄取，並可透過女人說的最後一句話 I filled the wrong application form.，知道女人填到了錯誤的申請表，因此選項 A. 及 C. 皆是錯誤選項。

exchange student program phr. 交換學生計畫　**Spain** n. 西班牙

reject v. 拒絕　**application form** phr. 申請表　**document** n. 文件

填寫表格的「填寫」，除了對話中出現的動詞 fill 之外，也經常會使用動詞片語「fill in/out＋要填寫的對象」，另外，complete 這個字，除了「完成」之外，也有「填寫完畢」的意思。

23. W: How would you like your eggs?

M: Sunny-side-up, please.

W: How about your steak?

M: I would like it to be medium-rare.

Question: Which of the following statements is true?

A. The man asks the woman to turn the cooked eggs upside down.

B. The man is asking the woman if the weather is nice or not.

C. The man doesn't like his beef well-done.

英文翻譯

女：您想要哪種蛋呢？

男：單煎一面的荷包蛋，謝謝。

女：那您的牛排呢？

男：我想要三分熟。

問題：下列陳述何者正確？

A. 男人請女人把煮好的蛋倒過來放。

B. 男人正在詢問女人天氣好不好。

C. 男人不想要他的牛肉全熟。

答題解說

答案：C.。題目要求考生依對話內容進行推論，並選出正確的陳述內容。對話中的女人正在詢問男人想要點什麼樣的蛋料理及牛排熟度，因此可先排除與點餐毫無關聯的選項 B.。男人在對話中表示自己想要單煎一面的荷包蛋，選項 A. 卻說「男人請女人把煮好的蛋倒過來放」，陳述內容錯誤。男人在最後一句話中提到牛排想要三分熟，符合選項 C. 內容，因此正確答案是 C.。

答題關鍵

本題的答題關鍵字之一的 sunny-side-up，意思是「單煎一面的荷包蛋」，選項 B. 利用發音相近的 upside down（上下顛倒）試圖混淆考生，要特別注意。另外，考生必須知道牛排熟度的 medium-rare 是指「三分熟」及 well-done 是指「全熟」，才能順利選出陳述正確的選項 C.。

sunny-side-up phr. 單煎一面的荷包蛋　　**medium-rare** adj. 三分熟的
upside down phr. 上下顛倒　　**weather** n. 天氣　　**well-done** adj. 全熟的

相關文法或用法補充

常見的蛋料理方式還有下面這些！

- 炒蛋：scrambled egg
- 全熟煎蛋：fried egg
- 水煮蛋：boiled egg
- 溏心蛋：soft-boiled egg
- 兩面煎熟，蛋黃不熟：over-easy
- 兩面煎熟，蛋黃全熟：over-hard

牛排熟度的說法常常會出現在各大考試之中，一定要記下來喔！

- 生的：raw
- 一分熟：rare
- 三分熟：medium-rare
- 五分熟：medium
- 七分熟：medium-well
- 全熟：well-done

24. M: Ma'am, may I have your passport, please?

W: Certainly. Here you are.

M: Is this you in the picture?

W: Yes. I just had a haircut last week.

M: No wonder I can't recognize you.

Question: What does the customs officer assume at the beginning of this conversation?

A. The passport doesn't belong to the woman.

B. The woman has a good hairstyle.

C. The woman is someone he knows.

英文翻譯

男：女士，可以請您給我您的護照嗎？

女：沒問題。這給你。

男：照片中的人是您嗎？

女：是的。我上禮拜剛剪了頭髮。
男：難怪我認不出您。

問題：海關人員在這次對話的一開始以為什麼？
A. 這本護照不是女人的。
B. 女人有好看的髮型。
C. 女人是他認識的人。

答題解說

答案：A.。題目要求考生依對話上下文推論出正確的選項內容，對話開頭男人向女人索取護照後，就向女人確認護照上的照片是否為本人，而在對話的最後，男人說 No wonder I can't recognize you.，表示自己認不出來照片上的是女人本人，代表男人在對話一開始對於護照是否是女子本人的存有疑慮，因此正確答案是選項 A.。

答題關鍵

這題的答題關鍵在於題目中的 assume 這個字，assume 的意思是「（自我的）推斷，以為」，所以 What does the customs officer assume at the beginning?，問的就是海關人員在對話一開始所做的自我推斷的內容。透過對話的上下文，再加上海關人員在聽到女人剛剪了頭髮後所說出的 No wonder I can't recognize you.，便可確認正確答案是 A.。

字詞解釋

passport n. 護照　**certainly** adv. 沒問題；毫無疑問　**haircut** n. 剪髮
assume v.（自我的）推斷，以為

相關文法或用法補充

certainly 這個字有兩種最常見的用法：

❶ 用在肯定的答覆或強調，意指「當然，毫無疑問」。

My sister certainly has a friend named George, but I'm not sure whether they are still in touch.
我姊姊確實有一個叫做喬治的朋友，但我不確定他們還有沒有聯絡。

❷ 用於對請求表示強烈同意，意指「沒問題，當然可以」。

A: Can I borrow your pen? I forgot to bring mine.
可以跟你借筆嗎？我忘記帶我的了。
B: Certainly.
當然可以。

25. M: It's 225.59.

W: I have some coupons here. Can I use them?

M: Everything is on sale in store today so we don't take coupons.

W: I see. I would like to pay with a check. I forgot my purse at home today.

M: Sure.

Question: What can be inferred from the conversation?

A. The woman wants to bargain with the clerk.

B. The woman has a check book in her purse.

C. The woman doesn't have cash at the moment.

英文翻譯

男：這樣是 225 元又 59 分。

女：我這裡有些優惠券。這些可以用嗎？

男：今天店裡的所有東西都特價，所以我們不收優惠券。

女：我知道了。我想要用支票付。我今天把我的皮包忘在家裡了。

男：沒問題。

問題：從對話中可推論出什麼？

A. 女人想跟店員殺價。

B. 女人的皮包裡放著支票簿。

C. 女人現在沒有現金。

答題解說

答案：C.。題目要求考生依對話整體內容進行推論，透過對話可以知道，女人因為把皮包忘在家裡，而想要以支票付款，因此可以合理推論，女人現在身上沒有現金，因此選項 C. 是正確答案。對話開頭時，女人想使用優惠券來減少消費金額，但在店員表示今天不能用優惠券後，女人說了 I see.，表示自己知道這件事了，並未繼續和店員殺價，因此 A. 不是正確答案。女人把皮包忘在家裡，但仍可用支票付帳，因此支票簿一定不會是在皮包裡，因此 B. 是錯誤選項。

答題關鍵

考生必須知道題目中出現的 infer 意指「推斷，推論」，且作答時必須理解對話整體內容，才能正確作答。此外，必須知道選項 A. 中的 bargain 是「殺價」的意思，且 check（支票）是要從 check book（支票簿）上撕下使用，才能確定選項 A.、B. 都是錯誤選項。

coupon n. 優惠券   **on sale** phr. 特價   **check** n. 支票   **bargain** v. 殺價

相關文法或用法補充

下面這些是常見的金錢相關單字，一起記下來吧！

• 股票：stock
• 自動櫃員機：A.T.M. ＝ Automated Teller Machine
• 黑市：black market
• 提領：withdraw
• 存錢：deposit
• 貨幣：currency
• 銅板：coin

第四部分：短文聽解

For question number 26, please look at the three pictures.

Question number 26: Listen to the following talk. Which picture best describes the talk?

A   B   C

I went out with my friends to celebrate my birthday today. We saw a family of four was having a picnic by the river. There were tomatoes in the basket. The parents were feeding the kids. Then, we took the MRT to downtown. There were a lot of passengers but everyone had a seat. Later, we decided to have dinner at a karaoke bar. Two of my friends suddenly went up to the stage and sang a happy-birthday song to me. I was really touched.

英文翻譯

請聽以下這段話。哪一張圖片最符合這段話？

我今天跟朋友出去慶祝我的生日。我們看到一家四口在河邊野餐。籃子中裝著番茄。爸媽正在餵小孩們吃東西。接著我們搭乘捷運去市中心。雖然乘客很多，但

所有人都有位子坐。然後，我們決定要去卡拉 OK 吧吃晚餐。我的兩個朋友突然跑上台對我唱生日快樂歌。我真的很感動。

答題解說

答案：C.。題目要求考生依照短文內容選出最符合描述的圖片，音檔播放前應先快速看過題目提供的三張圖片，務必注意圖片中的人物數量、地點、動作、狀態等細節資訊，並事先推想可能會出現的答題關鍵字。這段話描述女人跟朋友外出時的所見所聞，短文內提到一家四口在河邊野餐，但圖 A. 中只有三人，因此不符短文描述的內容。圖 B. 中的確有很多乘客，但仍有些人沒位子坐而站著，因此也不是正確答案。選項 C. 正確描述兩名友人於卡拉 OK 吧唱歌的景象，因此是正確答案。

答題關鍵

題目短文內提及的 karaoke（卡拉 OK）是第一個答題關鍵，接下來的 two of my friends suddenly went up to the stage and sang a happy-birthday song to me，則描述了各種作答的關鍵細節資訊，包括兩個人、唱歌等，作答時必須特別留意圖片中的人物數量、地點、動作、狀態等細節資訊是否符合短文所述。

字詞解釋

celebrate v. 慶祝　**picnic** n. 野餐　**river** n. 河川　**basket** n. 籃子　**feed** v. 餵食
passenger n. 乘客　**karaoke** n. 卡拉OK

相關文法或用法補充

「野餐活動」常常出現在各種測驗之中，一起把相關單字都記下來吧！
• 野餐籃：picnic basket
• 野餐墊：picnic blanket
• 冷藏箱：cooler
• 保溫瓶：thermos
• 野餐餐具（包含刀叉與湯匙）：cutlery
• 零食：snack

For question number 27, please look at the three pictures.

Question number 27: Listen to the following description. What didn't the family eat on Saturday?

A	B	C

It was a freezing Saturday. My parents and I decided to eat at home. First, for breakfast, we had some toast with handmade strawberry jam. I liked it very much. Second, we ordered a pizza for lunch. The pizza had pepperoni, mushrooms, and some onions. I really disliked the mushrooms because they made the pizza watery. Lastly, for dinner, my father wanted to have instant noodles. My mother thought they were unhealthy so she made beef noodles for everyone. We enjoyed the dish happily.

英文翻譯

請聽以下這段描述。這個家庭星期六沒有吃什麼？
星期六超冷的。我爸媽和我決定在家吃飯。首先，早餐我們吃了一些吐司配手工草莓醬。我真的很喜歡。然後，我們午餐訂了一個披薩。披薩上有義大利辣香腸、蘑菇和一些洋蔥。我真的很討厭蘑菇，因為它們會讓披薩濕濕軟軟的。最後，我爸爸本來想吃泡麵當晚餐。但我媽媽覺得泡麵很不健康，所以她為大家煮了牛肉麵。我們都吃得很開心。

答題解說

答案：A.。題目要求考生在聽完短文內容後，選出說話者一家在星期六沒吃的餐點。從短文內容中可知，雖然爸爸晚上想吃泡麵當晚餐，但媽媽不同意，所以後來吃的是牛肉麵，因此 A. 是正確答案。

在聆聽音檔前應先確認題目提供的三張圖片：instant noodles（泡麵）、pizza（披薩）、toast（吐司），並特別留意音檔中與這三種食物有關的資訊。本題詢問說話者家在星期六沒吃的餐點是什麼，短文內提及說話者一家在早上和中午分別吃了 toast 和 pizza，晚上爸爸想吃的 instant noodles 則因媽媽反對而沒吃成，因此正確答案是 A.。

字詞解釋

freezing adj. 非常寒冷的　　**pepperoni** n. 義大利辣香腸　　**mushroom** n. 蘑菇　**onion** n. 洋蔥　　**watery** adj. 濕軟的　　**unhealthy** adj. 不健康的

相關文法或用法補充

在傳達指令或表明事件發生時間時，常會利用序數做為轉折語，這些序數可以幫助考生辨別事件發生的先後順序，在聆聽短文內容時，應善用這些序數轉折語掌握事件的先後順序，幫助釐清時間點，常見的序數轉折語有：then（接下來，然後）、next（接下來，下一個）、first/second/third（首先／第二／第三）、lastly（最後）等。

For question number 28, please look at the three pictures.

Question number 28: Listen to the following talk. Which of the following animals does not exist in the zoo?

A　　　　　　　　　　B　　　　　　　　　　C

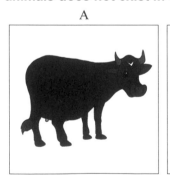  

Jane went to the zoo with her friend, Angela. Jane's favorite animal is the lion which originated from Africa. The lion, rather than using the tail to balance like a cat, used the tail to sweep away insects. Angela saw a deer without any spots on its body. Angela was disappointed because she wanted to see the sika deer. Finally, they saw an ox which had two sharp horns. The ox uses the horns to fight against its own kind or enemies. Jane and Angela were excited to know these animals.

英文翻譯

請聽以下這段話。這個動物園裡沒有以下哪種動物？

珍和她的朋友安潔拉一起去了動物園。珍最喜歡的動物是源自非洲的獅子。那隻獅子沒有像貓那樣用尾巴保持平衡，而是用尾巴來驅趕昆蟲。安潔拉看到一隻身上沒有任何斑點的鹿。安潔拉覺得很失望，因為她想要看梅花鹿。最後，他們看到了一隻有著一對尖角的牛。牛會用角和自己的同類或敵人打架。珍與安潔拉很興奮可以認識這些動物。

答題解說

答案：C.。題目要求考生按照短文內容，辨別出這個動物園中沒有的動物。雖然短文內有提到鹿，但安潔拉看到的鹿 without any spots（沒有任何斑點），而考生可清楚看見 C. 圖上的鹿有著明顯斑點，因此 C. 是正確答案。

答題關鍵

題目提供的三張圖片都是動物，因此可推知題目可能與牛（ox、bull、cow 等字）、獅子（lion）、鹿（deer）有關，考生須觀察三張圖片上動物的明顯特徵，才能順利作答。

字詞解釋

originate v. 源自　**sharp** adj. 尖銳的　**fight against** phr. 與～搏鬥
balance v. 保持平衡　**sweep away** phr. 驅趕　**insect** n. 昆蟲
sika deer phr. 梅花鹿

相關文法或用法補充

fight 的動詞三態是：現在式 fight → 過去式 fought → 過去分詞 fought

- 意指「鬥爭，對抗」時，搭配介系詞 against。
  Martin Luther King spent his whole life fighting against racism.
  馬丁・路德・金恩耗費一生對抗種族主義。

- 意指「與～打鬥，打架」時，搭配介系詞 with。
  The kids next doors are fighting with each other.
  隔壁的小孩正在打架。

- 意指「爭奪」時，搭配介系詞 over。
  The birds were fighting over some bread crumbs at the park.
  鳥在公園裡爭奪著一些麵包屑。

For question number 29, please look at the three pictures.

Question number 29: Listen to the following description. Which picture best describes the festival?

A   B   C

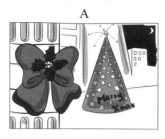  

This festival is usually celebrated when the weather is chilly, neither too hot nor too cold. On this day, people do a variety of activities. People eat special food, including a traditional pastry. The pastry can be sweet or savory. People can enjoy fireworks as well. It is a perfect time for families to reunite in many Asian countries, such as Taiwan, China, Japan, Vietnam, and South Korea.

英文翻譯

請聽以下這段描述。哪張圖片最符合描述的節日？
這個節日通常是在天氣涼爽時慶祝，不會太熱或太冷。在這一天，人們會進行各式各樣的活動。人們會吃特別的食物，包括一種傳統糕點。這種糕點可以是甜的或鹹的。人們也可以欣賞煙火秀。在像台灣、中國、日本、越南及韓國等很多亞洲國家，都會在這個絕佳的日子與家人團聚。

答題解說

答案：C.。題目要求考生依聽到的短文內容選出最符合描述的節日圖片，短文內容中提到了幾個條件：天氣不冷不熱、進行各種活動、吃傳統甜或鹹的糕點、欣賞煙火秀、很多亞洲國家都會藉此節日與家人團聚，符合這些條件的只有 C. 的中秋節。選項 A. 是聖誕節、選項 B. 則是端午節，均與描述內容不符。

答題關鍵

題目提供的三張圖片，明顯是三個不同的節日：Christmas（聖誕節）、Dragon Boat Festival（端午節）、Mid-Autumn Festival（中秋節），在音檔播放前，考生應先行推測可能會出現的答題關鍵字，如 present（禮物）、rice dumpling（粽子）、firework（煙火）等等，開始聽音檔時便可藉著答題關鍵字來提升作答速度與準確度。

neither...nor phr. 既不～也不～　**a variety of** phr. 各式各樣的　**pastry** n. 糕點
firework n. 煙火　**savory** adj. 鹹的

相關文法或用法補充

variety（多樣性；種類）這個字是非常常見於各大測驗中的關鍵重要字彙，一定
要好好學會怎麼用喔！

❶ a variety of：各式各樣的～，各種類型的～
She does a variety of exercises, including swimming, jogging, and trekking.
她會做各式各樣的運動，包括游泳、慢跑及健行。

❷ varieties of：不同種類的～，不同品種的～
This article was about the different varieties of entertainment.
這篇文章與不同種類的娛樂有關。

For question number 30, please look at the three pictures.

**Question number 30: Listen to the following description. Which of the
following activities does Louis not do?**

A	B	C

  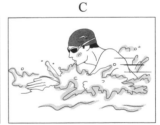

Louis always starts his day swimming in the gym. He is training for the National
Swimming Competition in Taipei next month. He doesn't sweat a lot because of the
air-conditioned atmosphere. After his swimming training, he joins his best friend to
play tennis. He always has a lot of fun. After school, he normally heads to the
supermarket to go grocery shopping. He buys some fresh vegetables, meats, and
fruits in order to maintain a healthy diet before the swimming contest.

英文翻譯

請聽以下這段描述。路易斯沒有做以下哪項活動？
路易斯總是以在健身房游泳來開始他的一天。他正在為了下個月在台北舉行的全
國游泳大賽進行訓練。因為是有開空調的環境，所以他沒有流很多汗。在游泳訓
練之後，他會和他最好的朋友一起打網球。他總是打得很開心。在下課後，他通

常會到超市買食品雜貨。為了在游泳比賽前維持健康飲食，他會買一些新鮮蔬菜、肉及水果。

答案：A.。題目要求考生依短文所描述的內容，選出路易斯沒有做的活動，短文中提及路易斯早上會在健身房游泳，游完泳後會和朋友一起打網球，因此圖 B. 及 C. 都是路易斯有做的活動。圖片 A. 中的人物正在買書，在短文內沒有提及任何與買書相關的資訊，因此 A. 是正確答案。

音檔播放前應先快速看過題目提供的三張圖片，必須特別注意圖片中的人物數量、地點、動作、狀態等細節資訊，並事先推想可能會出現在短文中的答題關鍵字。圖片 A. 中的人正在買書（buying books）、圖片 B. 中的人正在打網球（playing tennis）、圖片 C. 中的人則正在游泳（swimming），作答時應注意聆聽短文內是否出現了這些答題關鍵字，可加快作答速度與準確度。

competition n. 競賽　　**air-conditioned** adj. 有空調的　　**atmosphere** n. 環境
normally adv. 一般地　　**maintain** v. 保持；維持　　**contest** n. 比賽

做為形容詞的 V-ing（現在分詞）和 V-ed（過去分詞），不論是日常生活還是考試都常常出現，一定要分清楚兩者之間的差異，才不會用錯喔！

- V-ing 現在分詞 → **主動**做某個動作
  The smiling boy is my brother.
  那個微笑的男孩是我的弟弟。

- V-ed 過去分詞 → **被動**做某個動作
  Maria prefers handmade cookies.
  瑪莉亞比較喜歡手工餅乾。

全民英檢初級聽力模擬測驗
正確答案

1. B	2. A	3. C	4. B	5. C
6. A	7. C	8. B	9. C	10. B
11. A	12. A	13. C	14. B	15. A
16. A	17. B	18. C	19. A	20. A
21. A	22. B	23. C	24. A	25. C
26. C	27. A	28. C	29. C	30. A

模擬測驗

英語學習

英語實力全面提升！
單字記憶、文法理解、會話應用，

專為華人設計的全年齡英文學習書！
同時學會「字母、發音、句型、文法、聽力、會話」，自我學習、兼差家教、開班授課都能使用的英文課本！

★附母語人士發音 MP3 光碟

定價：399 元

分課帶領、融入會話、全面剖析，從基本知識循序漸進，讓你從詞性、句子結構、時態到片語、子句連結，建立文法藍圖，自學教學都好用！

★附 MP3 光碟

定價：380 元

第一本以「完全實用性」為目標的「語源」學習書，連初學者都能用，最簡單易懂的單字構成原理課本！

★附 MP3 光碟＋QR 碼線上音檔

定價：399 元

國際學村　LA PRESS 語研學院 Language Academy Press

語言學習 NO.1

學英語

全圖解
肢體動作
GESTURE
ENGLISH
英語會話

學韓語

看圖秒懂
韓國人天天在用的
擬聲
擬態語
精準理解、生動活用
讓你的韓語或更豐富

學日語

我的第一本
日語會話課本
自學、教學、旅遊、洽商、工作都實用的在地日本語！
JAPANESE
Everyday Life!

第二外語

專為初學者設計！
自學西班牙語會話
看完這本就能說！
只要直接套用本書會話模式，
一次學會日常溝通、必背單字與基礎文法！
SPANISH
Conversation

考多益

HACKERS × 國際學村
新制多益
全新！TOEIC
閱讀題庫解析
Reading
每月進場實測分析、完整傳授答題技巧
黃金證書手到擒來！

考日檢

N5-N1
新日檢
文法大全
精選出題頻率最高的考用文法，
一本全包全級數通用！
準確度破表哪級都可以

考韓檢
New
TOPIK II
新韓檢
寫作應考
祕笈
中高級

考英檢

NEW
GEPT
新制全民英檢
10回試題完全掌握最新內容與趨勢！
初級 聽力＆閱讀 題庫大全

想獲得最新最快的
語言學習情報嗎？

歡迎加入
國際學村＆語研學院粉絲團

台灣廣廈 國際出版集團
Taiwan Mansion International Group

國家圖書館出版品預行編目（CIP）資料

NEW GEPT 新制全民英檢初級聽力測驗必考題型 / 國際語言中心
委員會, 李佳靜, 林姿吟著. -- 初版. -- 新北市：國際學村, 2021.04
　面；　公分
ISBN 978-986-454-151-5（平裝附光碟片）
1. 英語 2. 讀本

805.1892　　　　　　　　　　　　　　　110002010

國際學村

NEW GEPT 新制全民英檢初級聽力測驗必考題型

作　　　者／國際語言中心委員會、　　編輯中心編輯長／伍峻宏・編輯／徐淳輔
　　　　　　　李佳靜、林姿吟　　　　　　封面設計／何偉凱・內頁排版／東豪印刷事業有限公司
　　　　　　　　　　　　　　　　　　　　製版・印刷・裝訂／東豪・紘億・明和

行企研發中心總監／陳冠蒨　　　　　　　線上學習中心總監／陳冠蒨
媒體公關組／陳柔彣　　　　　　　　　　數位營運組／顏佑婷
綜合業務組／何欣穎　　　　　　　　　　企製開發組／江季珊

發　行　人／江媛珍
法律顧問／第一國際法律事務所 余淑杏律師・北辰著作權事務所 蕭雄淋律師
出　　版／國際學村
發　　行／台灣廣廈有聲圖書有限公司
　　　　　地址：新北市235中和區中山路二段359巷7號2樓
　　　　　電話：（886）2-2225-5777・傳真：（886）2-2225-8052
讀者服務信箱／cs@booknews.com.tw

代理印務・全球總經銷／知遠文化事業有限公司
　　　　　地址：新北市222深坑區北深路三段155巷25號5樓
　　　　　電話：（886）2-2664-8800・傳真：（886）2-2664-8801
郵政劃撥／劃撥帳號：18836722
　　　　　劃撥戶名：知遠文化事業有限公司（※單次購書金額未滿1000元需另付郵資70元。）

■ 出版日期：2021年4月　　　　　　ISBN：978-986-454-151-5
　　　　　　2023年9月3刷　　　　　　版權所有，未經同意不得重製、轉載、翻印。